The Burnt Island Burial Ground

Lindsay Harding Mystery, No. 3

Mindy Quigley

For all Hohensteins and former
Hohensteins
And for anyone who has ever been
Hohensteined

Little Spot Publishing
http://littlespotforstories.com

Cover design by Genevieve LaVO Cosdon

Other novels in the Lindsay Harding series:
A Murder in Mount Moriah
A Death in Duck

Chapter 1

As far as chaplain Lindsay Harding could tell, the HVAC system that serviced the chaplains' offices at Mount Moriah Regional Medical Center had only two settings: "blast furnace" and "Siberia." It was late April, and despite the typically mild weather of the North Carolina spring outside, today was a Siberia day. Inside the small windowless office where she and her fellow hospital chaplains were based, the air conditioning units hurled out cold air with such vigor that Lindsay half-expected to see a team of sled dogs rocket through the door. When she settled down at her desk to complete her end-of-shift paperwork, Lindsay realized that she had lost track of her cardigan at some point during the day. She tried to tough out the cold as she filled in the first few patient contact reports, but quickly decided that without an extra layer on, she'd soon be frozen into a state of suspended animation.

Lindsay retraced her steps, working her way backward through the shift she had just completed. She'd spent the late afternoon in the Labor and Delivery Unit with an anxious first-time father who'd held her hand so tightly that her pinkie finger was still a little numb. Before that, she'd eaten lunch in the hospital cafeteria, during which time she'd been summoned to the Emergency Department to pray with a frantic couple whose son had swallowed half a dozen marbles. After the couple had been assured by the doctor that nature would eliminate the danger in due course, Lindsay had headed up to the oncology department. When the cardigan failed to materialize in any of those places, she walked to the chapel, where she'd conducted the usual Saturday morning service.

Mount Moriah Medical Center's chapel, a small interior room on the ground floor of the hospital, had been redecorated a few years earlier to transform it from an overtly Christian worship space into someone's idea of "interfaith," which, in this case, meant that the large wooden cross that formerly stood against the wall next to the pulpit had been replaced by a series of ill-conceived, wall-mounted quilts. The hangings were alleged to depict the sun and moon locked in an embrace, embodying, according to a small explanatory plaque, the themes of Hope and Peace. It was never entirely clear why Peace looked almost exactly like an angry pig dancing with an enormous banana.

The windowless chapel now stood in semi-darkness, with only two small floor lights on the dais providing illumination. Having spent time in this room almost every day during the four years she'd worked at the hospital, Lindsay knew the space almost as well as she knew her own house. She walked briskly past the rows of wooden chairs without pausing to switch on the lights, her footsteps echoing off the wood-paneled walls. She scanned the area around the pulpit, but her sweater was nowhere to be seen. As she turned to head back toward the door, she skidded to a halt, her heart thudding in her chest. Near the back of the room, a dot of glowing red light illuminated the outline of a seated figure. Lindsay pushed back her rising fear as she groped along the wall near the podium for the room's other set of light switches.

"Hello," she called out, her voice faltering slightly.

"Hey," a youthful female voice drawled back carelessly in return.

Everything's okay, Lindsay whispered to herself. *It's just a young woman. A hospital full of people is right outside the door. All you have to do is scream, and someone will come and help you.*

Any normal person might be taken by surprise at the unexpected presence of a stranger in a darkened room, but for Lindsay, the deep terror that engulfed her went far beyond the norm. A few months earlier, Lindsay's mother's psychotic ex-boyfriend, an ex-con named Leander Swoopes, had embarked on a violent rampage, brutally attacking Lindsay before disappearing in the aftermath. Ever since, she'd been left to wonder if he'd drowned in the ocean during an escape attempt or managed to get away. The thought of that dreadful time, and the idea that her attacker could still be hiding out somewhere, had turned every unexpected noise, every dark corner, and every encounter with an unknown person into a panic-inducing nightmare. Since that time,

2

Lindsay's nerve fibers had become like trip wires, set off with terrifying ease by even the slightest disturbance.

At last, Lindsay's trembling fingers found the switch, and the room was flooded with a bright yellow glow. The girl threw her arm over her face to shield her eyes.

"Can I help you with something?" she asked. "I'm in here trying to engage in quiet reflection or whatever, and you're kind of interrupting."

"Sorry," Lindsay said reflexively, her heart still pounding. "I didn't know anyone was in here." She caught sight of the object that had been glowing a moment before—the electronic cigarette in the girl's upraised hand. It appeared that the girl, like many people before her, had ducked into the always-unlocked chapel to "quietly reflect" on her nicotine habit in a place where she was unlikely to get busted for violating the hospital's smoke-free policy.

The girl lowered her hand from her eyes and glared at Lindsay. Even wearing a petulant scowl, her face was breathtakingly beautiful, with iridescent amber-colored eyes and a tawny complexion that looked like it had been retouched in Photoshop.

"Yes?" the girl asked, arching an eyebrow at Lindsay.

"Sorry," Lindsay sputtered again, realizing that she had been staring. The girl's flawless face and elegant, willowy figure had the peculiar effect of conjuring up an intense feeling of pity in Lindsay. Features like that must attract as many eyeballs as a burn victim's crepe-paper skin or an amputee's empty sleeve. Lindsay regained her composure, smiled at the girl, and gestured to the cigarette. "I'm afraid those aren't allowed in here. Not even the electronic ones."

The girl let out a world-weary sigh, flicked a switch on the device, and shoved it into her purse. "There. Happy now?"

"I'm Lindsay, one of the chaplains here," Lindsay said, in a softer tone.

Lindsay proffered her hand in greeting. The girl looked at it warily. Then suddenly the girl flashed a toothpaste commercial smile and extended her slender hand. "Jess."

The shift of expression had been so abrupt and complete, Lindsay momentarily wondered if she'd imagined the girl's initial hostility. Looking more closely, though, she saw that Jess seemed to have pulled her smile across her face—a thin, glossy covering for an ice sculpture.

"What brings you to the chapel, Jess?" Lindsay asked.

"Like I said, quiet reflection," Jess replied, arching a perfectly-shaped eyebrow.

"Or…whatever." Lindsay echoed Jess's words back to her and matched the girl's Mona Lisa smile. "Are you visiting someone in the hospital?"

"My grandfather's in here." She paused. "He's dying for real this time." For a moment, Lindsay thought she saw a flicker of grief or pain pass across Jess's face, but no sooner did the emotion register than it disappeared. Jess pressed her lips together, forming a slight pout. "My mom's probably gonna be here for *hours*, so now I have to wait until one of my friends can come and give me a ride home."

"You don't have your license?" Lindsay asked. Like many extraordinarily beautiful women, Jess had an ageless quality. She could've been fourteen or forty.

Jess shook her head. "It's super annoying because I already have a car and everything. I got it for my birthday when I turned eighteen in February. But the Driver's Ed teacher at school was trying to make me retake the course because she doesn't like me, and she's got this huge stick up her butt about it. My dad was gonna sue last year, but I told him to just chill out. I mean, I still have to go there all this year. But I'm graduating at the end of next month, so I'm taking private lessons now."

"Well, that's good, right?"

"Yeah, they're way better. The car we had to practice in at school smelled like cats, and Mrs. Travis doesn't let you play the radio."

"Is Mrs. Travis still teaching Driver's Ed?" Lindsay asked. "I graduated from Mount Moriah High School," she added, in response to Jess's upraised eyebrows.

Jess gave her a pitying look.

"What?" Lindsay prompted.

4

"Nothing. Well, it's just that you're a lifer. I thought maybe you weren't because your accent isn't very strong and you have hipster glasses. Most lifers wouldn't wear those."

Lindsay quietly registered the backhanded compliment, or was it a forehand insult? She asked, "What's a lifer?"

"You know, one of those people who never leave the town they grew up in. Settle down near their parents. Marry somebody they've known forever. That's what my mom and dad are—lifers. All the lifer women get their hair done at Violet's or the place in the mall and drive around in minivans with the little stick people family decals stuck to the back windows. And all the lifer men talk about high school sports like it's so freakin' amazing to watch some idiots in spandex toss around a stupid little ball." She paused to twist a tendril of her chestnut hair around the end of her finger. "No offense," she added.

"None taken," Lindsay replied evenly. "So I take it you're not planning to become a lifer?"

"I'm not staying a minute longer than I have to. Literally the second I graduate, I'm moving to New York to become an actress. I already have people interested in signing me to model, which should get me started."

"Wow," Lindsay said. "That'll be a big change from little old Mount Moriah. Do you think it'll be a culture shock?"

"Do you mean, will I be shocked that people up there actually *have* culture? Um, no." While she'd been talking, her large, satchel-like purse had tipped over, spilling a book and notepad onto the floor.

Lindsay picked the things up and handed them to Jess. The pad of paper was covered in triangles and angles, numbers and lines—it looked like trigonometry homework. Lindsay recited the book title out loud. "*Pocket Sky Atlas*. Are you into astronomy?"

Jess snatched it back. "It's for school. Just some boring homework." Her phone buzzed. She pulled it out of her purse and tapped out a message on the screen. "My ride's here." She tossed the phone back into her bag and extracted a little tube of watermelon-pink lip gloss and a small mirror. "Here, can you hold this a sec?" she said, not waiting for a reply before passing the mirror to Lindsay. Jess took hold of Lindsay's hand and

5

maneuvered it into position. Leaning closer to the small circle of her reflection, she dragged the colored wand across her lips. "There. Perfect." She smacked her lips together and took the mirror from Lindsay's hand. "Thanks. You're a star."

As Jess glided out of the room, Lindsay could almost feel a cool breeze wash over her. She sat there for a moment, wondering what car-crash combination of nature and nurture had given rise to such a creature. The mental chill from Lindsay's initial panic at encountering Jess in the dark chapel hadn't entirely abated, and it reminded Lindsay once again of her missing cardigan. She headed upstairs to the Geriatric Unit to continue her search, re-visiting patients she'd seen earlier that morning until she found herself standing in the doorway of one of the first patients she'd seen that day. She knocked gently on the propped-open door and stepped inside.

Mr. Meeks, an elderly man with smooth brown skin, a wild shock of white hair, and Coke bottle glasses looked up at her. He had the bedcovers pulled up right to his chin, his stubby fingers curling over the top of them like a mouse's paws.

"I'm glad you're here, doctor," he said. "This woman is trying to steal my television."

Lindsay cast a glance at the sturdy, dimpled nurse who stood at Mr. Meeks's bedside holding the television remote.

The nurse shot Lindsay an amused look and then turned to the old man. "Now, Mr. Meeks, you know I ain't trying to steal your TV. I'm Angel, remember? The nurse who takes care of you during the day."

The elderly man had undergone a knee operation a few days before. He was in the early stages of dementia, and the temporary move to the hospital from his familiar surroundings at Rest Haven, Mount Moriah's nursing home, had exacerbated his confusion.

"How are you feeling, Mr. Meeks?" Lindsay asked, smiling reassuringly.

Mr. Meeks pursed his lips and turned his myopic gaze on her. "Well, doctor," he said, "I don't like to complain, but my leg aches something fearsome."

"I'm sorry to hear that. The doctor will be in to see you later, and you can talk to her about your leg. I'm one of the hospital chaplains. We said a prayer together earlier today, and we talked about your grandson."

Mr. Meeks nodded his head but then immediately continued. "As long as you're here, doctor, I wanted you to look at that thing on my backside. It still ain't right," Mr. Meeks said as he began to wriggle out from under the covers.

Lindsay took a step forward and opened her mouth to protest, but the words foundered on her tongue when she observed that Mr. Meeks was wearing a green, wool cardigan several sizes too small for him. Despite being at least half a foot taller than the petite chaplain and of considerable girth, Mr. Meeks had managed to fasten all the buttons. The material encircled his torso like a sausage skin, and his wrinkled wrists protruded from the ends of the sleeves. "How did you..."

Mr. Meeks cut off the rest of Lindsay's question with a flick of his upraised hand. He looked at her closely, his eyes narrowing. "Hush up a minute. I just figured out you're not a doctor at all. You're that lady minister from the news. The one who escaped from the killer."

Lindsay blushed and shrugged. Much of the extensive news coverage that followed her confrontation with Leander Swoopes had focused on her, sensationalizing her role and attributing fake quotes to her that made her sound like a tough movie action hero. Although she'd avoided the press as much as she could and given no interviews, even after all these months, stories about her still seemed to emerge with disconcerting regularity.

"How come you were pretending to be a doctor?" he demanded. Before she could answer, he whipped his head back to Angel. "And how come you're still holding my television clicker, missy?"

"I'm just not sure this is the best program for you to be watching. Remember how upset you got yesterday when they showed that poor woman's dead body on this show? We talked about how maybe you didn't want to watch *CSI* no more. Why don't we turn on *Andy Griffith*? That's a real nice program. When you're hurting, laughter's the best medicine, isn't it?"

7

Mr. Meeks furrowed his brow as if giving the question deep consideration. "Is it really laughter? I'd have sworn it was penicillin. Because when I got the clap in Korea after the war..."

"Oh, look! They found bone fragments in the fireplace!" Lindsay practically shouted at the television screen.

"Christ Almighty! Will y'all keep it down over there? Can't a person just die in peace around here?" a low voice rasped from the far side of the room divider curtain.

Angel took advantage of Mr. Meeks's temporary distraction to flip the TV over to the soothing black-and-white world of Mayberry. Lindsay, meanwhile, crossed to the far side of Mr. Meeks's bed and stood in front of the drawn curtain.

"Sorry for disturbing you, sir." When her apology was met with silence, she continued, "Do you mind if I come in?"

"I'm not home," the voice replied testily.

Lindsay glanced at Angel, who just rolled her eyes and sucked her teeth.

"I understand if you want privacy. I just wondered if you might let me apologize face to face," Lindsay said.

"That's how you religious types work, isn't it? I once made the mistake of opening my door to some Jehovah's Witnesses. Next thing you know, I'm getting their newsletter every month."

"I promise I don't have a newsletter."

"You can't help me, so just leave me be," the man snapped.

"Okay. Just let Angel know if you ever think you might want somebody to talk to. That's what I'm here for."

When Lindsay's last entreaty was again met with a stony silence, she turned back to Mr. Meeks. "Mr. Meeks, do you think I could have my cardigan back?"

Mr. Meeks fingered the top button, which threatened to ping off at any moment under the strain. He regarded Lindsay suspiciously for a long moment. "No," he said. "Get your own."

"Now Mr. Meeks..." Angel began.

"Don't know why she's talkin' to him anyhow," Meeks said. "That man is a stone cold killer. I heard him say so with my own two ears. He thinks I don't hear him talkin' to hisself, but I do." He turned his head toward the curtain that separated the room in half. "I hear you talking, murderer!" he shouted. "And you and you," he

8

said, pointing to Angel and Lindsay in turn, "are thieves." He snatched the remote from Angel's hand. "Keep your thieving hands off of my television, and tell that pretend doctor over there to stop trying to steal my very best sweater."

***

Angel had also tried and failed to convince Mr. Meeks to relinquish Lindsay's sweater, but ultimately she and Lindsay decided to chalk it up as a loss and retreat to the nurses' station to draw warmth instead from hot cups of coffee.

"So who's the other patient in Mr. Meeks's room?" Lindsay asked, pouring half a plantation's worth of sugar packets into her cup. "He wasn't there this morning."

"You mean Little Mister Sunshine?"

"Yeah, the one who's part of our criminal band of thieves and murderers," Lindsay said wryly.

"That's Otis Boughtflower. He just got moved up this afternoon."

"Otis Boughtflower. Why does that name sound familiar?" Lindsay searched her mental Rolodex. Having spent most of her life in Mount Moriah, she usually knew, or knew of, the local patients. However, the hospital drew patients from all over central North Carolina, southern Virginia, and beyond, so it wasn't uncommon for her to lack the usual small-town, one-degree-of-separation nexus of connections.

"You ever drive past Boughtflower Hosiery outside Burlington?" Angel asked. She jerked a thumb toward the room from which they'd just emerged. "That's him. The king of socks."

"I remember driving past there when I was little. I used to think they made hoses. I always pictured some kind of machine, like a gigantic version of a pasta maker, with strings of hoses coming out that they chopped into littler hoses." She stirred her coffee. "It's so depressing going past there now. All those lost jobs. They went bankrupt, didn't they?" In her mind's eye, Lindsay saw the huge crumbling brick building surrounded by vast swaths of empty, cracked parking lot. Its doors had been shuttered for at least a dozen years.

"Bankrupt?" Angel flattened her lips and made a long "*mmm*" sound. "That's what they told people, but that ain't what happened. Our friend in there sold off the company and all the equipment to a big Chinese company. That man's got enough money to burn a wet mule, and then some. My cousin was his home health aide and she nursed him up until he got admitted. I dropped her off for work a couple of times at Mr. Boughtflower's place. You know that turn-off with the fancy gates when you get down past where the old middle school was on the other side of New Albany?"

Lindsay nodded. Like most small-town folks, she could navigate just as easily by landmarks that used to be there, as by ones that still existed.

"Well," Angel continued, "that's his house. The driveway goes on for about a million miles. Not gravel, neither. It's all paved just like a real road. Even got those old-fashioned kind of streetlights when you get up close to the house. I went inside one time to use the restroom, and, honey, you could've parked a truck in that bathtub. Everything was made out of this sparkly marble. I felt like I was peeing in a museum."

"I always wondered what was back there," Lindsay said. She glanced toward the room that Meeks and Boughtflower shared. "How long will he be in the hospital?"

"I don't think he's going home again. He's diabetic, already was on dialysis three times a week, and has congestive heart failure and COPD. Now all the other organs seem to think it's quitting time, too. It's just a matter of time, and he knows it. Dunette—that's my cousin—offered to take him home and get the hospice people to come to him, said she'd stay with him 24-7, so he could spend his last days at home, but he said no."

"That is weird," Lindsay said. "But what's even weirder is that he's in a regular room. If he's such a big shot, why doesn't he pay for a private room?"

Angel shrugged. "When Dunette asked him about it, the old man said this seemed as good a place as any to kick the bucket. Just yesterday he told Dunette he wouldn't be needing her anymore. Just like that," she said, snapping her fingers. "No severance pay or nothing. And you should see the family. Don't even need to watch the soaps with them around. His daughter's meek as a church mouse, tiptoeing around here like she wants to say she's sorry for taking up a share of the world's oxygen by breathing. Her husband, the son-in-law, is a purebred, grade-A baloney artist. And the teenage granddaughter? Prettiest little thing you ever saw and smart, too, but more spoiled than last week's egg salad. Thinks the sun comes up just to hear her crow."

"Ah," Lindsay said. "I think I met last week's egg salad downstairs. Long, brown hair? Seems to hate everything?"

"That's the one. She could give old Otis a run for his money in a pig-headedness contest. I guess orneriness must skip a generation, like red hair. My cousin feels sorry for him, but I can't see why. That old man's only been here half a day and I'm ready to pull out my hair."

"Wait," Lindsay said suddenly. "Did I hear right that your cousin's a home health aide? And that Boughtflower let her go? What company does she work for?"

"She's been doing private work, just part-time the last few years. She needs the flexibility because she's studying to be an RN," Angel said.

"Does she have another job yet?"

"No. I told you, she only got her walking papers yesterday."

Lindsay lurched forward, nearly spilling her coffee on Angel. "You've got to give me her number!"

Angel raised her eyebrows.

"You have no idea how hard it is to get a decent home health care worker who does flexible hours!"

"What do you need a nurse for?" Angel asked.

"Simmy is supposed to move in with me next week and I still haven't found anybody."

"Who's Simmy?"

"Sorry," Lindsay said. She paused for a moment, allowing her brain to catch up with her mouth. "Chrysanthemum Bennett. She's my great grandmother."

"And she's gonna live with you?" Angel asked.

"Yes, I've had an addition put on my house and everything, but I still haven't found anybody to help out with her while I'm at work. She got beat up pretty bad during that whole…thing I was involved in. She was in the hospital for a long time, and then a rehab place. She's supposed to move in with me next week when she finishes her in-patient rehab."

"Wait a minute. I remember hearing about this now. Didn't you just find out she was related to you? How come you're letting her live with you?"

"Yes, but I've known her my whole life, and we've always gotten along," Lindsay said. "Because of what happened, she has dizzy spells and falls a lot, so she can't live by herself. I couldn't let them put her in a nursing home. She's just not nursing home material. She keeps complaining that everyone in the rehab place is "old," and that all the attractive men either have dementia or are only interested in long-term relationships, which are not her thing. And she can't go back to her place on the Outer Banks because she can't drive herself around anymore. She really needs someone to be there a lot of the time."

"Still, that's a lot to do for a grandma you just discovered," Angel said. "Lotta folks wouldn't do that."

"It's kind of for me, too. Simmy's the only one who really understands what I went through." Lindsay looked off down the hallway, momentarily lost in her thoughts.

Angel squeezed Lindsay's arm and let a moment pass before prompting, "So you wanted to know about Dunette?"

"Oh, yeah. I've interviewed so many home health aides—I've lost count, but I think it's somewhere around eleventy jillion. Because I work shifts, I need somebody who can help out during the times when I can't be there. I'd really like to have just one person, rather than a bunch of different people. And ideally I don't want to hire some psycho who was voted 'Most Likely to Hogtie an Old Lady and Rob a Minister's House' in high school."

Angel laughed. "Well, I can vouch for Dunette. She took care of my grandma when she was dying, and her own mama when she was sick with stomach cancer. I'm the one who told her she should be a nurse. She's just got that caring nature, you know? You gotta have that caring nature if you're gonna put up with mean old so-and-sos like Mr. Boughtflower and still keep a smile on your face. And you really gotta have it if you're gonna be looking at Mr. Meeks's backside ten times a day." She shook her head. "Honey, what that man's got going on back there would peel the smile off anybody's face."

Chapter 2

The Mex-Itali Restaurant had a reputation for serving the best Mexican food in Mount Moriah. It also had a reputation for having the town's best Italian food. Although its eminence was due, at least in part, to the fact that it was the only Mexican or Italian restaurant in that part of the state, it was nonetheless true that to get a more authentic ethnic food experience, you'd have to drive all the way to the Olive Garden in New Albany or even as far as the Taco Bell down off of I-85.

The restaurant's unique position in the local culinary landscape, coupled with its Saturday night margarita special, made it the obvious choice for Lindsay to celebrate her thirty-first birthday with her boyfriend, Warren Satterwhite. However, when she arrived at the Mexi-Itali at five minutes before 6 p.m. on the evening of the Great Cardigan Theft, she found a nearly-empty restaurant and no sign of Warren. At the table nearest to the door, a wide-bottomed woman was attempting to wrestle her squalling baby into a high chair. Her two older children laughed hysterically as they draped spaghetti across their upper lips to create Fu Manchu mustaches. The children's father sat across from them, oblivious to the red sauce covering their faces and dripping onto their shirts. He fixated on his cell phone, his thumb darting back and forth across the tiny screen like an inchworm on amphetamines.

"Well, hey, Miss Lindsay!" The restaurant's proprietor, Clydetta Stockton, spied Lindsay through the pass-through opening between the kitchen and the dining room. Clydetta waddled out through the swinging door and folded Lindsay into an embrace heavily perfumed with hairspray and garlic. Lindsay had been coming to the Mex-Itali since childhood, and had watched as Clydetta grew shorter and thicker with each passing year. Now, as her seventh decade approached, the little woman had settled into the shape of a garden gnome.

Lindsay returned the greeting as Clydetta released her. "Hey, Miss Clydetta."

"Now don't you look just as pretty as a picture? Your hair looks so nice fixed like that," Clydetta gushed.

Lindsay knew the compliment stretched the truth. She had the kind of fine, curly hair that resisted all but the most forceful attempts at styling. If she tried to pin it up, she always ended the day taking out at least a dozen fewer hairpins than she'd put in. That was the kind of hair she'd been born with—the kind that was capable of actually devouring metal hairpins. Still, she'd made a special effort to tame her wild mane. Warren had had flowers delivered to her at the hospital, along with a little card saying how much he looked forward to celebrating with her that evening. When your boyfriend sends you flowers, she'd reasoned, the least you could do was try not to look like an alpaca in need of shearing.

"Warren called ahead to let me know it was your birthday," Clydetta said. "I saved a romantic table for you." She winked one of her heavily-mascaraed eyes.

Lindsay cast a quick glance around the restaurant, wondering which of the Formica-topped tables could possibly have aphrodisiac properties. Clydetta led her to a booth in the corner furthest from the other diners. The neon glow of a wall-mounted Budweiser sign revealed that all the cracks in the vinyl upholstery of the bench seats had been covered with electrical tape. Clydetta hefted her ample self up on the back of one of the seats and flicked a switch to turn off the sign. She climbed down again with a deep "oof" sound. She extracted two LED candles from her pocket, turned them on and plunked them side by side in the middle of the table.

"Thanks, Clydetta. That's real sweet of you."

"Least I can do for one of my favorite couples. I remember when y'all used to come in here after school sometimes," Clydetta said.

"Well, we weren't dating back then. We were just friends," Lindsay replied quickly. She realized with annoyance that Jess's comments about "lifers" had gotten under her skin more than she'd like to admit. Even though she'd left Mount Moriah for college, and had even moved to Ohio briefly with her former fiancée, the truth of the matter was that she was now sitting in the same restaurant she'd been sitting in for decades, getting ready to eat the same food with the same guy.

Lindsay cast another glance around the restaurant. "Is Warren in the bathroom or something? I saw one of the New Albany unmarkeds out front." As a detective for the police force in the neighboring town of New Albany, Warren drove a constantly-shifting array of vehicles. Depending on the task, he might show up in a patrol car, one of the force's rugged SUVs, his personal vehicle, or, like today, an unmarked, black Ford Crown Victoria.

"He came in about an hour ago, but he said he had some business to take care of with a friend of his. He did say to let you know if he was running a couple minutes late just to sit tight. I'll bring you a margarita while you wait. On the house," she said, winking again.

***

At 6:22pm, Lindsay was still alone, working her way through her second basket of the Mex-Itali's signature appetizer—tortilla chips with marinara and parmesan queso dipping sauces. She was well into her third complimentary margarita, and the tequila was making her head feel like a balloon about to rise off the top of her shoulders. If Warren arrived much later, she wasn't sure if he'd find her at the table or under it.

The little bell over the front entrance dinged, and Lindsay looked up expectantly. Warren cast a glance around the room. When his eyes settled on Lindsay, a warm smile lit up his face.

"I'm so sorry I'm late," he said when he reached the table. He bent down and brushed his lips briefly across her cheek. Warren's reserved nature and police-issue professionalism presented a huge barrier to any kind of public display of affection. The few times Lindsay had tried to kiss him or hold his hand in a public place, his whole body had become as rigid as a Ken doll's.

"That was some greeting, Romeo," Lindsay said, smiling at him. She noticed that he wore his "party shirt"—a subtle green and grey striped pattern that represented the only button-down shirt he owned that wasn't solid grey, white or blue cotton. His copper-colored hair curled softly away from his handsome, open face.

"Well, you're some gal," Warren said, winking in response to the good-humored sarcasm in her tone. He took the seat opposite hers and exhaled. "Happy birthday."

Lindsay was about to reply when the bell over the door tinkled again and a pretty, well-manicured woman entered. It took Lindsay half a beat to recognize her as Cynthia Honeycutt—the woman who, in the eyes of the law and the drag queen who had performed their wedding ceremony in Las Vegas, was Warren's wedded wife.

Cynthia made a beeline for their table, her steps clicking across the floor as her sleek, strawberry-blonde hair swished around her face. "Hey, y'all. I'm sorry to interrupt. Warren, honey, you forgot your sunglasses in my car."

Warren frowned and reached out for Lindsay's hand.

Cynthia held out the glasses as if to set them on the table, but then paused and said, "Warren told me y'all are celebrating your birthday. It's always nice when your birthday falls on a weekend, isn't it?"

Lindsay smiled tightly. She had nothing against Cynthia. At least nothing any person with a pulse *wouldn't* have against the very attractive woman who was legally wedded to her boyfriend. The pretty nurse and Warren had tied the knot during a drunken night in Vegas the previous year, before Lindsay and Warren had started dating. The rash marriage, which took place during a weekend of wedding festivities for Warren and Cynthia's mutual friends, was entirely uncharacteristic of the soft-spoken, straight-laced detective. Warren never discussed the circumstances, but ever since that night, he had scrupulously avoided hard liquor, the state of Nevada, and drag queens invested with the legal authority to perform wedding ceremonies.

Warren had always intended to have the marriage annulled, but his perpetual failure to do so had become a sore spot between him and Lindsay. When Cynthia and Lindsay occasionally ran into each other at the hospital, Cynthia seemed to find it endlessly amusing to say—usually in front of elderly townswomen or hospital administrators—"Hey, Reverend, I heard you went on another date with my husband last night!" and flash Lindsay a melodramatic, icy glare. She would follow this up with a mischievous wink that only Lindsay could see. If that wasn't bad enough, from the few times Lindsay had seen Warren and Cynthia together, she got the distinct impression that Cynthia wouldn't have minded consummating the sham marriage.

"Well, my actual birthday isn't until tomorrow," Lindsay said, trying to keep a note of irritation out of her voice.

"Any big plans?" Cynthia asked, clearly in no hurry to make an exit.

"I'm going out to breakfast with my dad in the morning before church, and then I'm driving to Troy to visit my mother."

"Troy, Virginia or Troy, North Carolina?" Cynthia asked.

"North Carolina."

"Oh. Does she live there?"

Lindsay nodded, her eyes locking with Warren's.

"I've got family down there, too. Near the Country Club at Seven Lakes? I wonder if they know each other?" Cynthia speculated, tilting her head to one side.

"I doubt it. She was only just transferred there," Lindsay said. She immediately realized she'd said too much. If she had known that Warren's Vegas wife was going to quiz her about her mother, she wouldn't have had so many margaritas.

"Transferred? Is she in the military?" Cynthia asked, her round, baby-doll eyes widening with interest.

"Lindsay's mother is incarcerated in the Southern Correctional Institution for Women to serve the rest of her sentence for aiding and abetting a fugitive," Warren said evenly. "I'm surprised you didn't read about it in the papers or hear about it around town." He paused and widened his eyes to mirror Cynthia's expression. "Or maybe you did, and just forgot?"

Warren wasn't given to cattiness, and passive aggression was as foreign to him as souvlaki, but Cynthia's insistent questions had clearly pushed him over the edge. Using the brief moment of silence his words engendered, he rose and removed his sunglasses from Cynthia's slackened grip. He put his hand on her back and spun her toward the door. "Thanks so much for dropping these off. I'm sure we'll see you around town."

"Bye!" Lindsay called after her.

When Warren took his seat again, Lindsay furrowed her brow and leaned her elbows on the table. "You know I'm open-minded, or, as my father lovingly says, 'one of those anything-goes liberal types,' but even I have to wonder why you had your Vegas wife drop you off at my romantic birthday dinner."

"I didn't," Warren said.

"Look, my blood is at least 30% margarita at this point, but you can't tell me that I didn't just see Cynthia Honeycutt, a.k.a. Mrs. Wannabe Warren Satterwhite, standing there."

"That was her, all right," Warren said. "But she's not my wife. Not anymore. That's why I was late. I've been trying for months to get her to do her side of the paperwork for a no-fault annulment. We needed to get sworn affidavits from all the people who were partying with us in Vegas saying that we were both too drunk to consent, and we had to show proof that we'd never cohabitated. She said she didn't want to do it because she thought it might look bad if her boss or the people at her church found out."

"How does that look any worse than marrying a stranger in Vegas?"

Warren shrugged. "You got me. Anyway, I had to promise to help her brother get out of a citation he'd been issued for not cutting the grass at his rental properties."

"Can you even do that?"

"No. The town issues those tickets, not us. I just paid the fine and hired a guy to take care of the lawns. Anyway, she's happy and it's over now. An annulment means it's gone. It's like the whole marriage never happened."

Clydetta approached them, balancing a large serving tray on her shoulder. "Get it while it's hot," she said, setting a plate in front of Lindsay.

"But we didn't even look at the menu yet," Lindsay protested. Before she could utter another word, though, she noticed that the plate was totally empty save for a small velveteen jewel box.

"Enjoy," Clydetta said, winking at Warren before she padded quietly back to the kitchen.

"Now, before you say anything," Warren began, holding up his hands to preempt any argument. "I know that the Mex-Itali isn't the most romantic place for a proposal. I know that Miss

Clydetta and all the cooks are spying on us from the kitchen. I know that that Taylor Swift song you hate is playing on the radio. But I also know that this is where we came on our first real date, and that ever since that night I was sure that I wanted you, Reverend Lindsay Harding, to be my wife." He lifted the box off her plate and opened it. A simple white gold band with a round inset diamond nestled inside. "Will you marry me?"

Lindsay stared at him, suddenly feeling as if the walls had become liquid and begun to undulate around her. She took the ring out of the box and peered at the glistening jewel. She looked back at Warren, trying to keep his expectant face in focus as the room rolled and churned. "I…" she began. "I think I'm gonna barf."

The ring clattered down onto her plate as she bolted to the bathroom, where she proceeded to heave up two and two-thirds margaritas, a basket and a half of chips, and assorted dipping sauces. Once she was certain that her whole upper digestive tract had been cleared of any trace of Italian-Mexican fusion cuisine, she removed her glasses and splashed cold water over her face. In the mirror, she could see that her hairpins had come loose at the sides. Blonde curls pinwheeled around her face and clung damply to her forehead.

A gentle knock sounded on the door, and Warren called softly, "Linds? Are you okay?"

She opened the door and leaned against the doorframe.

Warren stood there, his brow creased in an expression that mingled concern with amusement. "That's not really the reaction I was hoping for."

She smiled wanly. "Sorry. I had too much to drink, and then you kind of caught me off guard. I'm going to need a lot more warning next time you propose. Like maybe you could wear some kind of explanatory sign for a couple days beforehand?"

"You mean you're going to make me propose a third time?" Warren asked, arching his eyebrows.

"Oh. I wasn't sure if that first one counted." Over the Christmas break a few months previously, Warren had, with an almost manic urgency, asked her to marry him. The circumstances—she was headed to the hospital after narrowly escaping from a murderous psychopath—had been even less romantic than a 6 p.m. Saturday dinner at the Mex-Itali. At the time, she had feebly asked him for a rain check, and now he was apparently ready for that check to be cashed.

"You know what?" Lindsay said. "Let's definitely not count that first one. I never want to think about that night again. Let's…annul it. This is the real proposal." She leaned into his chest, burying her face and inhaling the warm soapy smell of him. He stroked her back and a very unladylike belch escaped from her lips. "Actually, maybe let's annul this one, too. Do you have any gum?"

Warren took a pack of gum out of his pocket and offered it to her. "You want to go home?"

"No, I feel fine now."

They walked back to the table and sat down. The ring still sparkled from the center of the white dinner plate. Lindsay picked it up again and slipped it on her finger.

"Is that a yes?" Warren asked, looking at her uncertainly.

Lindsay admired the ring for a moment, but then abruptly twisted it off and returned it to the plate. "Wait. What about Simmy?"

"What about Simmy?" Warren responded.

"Well, I can't ask her to move in with me and then run off to get married and leave her there alone," Lindsay said.

"I know. But I thought we could figure all that out later. We can all live in my house, if you want," Warren said.

"But all the bedrooms in your house are upstairs. She has problems with her balance. I don't think she can live in a house with stairs."

"We don't have to figure it out now, Linds. There's no rush. If you want, I'll move in with you and Simmy. Or we'll buy a bigger place all together," Warren said.

"It wouldn't be fair to have her live with newlyweds."

Warren let out an exasperated sigh. "Look, we don't have to get married tomorrow. We can wait until things with Simmy are more settled. All I'm asking is that you hitch your future to mine so that wherever you go, we go together. That's all I'm asking."

Lindsay smiled at him. "You're right. Thank you. I'm just nervous." She picked up the ring and slipped it back on her finger.

The proposal suddenly felt like a tightrope stretched out before her. She could almost picture Warren standing on the far platform, urging her across to safety and reassuring her that all she had to do to reach him was put one foot in front of the other; almost as if he were unaware of the heavy pull of gravity and the dizzying fear of heights.

"You look like you're gonna puke again. Are you sure you're okay?" Warren asked.

Lindsay nodded quickly. "I'm fine. I'm good. Great, in fact. This is great. Really, really great. Thank you." She reached out and squeezed his hand.

Clydetta's steps squished across the linoleum toward their table; again she carried the large serving tray. "Can I assume congratulations are in order?" she asked.

Lindsay nodded again. "Yes. We're going to get married."

Clydetta let out an excited squeal, rested the edge of the tray on their table, and began to lay plates in front of them. "I'm over the moon for y'all. You make a lovely couple. Look here, I brought your favorites—meatballs marinara, pinto bean lasagna, barbecue parmesan…" She paused and scrutinized the portion of lasagna. A small plastic figurine of a groom stood alone on top of it. "Now what happened to the bride?" she wondered aloud. She looked back toward the kitchen, but it was nowhere to be seen.

"Don't worry about it," Warren said. "That was real nice of you."

The mother from the other table passed them, diaper bag slung over her shoulder, baby writhing on her hip like a contortionist. Lindsay glanced at them and saw, clutched firmly in the baby's tiny fist, a miniature plastic bride. Over the mother's shoulder, Lindsay made eye contact with the baby as the infant lifted the figure to her mouth and began to gnaw on it with her small, sharp teeth.

Chapter 3

"Is my wig on straight?" Lindsay's great-grandmother folded down the sun visor in Lindsay's car and flipped the mirror open.

"You look great," Lindsay reassured her for the tenth time.

Dull, gray mist, a remnant of an earlier rainstorm, hung around Lindsay's mint green Honda Civic. It was shortly before 11 a.m. on the morning of Lindsay's thirty-first birthday, and Lindsay and Chrysanthemum "Simmy" Bennett sat in the parking lot of the Southern Correctional Institution for Women. The gigantic, yellow brick facade of the prison sprawled out before them, looking as if someone had set out to build the most architecturally uninteresting building the human mind could conceive, and then ferociously safeguard it with miles of chain link fence and unspooled razor wire.

"You sure I look all right, honey? Did I draw my eyebrows on too high? I don't want to go in there looking like a geisha girl who's just seen a ghost." Simmy scrutinized her reflection in the tiny visor mirror.

"Relax, Simmy," Lindsay said, taking the older woman's hand. "You look fine."

Simmy returned the gentle pressure of Lindsay's squeeze. "You're right. I don't know why I'm so nervous. It's a jail visitation, not the junior prom. I'm being an old ninny."

"It's normal to feel a little nervous. You haven't been out in public for a while, and visiting your granddaughter in prison isn't a very relaxing first outing."

Despite her outward reassurances, inwardly Lindsay shared some of Simmy's concerns. The elderly woman had taken a fierce beating during the same kidnapping and robbery attempt that had left Lindsay and her mother near death a few months before. Like Lindsay, Simmy had initially been paralyzed by anxiety, afraid to leave the confines of the rehab center where she'd been staying. She had only recently worked up the courage to make the visit to

Sarabelle. Lindsay wondered if Simmy would ever again be the self-reliant, age-defying octogenarian Lindsay had previously known. In place of that spry, zippy woman, the Simmy sitting next to her now was a slower, more cautious elderly lady—prone to falls, worries, and aches of unknown origin.

"Should we go in?" Simmy asked.

"They won't start letting people in until 11 o'clock on the dot," Lindsay said. "Then they'll have to do all the search and screening procedures on us."

Simmy began to drum her fingers impatiently on the door's armrest.

"We can get out and stretch our legs if you want," Lindsay offered.

"We'd better not. It's so humid." Simmy cast a surreptitious glance at Lindsay's hair, as if it were a Gremlin that might turn from soft and fuzzy to downright diabolical at the mere touch of a raindrop. Which, as it happened, wasn't too far from the truth. Simmy caught her eye and smiled, seeming to read Lindsay's thoughts. She reached up and smoothed Lindsay's curls. "You're gonna make such a pretty bride, honey. Have y'all talked about a date yet?"

"I told you we're not planning anything yet—not for a long time," Lindsay said.

Simmy raised her eyebrows, which were in fact drawn on just a smidge too high and did, in fact, give her a quizzical, geisha-like expression. Lindsay realized that her reply to Simmy's question had tumbled out of her mouth with unexpected sharpness, and she shifted her gaze to avoid Simmy's questioning look. Long accustomed to feeling her way sensitively around other people's hot button issues, Lindsay silently noted the emergence of this new hair-trigger emotional topic of her own—her engagement to Warren Satterwhite.

Simmy settled back into her seat and shifted the conversational gear into neutral. "Are you looking forward to getting back into your own house?"

"Yes," Lindsay answered, grateful that Simmy wasn't the kind of person to blunder blindly into uncertain emotional territory. "It'll be nice to sleep in my own bed again." Lindsay had spent the last three months staying with her father while the extensive renovations on her house were completed. A new addition, with a handicapped-accessible bedroom and bathroom had been built to accommodate Simmy, and all the old hardwood floors leveled out to prevent the already-wobbly older woman from falling.

"I know it must be tough for you, living at your daddy's house," Simmy said. "I really can't thank you enough for what all you're doing for me. All this upheaval!"

"I want to do it," Lindsay said, and she meant it wholeheartedly. Despite all they had been through, Simmy seemed to wake up each day determined to move steadily forward, even if those movements were slower and wobblier than they used to be. Lindsay had never known anyone so disinclined to judge others and so quick to accept people and situations as they were. When Lindsay was a child, she'd often wished that Simmy—fun-loving, affectionate Simmy—could've been her caregiver, instead of her wildly mercurial mother Sarabelle, her often-critical and sometimes-pigheaded father Jonah, or her frosty Aunt Harding. Ever since she'd found out that Simmy was in fact her long-lost great-grandmother, she'd latched onto her with both hands. Simmy returned the affection, seeming to revel in finally having real family ties.

"Still," Simmy continued, "you and your daddy haven't always seen eye to eye. It can't be easy for a grown woman to be sleeping in her childhood bed."

"Living with my dad hasn't been as bad as I thought. He's really mellowed. And it helps a lot that I'm not going out every night in a miniskirt to raise hell the way I did when I was a teenager. If anything, I feel like I'm cramping *his* style. He seems to have a very active social life."

"Is he seeing somebody?" Simmy asked, her eyes lighting up with interest.

"To tell you the truth, I wouldn't know. For a middle-aged preacher, he sure seems to have an awful lot of late night phone calls and meetings, but if I ask anything about it, he just dodges the question. Maybe he's trying to pay me back for all the sneaking around I did when I was a teenager. Anyway, I think we can tough it out for a few more days."

Simmy smiled. "I promise I'm gonna think of some way to pay you back. And I'm gonna get myself better just as soon as I can so I can get out of your hair and back to my own house."

"There's no rush. You know I'm glad to have you," Lindsay said.

"You're young, and you and Warren have got to get on with your lives. You don't need a little old lady doddering around underfoot."

"Warren loves you, too."

"Y'all are too good to me. Did you know Warren stopped in the other day with a box of Krispy Kremes for all the nurses at my rehab place? He's a sweetheart." Simmy smiled. "I don't know what I'd have done without you. Ever since the accident, I feel like I'm not myself. Everything's so caddywumpus, I don't know which end of the hog to feed."

Lindsay noticed the way Simmy used the word "accident" to describe the series of terrible events that had befallen them a few months before. It seemed an odd euphemism, but Lindsay couldn't really find the right words either. What words could describe her great aunt's violent death and the exposure of the painful secrets the old woman had tried so hard to hide? What simple phrase could sum up the savage attack that followed—an event that still made Lindsay sit bolt upright in the middle of the night and clutch her heart to keep it from pounding right out of her chest?

"Do you want to talk about it?" Lindsay asked gently. She had tried to coax Simmy into talking about those terrible days so many times she'd lost count. Talking through other people's crises and traumas had formed a large part of her chaplaincy work, and had become almost second nature to her. Following the incident with Swoopes, Lindsay herself had undergone several intense weeks of crisis counseling before she'd been able to return to work. And even in spite of receiving professional help, her emotional state had remained precarious. Simmy, by contrast, had always been the kind of person who marched relentlessly forward through life, without pausing for nostalgia or deep reflection. She'd made it clear that psychoanalysis didn't interest her in the least.

"You know, I hardly remember anything from that night, which is a blessing. I can't see why you keep wanting to hash through all that mess again. It's morbid." Simmy flipped open the visor and checked her wig again. "We've got happier things to talk about anyway, like your birthday and your wedding and moving back into your house."

Lindsay sighed. A part of her wished that Simmy would open up to her. If the older woman could share her feelings about what happened, Lindsay selfishly hoped she might at last be able to heal some of her own psychological wounds. But she'd have to resign herself to defeat on that score.

"How's Kipper doing, honey?" Simmy asked.

"Kipper's great," Lindsay answered. "He's coming to stay next weekend."

"Oh, I'd clean forgotten about that shared custody arrangement y'all have. Is that working out all right?"

"I suppose so. Kipper always has trouble settling for the first day or so when he visits me. I don't know if it's all the table scraps Tanner feeds him, or the stress of being around those weaselly little Pomeranians. And then, just as soon as he's back on track, I have to take him back there."

Lindsay's part-owned dog, Kipper, had come into her life a few months before in the most roundabout way imaginable, but he was now such a firmly entrenched part of her life she couldn't imagine being without him. The large, black-and-orange Doberman had become her most loyal companion, and had even taken a bullet trying to save Lindsay's life. The dog had originally been owned by Warren's father, but when Warren Sr. passed away, Kipper ended up in the care of Warren's sister, Tanner, and her husband, Gibb. It was never entirely clear what happened next. To hear Lindsay's mother tell it, Sarabelle had rescued Kipper from death's door after a hurricane. Tanner's version cast Lindsay's mother as a dog-napper, who used the hurricane as cover to abscond with him. Whichever version hewed closer to the truth, somehow the dog wound up living with Lindsay's great aunt and her mother on North Carolina's Outer Banks until "the accident" had left her great aunt dead and her mother in jail. Lindsay brought the Doberman back to Mount Moriah in the aftermath and reunited him with Tanner, who insisted that she was his rightful owner. Knowing how much the dog meant to Lindsay, Warren managed to negotiate a joint-custody arrangement that allowed Kipper to stay a part of her life.

"Oh, look," Simmy said, pointing excitedly. "They're letting everybody in."

Twenty-five minutes later, Lindsay and Simmy sat in the prison's waiting room, perched on the kind of butt-numbingly uncomfortable plastic chairs that seem to exist only in government buildings. They'd heard Sarabelle Harding's name called over the intercom several minutes earlier, but she had yet to emerge from the metal door that led to the prison's main living and working areas. Lindsay silently marveled that even in an environment that was regimented down to the minute, her mother still managed to be late.

At long last, the large metal door clanged open and Sarabelle emerged. They each gave her the brief hug permitted by prison policy and took their seats opposite each other.

"Honey, you look wonderful," Simmy said to her. And indeed it was true. Sarabelle had always possessed a fine-boned beauty, but in recent years, her bad habits—excessive smoking, drinking and sunbathing—had begun to catch up with her. However, an unexpected silver lining of the brutal beating she'd endured at Leander Swoopes's hands was that her facial injuries necessitated extensive surgery. The two reconstruction procedures had restored a large measure of her youthful good looks. Lindsay's mother also wore full makeup, which looked strangely at odds with her shapeless, dun-colored prison clothes.

"I been trying to make a little bit of an effort to look good, even though the only men you see in here are the guards." Sarabelle lowered her voice to a whisper. "You know I used to have a thing for men in uniform, but I swear I ain't never seen a more pig-ugly collection of the male species than what's on display here."

Simmy gave a deep, hearty laugh, but Lindsay twitched her eyes around the room, wondering if the "pig-ugly collection" had a way of eavesdropping on them and punishing Sarabelle for her comments. She had visited Sarabelle a few times during her incarceration, and had found that, just as in the outside world, she could never be sure which personality her mother would present. A few times, Sarabelle had been pathetic and needy, bemoaning the unfairness of her fate and sniffling into her sleeve like a small child. Other times, she sat with her arms tightly crossed, her face full of resentment. But usually, like today, she was the happy-go-lucky, good-time girl, determined to show that she was still having fun despite how The Universe had wronged her.

"And speaking of ugly," Sarabelle continued, "most of the girls in here could *be* men."

Sarabelle and Simmy's muffled snickers sounded nearly identical, and the same impish glow lit up their faces. Lindsay smiled, too, but she felt a familiar wall of exclusion emerging. She knew it wasn't intentional, but any time Simmy and Sarabelle got together, it became clear that while the two of them naturally surfed along on the same carefree wavelength, the more introspective, analytical Lindsay would be left dogpaddling in their wake. They were just built differently. Having grown up with only her aloof great aunt and her distracted, disciplinarian father in her life, Lindsay still found herself at sea when trying to understand the intricacies of family dynamics. It was something she'd always felt she had to study, like algebra. And as ever, she was astonished by her mother's capacity to be so totally self-centered that she failed to notice Lindsay's sparkling engagement ring, or even mention the fact that today was her only child's birthday.

When Lindsay shifted her attention back to the conversation, Simmy and Sarabelle had moved on to a new subject.

"While I'm thinking about it," Sarabelle said, snapping her fingers, "I meant to tell y'all something. I have a pen pal. You'll never guess who." She waited for a moment, allowing the suspense to build. "Christopher Sikes."

Simmy and Lindsay looked at her blankly. "Who's Christopher Sikes?" They asked in unison.

Sarabelle's eyes widened and she leaned closer, like a little girl about to whisper a secret. "Lydia Sikes's son."

"Who's Lydia Sikes?" Simmy asked.

Lindsay almost didn't hear the question, though. The sound of her own blood pumping through her body seemed suddenly deafening. Lydia Sikes's murder the previous Christmas had launched a chain reaction of terrible events. The mention of her name stiffened Lindsay's spine and caused her to grip the edge of the table for support.

"Don't you remember that woman who shacked up with Leander? The one that died?" Sarabelle said. "Well, her son, Christopher, wrote to me."

"What did he want with you?" Lindsay asked, recovering the power of speech.

"I can't be sure. His letters were real nice at first. Asked me if I was doing okay, and if they were treating me good in here. But I think that was all just buttering me up, because eventually, he got around to asking me if I knew something about where Leander might be hiding out. I wrote back and told him point blank that I hoped to God that Leander was at the bottom of the ocean, and that's the honest truth."

"Did he write again?" Lindsay asked.

"Yes, but I'm not sure he believed me." She held her hands to her chest and frowned, looking at them for sympathy, as if the idea of someone not believing a convicted felon and serial liar like her should strike them as utterly improbable. "He was still real polite and friendly, but I got the impression that he thought Leander was just waiting in the wings, and he and I would run off together as soon as I got out of here. Course I told him that I ain't seen a trace of that rat bastard since that whole mess."

"That's terrible for him to think that after what that man did to you," Simmy said.

"I know!" Sarabelle agreed.

Lindsay interrupted. "If Lydia's son followed your trial, he'd know that a big part of your defense, and the reason you got off so lightly, was that you said Leander had you under his thumb completely. And he'll also know that you stayed in touch with Leander even when he was in prison and the entire time he was living with Lydia Sikes."

"Well, that doesn't mean I'm *still* in touch with him," Sarabelle said. "There's no reason to think he's even still alive."

"No, but he's been known to go underground before when the heat was on him. And you're in prison right now, serving a sentence for helping him get and then dispose of a gun that was used to kill Christopher's mother," Lindsay said flatly. "You can see where he might get the wrong idea."

Sarabelle slumped in her chair, crossed her arms, and pouted. "Did you come all the way here just to be mean to me? I thought we were gonna have a nice visit. Can't you just try to be nice to me for once? It's your birthday, after all. We should be celebrating instead of arguing. I just wish I wasn't cooped up in here so I could've made you your favorite red velvet cupcakes. I know how much you love them."

Lindsay refused to go on her mother's guilt trip. Leave it to Sarabelle to acknowledge her birthday in such a manipulative way. "I'm not being mean," Lindsay said firmly. "I'm just wondering what he really wanted. Don't you think it's a little weird that he got in touch with you? Especially if he thinks you're in league with the man who killed his mother?"

"He's harmless," Sarabelle said, with a dismissive wave of her hand. "Poor, white trash, just like his mother. I know the type."

Lindsay raised an eyebrow, but managed to refrain from pointing out the irony of the insult, coming from a woman who'd spent the better part of her adult life living hand-to-mouth on the fringes of polite society.

"Let me know if he gets in touch again, okay?" Lindsay said. "Anything that has even the slightest connection to Leander Swoopes gives me a very bad feeling."

Chapter 4

At 10 o'clock that night, Lindsay was splayed out on her father's couch watching WWE wrestling. As if the visit with Sarabelle hadn't been exhausting enough, after Lindsay dropped Simmy off at the rehab center where she was living, she'd ended up working most of the afternoon and evening, covering a shift at the hospital for her friend and boss Rob, who had come down with a stomach virus. The afternoon had been among the most miserable she could remember—two long-time patients, including a young mother in her thirties, had died, and she'd been required to help one of the hospital's oncologists break the news to a teenage patient that his latest round of chemotherapy had failed to check the fast-growing tumors that were destroying him from the inside. While her own body might have come away from the shift unharmed, Lindsay felt like her soul had been on the losing side of a fistfight.

Although Warren had swung by the hospital briefly to bring her dinner during her shift, he was busy that night helping out with the investigation of an armed robbery case in the neighboring county. She had yet to see her father, who still wasn't home after conducting the evening service at his church. All in all, she was totally drained of energy and lacked the mental capacity to watch anything more taxing than a bunch of greased-up gym rats hurtling themselves around on a rubber mat. Neither she nor her father had had time to do the dishes that day, so she also lacked clean bowls and spoons, which meant that when the phone rang, she was eating Apple Jacks straight from the box.

Even before the word "hello" was fully out of Lindsay's mouth, Tanner's voice screeched, "You need to come and get the dog. Something's wrong with him!"

Lindsay snapped to attention, overturning the cereal box that had been perched on her lap. "Are you at the vet?"

"It's not that," Warren's sister said. "Just get over here."

Lindsay began to ask another question, but the sound of the dial tone let her know that Tanner had already hung up the phone.

When Lindsay pulled up in front of Tanner and Gibb's house twenty minutes later, Tanner immediately emerged from the front door and accosted her as she stepped out of the car.

"What took you so long?" Tanner demanded.

"Well, my dad's house is nineteen minutes' drive away from you, and it took me 60 seconds to get my keys and coat," Lindsay said irritably. "What's going on with Kipper? Is he okay?"

Tanner's coal-black eyes flashed at Lindsay. "Why didn't you tell me he'd been corrupted?"

"Corrupted?"

"Yes, corrupted. He *peed* on Ringo." Ringo was the yappiest of Tanner and Gibb's quartet of Pomeranians: John, Ringo, George and Muffin. "I let them out in the yard to do their business and I saw him lift his leg and aim right for Ringo."

"Are you sure? I mean, Kipper's a lot taller than they are. Maybe Ringo just wandered into his line of fire." At times like these, Lindsay was immensely grateful for the years of chaplaincy experience that allowed her to maintain a neutral expression even when she was talking to someone unhinged by grief, anger or, in Tanner's case, a natural tendency toward melodrama.

"This is the last straw! I've suspected that something was off with him ever since he came back. It's bad enough that him being in my house endangers my life, but since that wasn't his fault, I was willing to try to overlook it."

Lindsay leaned wearily against the hood of her car. "Tanner, please try to help me understand what we're talking about. How is the dog endangering your life?"

"Obviously, him spending six months in the company of hardened criminals was going to have an effect." Tanner's eyes darted from side to side as if to ensure that no invisible person on the totally empty street could overhear them. "But I think he might have Swedish Syndrome."

"Swedish Syndrome?" Lindsay repeated. "Do you mean Stockholm Syndrome?"

"Yeah, that thing where the kidnapped person starts to identify with the person who took them. I think he has that. Ever since he came back, he just mopes all the time. He never really played with the other dogs, but now he'll go in the bedroom and actually close the door behind him to keep them away. It's awful. They just stand there and bark and scratch and cry, like they're trying to ask their big brother what's wrong and how they can help him. But he just ignores them! And I don't like the way he looks at me lately. Like he's plotting something."

"Maybe he just got used to a quieter lifestyle when he was on the Outer Banks. It'll probably just take him a little more time to readjust," Lindsay said.

"It's been four months. If anything, he's getting worse."

"I still don't understand what you mean about him being dangerous. He'd never hurt any of us," Lindsay said.

Tanner sniffed. "How can you be so sure? He's got that big scar on his side from where he got shot. It looks just awful, and I don't like having to explain to everybody who sees him about him being kidnapped and forced to live with criminals. After all, your mother was in league with that murderer, Leander Swoopes. She was basically his Bonnie."

Once again, the sound of Swoopes's name made Lindsay almost physically sick. She swallowed hard, trying to keep her voice steady. "His Bonnie?" she asked.

"Yeah, as in Bonnie and Clyde. Your mother already stole the dog once. For all I know, she might be on the phone to Swoopes right this minute telling him to kill me so she can keep him for herself."

"Sarabelle's in jail, and will be for a long time. Swoopes is probably at the bottom of the Atlantic. Even if he's alive, there's no way that Sarabelle would be in touch with him. He tried to kill us both," Lindsay said, working hard to convince herself of something that was by no means certain. Too many times before, she had placed her trust in her mother, only to see her naïve belief torn to shreds by betrayal.

Tanner crossed her pale, freckly arms over her chest. Her skin seemed to glow in the porch light. "My mind's made up. You need to take him. Permanent." Tanner turned on her heel and led the way into the house. "I'll get his stuff packed. He's in there," she said, walking past Lindsay and gesturing to the living room.

Tanner's husband, Gibb, slumped on the couch in front of the TV. He wore a stained Carolina Panthers sweatshirt, which had inched up to reveal the pale, hairy expanse of his lower belly. With his fat-fingered paw of a hand, he shoveled cereal into his mouth straight from the box. Gibb grunted a greeting and held out the box to offer some Cap'n Crunch to Lindsay.

She held up her hand to decline. "I'm good, thanks." Casting a quick glance down at the stained Elon College sweatshirt she was wearing, Lindsay silently resolved to change into clean pajamas and wash the dishes the moment she got back to her dad's house.

Kipper lay on the floor at Gibb's feet. He looked up at her helplessly. He wore an orange and pink argyle dog sweater, and all four Pomeranians stood on and around him like Lilliputians conquering a giant.

"Hey, buddy," Lindsay said, kneeling next to him and shooing the small dogs away. Kipper rose and nuzzled Lindsay's chin as she petted him. She buried her face in Kipper's fur to hide her huge grin from Gibb. She'd endured the heartrending pain of having to return the dog to Tanner after all he'd meant to her, and now Lindsay was overjoyed that he was coming back to live with her permanently. If she'd known that all he had to do to be banished from Tanner's house was to urinate on one of those furry little dog-shaped horror shows, she would've trained him to do it long ago.

At eye level with the coffee table, Lindsay caught sight of two framed pictures sitting side by side. One showed Gibb and Tanner on their wedding day—Gibb wearing a too-small tux, while Tanner clutched his arm tightly, her Day-Glo white skin making her bridal gown look almost dingy by comparison. The other picture showed a beaming Gibb kneeling behind a dead stag, holding its head up by the antlers. Lindsay couldn't recall ever seeing such an expression of pure, unadulterated joy on his face before.

"When was this taken, Gibb? You look really happy," Lindsay said.

Gibb cast his eyes toward the door. Usually, he spoke like he was being charged by the word, mostly communicating by pointing to the things he wanted and grunting. Tanner did the talking in their relationship, and without her there, he seemed slightly unsure exactly how this whole adult conversation thing worked.

"Me and my buddies head down to Robeson County a couple times a year."

"That's right on the border with South Carolina, right?"

"Yep. Porter's brother's got a cabin down in the swamps. We hunt deer and wild pigs mostly. Sometimes we fish," Gibb said.

There was a brief silence, and Gibb seemed in no hurry to fill it. Lindsay glanced back at the photo. "That's a really huge deer."

Gibb's eyes kindled into life. "That there's a 14-pointer. Bet you never seen one that big."

"Nope," Lindsay agreed. She'd never been one for hunting, but she knew that laying around the woods and killing whatever warm-blooded animal happened across your path was akin to a religion for many Southern men. "Do you use arrows or guns?" she asked.

Gibb scoffed. "Crossbow. Guns are for sissies. Last year, I had to take out a wild boar with just my bowie knife. Damn thing got up under the blind and just jumped at me when I was climbing down. Gave me this." He rolled up his pant leg to reveal a livid, red scar across his shin. "You shoulda seen the way..." Gibb stopped speaking abruptly when Tanner entered the room carrying two overflowing sacks.

"Is he boring you with his war story about killing that pig?" she asked, rolling her eyes. "Gibb, I told you, nobody wants to see your dumb old scar."

"Not at all," Lindsay said. "I want to hear the rest of the story."

"You don't have to humor him just to be polite," Tanner said. "We're practically family. Pretty soon you and Warren will be as happy as me and Gibb. Right, baby?" She puckered up her lips and blew a kiss through the air at her husband.

Lindsay expected Gibb to show some sign of annoyance at his wife's condescension, but instead he held up his hand like a catcher's mitt and caught her imaginary kiss. He looked at Tanner with an odd sort of gratitude, as if he were a not-wholly-competent soldier whose commander had just given him clear marching orders. The dynamics of their relationship both fascinated and repelled Lindsay.

"Anyway," Tanner said, "here's all the dog stuff. I bought him a bunch of sweaters so nobody would have to look at that ugly gunshot scar all the time. There are some lighter-weight ones in there, too, for when it gets to be summer. The mesh tank top is for if he goes to the beach," Tanner said.

Lindsay rose and took hold of the bags, her movements setting off a volley of percussive barking from John, George, Ringo, and Muffin. She glanced back at Gibb, but his dull gaze was planted firmly on the TV.

***

It was nearly 11 p.m. by the time Lindsay and Kipper returned to the quiet street of small, brick bungalows where her father's house stood. As she approached the house, she saw a dark-colored sedan back out of the carport and head off toward downtown Mount Moriah. The car looked familiar, but in the darkness Lindsay couldn't make out the details clearly enough to place it.

Once inside the kitchen, Lindsay found her father, Jonah, standing at the sink and washing the dishes that had been left piled there.

"Hey, birthday girl," he said, drying his hands on a dishtowel. "I was wondering what became of you."

"There was a Kipper situation," Lindsay replied, kneeling to remove Kipper's sweater. Once free, Kipper waggled his whole body as if trying to dry himself. "I hope you don't mind having a new roommate, because it looks like he'll be a permanent fixture. Tanner's worried that he's plotting to kill her, so she sent him packing."

Jonah smiled, a network of laugh lines fanning out from his warm, brown eyes. "That's great, sweetheart. I know how much he means to you. Looks like God answered your prayers. And He did it on your birthday."

"Just like Santa." Lindsay arched toward the ceiling and gave a double thumbs-up sign to the heavens. "Thanks for the birthday dog, Big Guy."

"I'll let your new mother get away with that blasphemy because it's her birthday," Jonah said, leaning down to pat Kipper on the back.

Lindsay poured herself a glass of sweet tea from the ever-present pitcher that resided in Jonah's fridge. She jokingly referred to it as the "fishes and loaves sweet tea," because, like the miraculous meal that fed the multitude, the tea seemed to remain undiminished, though she drank it every day. She knew that Jonah replenished the supply each morning before she woke up, but she'd never yet caught him in the act.

"Was somebody here just now?" she asked. "I thought I saw a car drive away."

Jonah turned back to the sink and began rinsing a plate. "That was a parishioner."

"At 11 o'clock at night? I don't remember you having so many late-night house calls and visits when I used to live at home."

Jonah turned off the tap and pivoted around to face her. He opened his mouth to say something, but then seemed to mentally recalibrate. "Did you have a nice visit with your mother?" he asked.

"I suppose it was as nice as spending your birthday visiting your mother in prison can be," Lindsay replied.

"I'm really glad that you've patched things up with her. Your mother is your mother, no matter what she's done."

"Hold your horses," Lindsay said. "I wouldn't go as far as saying we've patched things up. Once she's back on the outside, if she can manage to go a few months without endangering my life or getting me or herself into trouble with the law, maybe we can talk about starting to make peace. It was really Simmy who wanted to go."

"Still, it was the right thing to do. People often go about their business forgetting that the Book of Matthew commands us to tend to the sick, clothe the poor, and visit those in prison."

"Well, if I swing by Goodwill to drop off all these stupid dog sweaters, I'll have done all three in one day. New Testament Trifecta!" Jonah shot her a sharp look, but she held up her hands to ward off his rebuke. "Hey, I have birthday blasphemy immunity for another 45 minutes. Anyway, you still haven't told me who was in the mystery car."

Jonah grabbed a clean plate from the drying rack and walked over to the sideboard, where a large paper box rested. Lindsay tried to see what he was doing, but he used his body to shield his actions. At last, he turned around. A large icing-covered cinnamon bun stood in the middle of the plate with a lit candle mounted on top of it.

"I asked Mrs. Bugbee to bake a special batch of nutty buns for your birthday."

"Aww, thanks, Dad," Lindsay said, holding her hair back with both her hands and puffing out the candle. "This is way better than a birthday cake."

Mrs. Bugbee, a plump, middle-aged parishioner at Jonah's church, held the secret recipe for Lindsay's favorite food of all time. Her nutty buns had won first prize at the Alamance County Fair three times and were the pride of the mid-Piedmont evangelical church bake sale circuit.

"That wasn't her dropping these off, was it? I thought she drove that huge A-Team conversion van thing."

"No, that wasn't her," Jonah said. His eyes travelled from Lindsay's face down to her hands. She was twisting her engagement ring around and around. "Is everything okay with your ring?" Jonah asked.

Lindsay looked down at her hands. "It's been really itchy all day. My skin is probably irritated from all the extra hand washing I've been doing to try to avoid catching this stomach thing that's going around."

Jonah stepped closer. "Why is your ring finger so red? Maybe you should quit messing with it."

"I guess I'm just not used to it yet," Lindsay said, closing her right hand over her left. She'd been incredibly relieved at how well Jonah had responded to the news of her engagement. Although he had never given any indication that he didn't like Warren, his natural tendency had always been to subject her potential suitors to withering examinations. She didn't want to say or do anything that might draw his scrutiny.

"So if that wasn't Mrs. Bugbee in the car, who was it?" Lindsay asked, as much to distract her father's attention as out of genuine curiosity.

Jonah lifted his Bible from the countertop, sat down at the table and folded his hands over the top of the book. The house phone began to ring, but he ignored it. When Lindsay rose to answer, Jonah gestured for her to stay seated.

"Lindsay, honey. If you're gonna get married to Warren Satterwhite, there's something we need to talk about."

Lindsay looked worriedly at the earnest expression on her father's face and then at the Bible. She involuntarily scooted her chair away from him. "Whoa, Dad. Is this going to be gross? I'm thirty-one, remember? And I've had boyfriends. Like really *had* boyfriends," she said, laying special emphasis on the word.

There was a second of silence and the phone began to ring anew. Lindsay practically vaulted up from her chair to answer it.

The caller turned out to be another of her chaplain colleagues from the hospital, Geneva Williams. Geneva had been stricken by the same virus that knocked Rob flat earlier in the day, and she'd been calling around to try to find someone to take over her shift.

"I don't even wanna ask you when you already worked all day, and with it being your birthday and all, but I can't reach nobody else. I know you and I both thought Rob was just being his usual big baby girl self when he went home, but, child, this bug ain't playing around. Seems pretty quiet here, so you can just curl up in the chaplains' room and get some sleep."

"Hmm..." Lindsay said. "I'll come in, but it sounds like I might want to avoid being in the chaplains' room if you and Rob have been there."

"No lie. Bring some bleach and a surgical mask. Maybe two surgical masks. This ain't no joke. I just threw up something I ate *last* week."

Chapter 5

The uneventful shift Geneva promised failed to materialize. In its place came a frenetic night—the aftermath of a multicar wreck tumbled into the hospital and left Lindsay splitting her time between injured patients, anxious families, and traumatized first responders. She had been exhausted even before her shift began, and it was only through sheer determination that she was able to appear to be a serene presence amidst the whirlwind of tragedy. By dawn, things had finally calmed down enough to allow her a momentary respite. Still avoiding the chaplains' room, she headed for the chapel, hoping to find a quiet place to rest her eyes. Instead, she was surprised to find Angel Bledsoe, the nurse from the geriatric ward, and another woman with a similarly sturdy build, sitting in the front row of chairs near the pulpit.

The two turned, startled, at the sound of Lindsay's entrance. When Angel recognized the chaplain, she greeted her with a wave and a heavy sigh. She turned to her companion and said, "This is who I was telling you about. The one whose grandmother needs taking care of."

"Hey," Lindsay said, extending her hand in greeting. "You must be Angel's cousin."

"Dunette Oxendine. Pleased to meet you, Reverend," Dunette said, in a voice like velvet. Her hand, when it met Lindsay's, was every bit as soft and warm as her voice. Everything about her exuded a comforting wholesomeness; she was like a chocolate chip cookie in human form.

"I've been meaning to call you and arrange a meeting, but it's been a crazy couple of days," Lindsay said.

"I suppose the fact that we're all in a hospital chapel in the middle of the night, looking like we've been rode hard and hung up wet, attests to that fact." Dunette smiled, her eyes shrinking into little crescent shapes above her round, honey-colored cheeks.

Lindsay noticed that Angel managed only the slightest of smiles in response to her cousin's good-natured joking. Her usually pristine uniform was a mass of wrinkles and her eyes were swollen with fatigue. Lindsay knew that the demands of patient care could be overwhelming—part of her job as a chaplain was to see that the hospital's staff didn't burn out under the emotional strain.

"Is everything okay?" Lindsay asked her. "Don't you usually work the day shift?"

"Dunette's here to take me home. I was too tired to drive. We were just offering up a prayer for poor old Mr. Meeks before we go," Angel replied. "He passed on."

"I'm sorry to hear that," Lindsay said, remembering the white-haired man who'd been wrapped tight in her sweater only a few days before. "What happened?"

"Just one of those things. He'd been fighting kidney infections off and on for a long time, but we had it under control before the knee operation. Labs looked clean as a whistle. But it had started to flare up again a few days ago. We thought we had it licked, but it just grabbed ahold of him and wouldn't let go. Got into his blood. By the time I got in this morning, he'd already been moved to the ICU. I called his son to tell him what was going on. His car couldn't make the trip, so he had to catch a bus up from Georgia and couldn't get here until later. He asked me to stay with his daddy until he got here so he'd have a familiar hand to hold. So I stayed."

"She's been here since 8 o'clock yesterday morning," Dunette said, stroking Angel's hand.

"You must be exhausted. Did his son make it in time to say goodbye?" Lindsay asked gently.

"Yes. He got here about an hour ago, and Mr. Meeks passed on not 20 minutes later. It's probably a blessing for him to go downhill so quick, you know? All three of us have seen enough to know what it gets like with these dementia patients toward the end."

Lindsay was quiet for a moment, allowing space for their shared sadness. Death was rarely pretty, but she had to agree with Angel that the way dementia could rob a person's humanity with such cruel relentlessness was especially terrible to behold.

"Should I go up and check on Mr. Meeks's son? Is he still here?" Lindsay asked.

"That might be nice. He was going to stop upstairs to pick up his daddy's things from the nurses' station. It all happened so fast they didn't even get a chance to bring it down for him. You might catch him if you go now. I'm just gonna stay here for another minute."

Lindsay promised to get in touch with Dunette about the home health care job later that day, and then headed up to the geriatric department. The ward was unusually quiet, and the lights had been dimmed to give the patients a better chance of catching whatever fleeting moments of sleep were possible in the hospital. The nursing station was empty and Mr. Meeks's son was nowhere to be seen. At the far end of the hall, she could see a nurse fiddling with the wires on an ECG machine. He didn't seem to notice her, so Lindsay leaned heavily against the desk for a moment and closed her eyes.

"Is that you?" A raspy voice cut through the stillness. Lindsay's eyes flew open. She looked around, but saw no one. "I'm talking to you, preacher lady," the voice said. Lindsay pivoted around and saw an enormous mountain of a man filling the dark doorway of what had been Mr. Meeks's room. He leaned heavily on the door handle with one hand and the frame of a walker with the other.

"Mr. Boughtflower?" Lindsay ventured uncertainly. Although Angel had told her the man whose voice she'd heard behind the curtain was gravely ill, Lindsay had expected someone with Boughtflower's vast wealth to possess the sleekly polished look that money often enabled. The man standing before her, however, looked like a city that had been brought down by an earthquake—an immense ruin. Brittle, jaundiced skin covered his body. His enormous belly hung in front of him like an ill-fitting apron.

Boughtflower nodded and gestured for Lindsay to follow him into his darkened room. He turned his walker away from her and headed back toward his bed. Lindsay gave a quick, almost involuntary glance around her, but no one was in sight. Boughtflower listed slightly to one side and Lindsay rushed forward to steady him, but before she even touched him, he swatted her away as one might shake off a buzzing insect. She took a step back and allowed him to make his way across the room unaided. The only sounds that filled the space were the rattle of his breathing and the muffled scrape of his walker against the linoleum. After several minutes of hard work, he reached his bed and settled onto it. With his hands, he physically lifted each of his tree-trunk legs from the floor onto the mattress. He lay there a moment, staring at Lindsay, his huge chest heaving, eyes bright from exertion.

"Shut the door. I feel a draft," Boughtflower said.

Lindsay paused for a moment. The idea of closing herself into a room with this man filled her with revulsion. Her reluctance wasn't simply a reaction to his vast, disintegrating body. Rather, a creeping pinprick of anxiety, a feeling that she was being lured into danger, caused her to hesitate. This shapeless dread had dogged her for months, and she inwardly berated herself for letting her outsized worries about Leander Swoopes control her. Boughtflower could barely move. There was certainly nothing he could do to harm her.

She shut the door with a soft click. With the door closed, the room was thrown even deeper into shadow. Lindsay's hand moved to the light switch, but Boughtflower stopped her.

"Leave it," he demanded. "The light hurts my eyes."

"How did you know who I was?" Lindsay asked. "Have we met before?"

"I heard you passing by. Recognized your squishy shoes," Boughtflower told her.

"Oh," Lindsay said, making her way to the chair next to Boughtflower's bed. "Did I wake you?"

He ignored her question and continued, "Hope you're not looking for him." He jerked his thumb toward Mr. Meeks's empty bed.

"No. I heard what happened," Lindsay replied. "I was looking for his son. I wanted to check that he was all right."

"He already left. One of the nurses walked him down to the lobby."

"Do you want to talk about anything…?" When Lindsay was working, this was a question that she asked a dozen times a day, but now it came out of her mouth with unaccustomed timidity. Something was clearly on Boughtflower's mind for him to summon her into his room, especially given his vehement dismissal of her a few days prior. And yet his continued posture—an almost menacing hostility—made her question just what, if anything, he planned to share with her.

"Lucky bastard got off easy, if you ask me." Boughtflower had a husky smoker's voice, and when he spoke, his mouth revealed a set of bright-white dentures that glowed in the dim light like highway reflectors.

"Oh?"

"Yeah, Meeks had nothing going on upstairs." He tapped his temple with his index finger. "Not a care in the damn world. Yesterday afternoon, he was eating vanilla pudding and laughing his head off at Howdy Doody."

Without warning, a coughing fit seemed to bubble up from somewhere deep within Boughtflower's body. For several moments, his whole body shook with violent spasms of coughing. Lindsay instinctively reached toward him, but he waved her away. After the coughing finally subsided, Boughtflower wiped the beads of sweat that had formed on his face and placed an oxygen tube that had been lying next to him under his nose, hooking it around his ears.

Lindsay waited for Boughtflower to say more, but when it became clear that he didn't plan on adding anything else, she spoke again. "Mr. Meeks did go quickly."

"I heard you praying with him the day before yesterday. He didn't even ask forgiveness for anything. Like he hadn't ever done anything to be sorry for. Or maybe he had, but he'd already forgotten," Boughtflower said bitterly.

"Well, Mr. Meeks didn't know he was dying. And even if he had, who's to say whether he would've prayed any differently?"

"Maybe it wasn't anything he did directly, but sins he carried with him."

Boughtflower's words were dripping with a hidden meaning. Lindsay, however, was still mystified about what that meaning might be.

"People have lots of different ideas on how to apologize and who to ask for forgiveness," she said, looking at him for some reaction that would help her understand his urgency and vehemence. "Some people pray. Some people talk to a minister or confess to a loved one. Some go straight to the people they think they've wronged and ask their forgiveness, or do good deeds to try to outweigh the bad. Others don't think any of that is necessary."

Boughtflower pounced on this last statement. "They're fools then. I know enough to know that if you take sins with you when you die, nobody can save you from punishment."

The old man again lapsed into bitter silence.

"Is something on your mind, Mr. Boughtflower? God's very good at forgiveness. You could say that it's an area of special expertise," Lindsay said.

His eyes darted around the room, seeming unable to focus on her face. "I've decided to do something good, something to save my family, maybe something that'll even help me when I go to meet my maker. I need your help seeing it through."

"Me?" Lindsay asked.

"I heard Meeks say you're the preacher from the news, so I had my granddaughter look you up on the computer. Is it true? That you got the better of that crook, Swoopes?"

"I suppose it is. Mostly I got lucky."

"That's not how it sounded on the news," Boughtflower said. "It sounded like you're somebody who can do what needs to be done. And you're a minister, so you won't tell nobody nothing about it."

"I'm happy to help in any way I can."

"I made a will that'll give all the money away when I go. All of it. They don't know about it, but I'm telling you it's for their own good. I want you to see that it gets done how I want it. The lawyer said the will was all copacetic, but he's a *lawyer*." He invested the word "lawyer" with such disdain that it came out of his mouth like a curse. "I need somebody with no skin in the game, somebody tough, to make sure it gets done exactly like I say. That's you." He pointed a stubby finger to Lindsay's chest.

"I'll try, Mr. Boughtflower, but from my experience it's better not to leave behind surprises for your loved ones to find after your death. It can be confusing and painful. If it helps, I can set up a time for you to talk with your daughter and her family about your wishes."

46

"You don't understand," he said, with growing intensity. "We hid the body. The money belonged to everyone, but we stole it for ourselves. I've been wrong. I've done wrong. My whole life, it's weighed me down. You gotta help me give it back before it's too late. If I don't stop this, that money's gonna drag us all straight down to hell." As he spoke, Boughtflower reached out and grabbed Lindsay's thin wrists. The pressure of his grip was like a vice, a burning vice.

"I don't understand what you mean. What body?"

"Just do this," he growled.

Lindsay shook her arms free and put her hand out to touch Boughtflower's forehead. "You're burning up with fever, Mr. Boughtflower. I need to get the nurse." She reached out and pressed the nurse call button on the bedrail.

"Promise me," the old man wheezed. Another coughing fit seized him, and, as he choked and struggled for breath, further conversation became impossible. The nurse rushed in to help him, and quickly summoned more medical personnel for assistance. As doctors and nurses rushed in, Lindsay was pushed back toward the door. Even as she left, she knew it would be a long, long time before she'd be able to forget the vivid intensity of Otis Boughtflower's eyes as he lay gasping on his hospital bed.

Chapter 6

"You've got to be kidding me." Lindsay emerged from her car and circled to the passenger's side to inspect her tire. She'd finished her nightmarishly long double shift and was still reeling from Boughtflower's strange confession about hiding a body and stealing money. He was by no means the first patient she'd tended to who felt the crushing weight of remorse and fear as the end of life drew near. But he was definitely the first who'd confessed to being involved in hiding a dead body. She'd already done a quick internet search on her phone to see if he'd ever participated in any kind of crime that could explain his statement, but found nothing. Now, as she was finally heading home, she felt the telltale drag of a flat tire as she backed out of her parking space. Sure enough, the rubber of her right front tire clung limply to the rim.

She hobbled the car into an open space and popped the trunk open to remove the spare. She hadn't changed a tire in more than a decade and wasn't looking forward to the prospect of doing so in the hospital parking lot at 20 minutes past 7 a.m. on a Monday morning. She called AAA—the membership was a standing Christmas present from her father—but the dispatcher who answered told her it'd be at least an hour before a mechanic could get to her. Next, she put in a call to Warren. He picked up on the first ring.

"Hey," he said. "How was your shift?"

"If I were ranking all chaplain shifts in the universe, ever, it would be runner-up in the Weirdness category and definitely in the top ten for Suckiness," she replied grimly. "You know it's bad when you're actually jealous of your colleagues who are home with a stomach virus."

"Sorry to hear that," Warren said. "Why don't you get some sleep, and I'll pick you and Kipper up after work tonight. We can sit on my couch and share a pizza."

"I was hoping I could see you sooner," Lindsay said. "Like right now, for example. You'd look awfully sexy lying on the ground changing my flat tire."

"'Fraid I can't. I'm on my way out to Lake Cammack to check out a burned out truck. Do you want me to send Vickers over to give you a hand? He was just eating his first Croissan'wich of the day when I left the station."

Freeland Vickers was the longest-serving member of the New Albany force. From everything Warren told her, Lindsay was fairly certain his long law enforcement career could be attributed to the careful way in which he conserved his energy by never doing anything that wasn't absolutely required.

"No, thanks," Lindsay sighed. "Triple-A will probably be here before Vickers even finishes his coffee. I'll give it the old college try, and when I inevitably make it ten times worse, I'll hide all the tools and tell the triple-A guy it was like that when I found it."

"Good plan," Warren laughed.

"Probably not what Jesus would do, but there's surprisingly little biblical guidance on saving face in front of a car mechanic."

"Text me later so I'll know you made it home. And call me if you change your mind about Vickers."

"Aye-aye," she said. "I'll see you tonight. As a matter of fact, we might even be able to have our pizza-and-couch time at my house. The final inspection is supposed to be this afternoon." She paused. "Hey, if you have time today, can you use your fancy policeman skills to look into something for me? You know Otis Boughtflower, the sock factory guy I told you about? I think he may have confessed to a murder and robbery."

"What? It seems like everybody would've heard about something like that."

"I know," Lindsay said. "He had a really high fever when I talked to him, so maybe he was delirious. But he seemed pretty convinced it happened."

"I'll see what I can find out," Warren said. "Maybe something happened when he was still a juvenile. Sometimes even serious crimes used to be swept under the rug if the family was well connected."

49

Lindsay signed off and let out another deep sigh. She shifted the stacks of papers, pairs of running shoes, and other detritus that littered the trunk, flipped open the trunk floor and began trying to heave the spare out of its resting place. It didn't budge.

"Need a hand?"

Lindsay spun around. She'd been vaguely aware of the sleek, silver Mercedes pulling up alongside her, but she'd been too engrossed in her task to notice the driver rolling down his window and leaning out to offer his assistance.

"Uh, sure. I'm usually a do-it-yourself kind of gal, but I seem to have fallen at the first hurdle here." She gestured to the spare, still firmly wedged in its holding well.

The man turned off his engine and got out of the car. He was so absurdly handsome that Lindsay almost laughed out loud—chiseled jaw, wavy black hair, tanned skin, and sparkling eyes the color of cinnamon sticks. Almost literally a knight in shining armor, though in his case, his "armor" was a $40,000 car. Lindsay had an odd, fleeting thought that he and Otis Boughtflower's haughty granddaughter would have impossibly beautiful children.

The man extended his hand. "Adam Tyrell."

"I'm Lindsay Harding. This is so nice of you. But before you do anything—full disclosure: I have Triple A coming in about 45 minutes. But in my experience, that could mean anything from an hour to next Thursday, and I'm really impatient."

He smiled the kind of smile that probably caused susceptible women to fall into a dead faint. Even Lindsay found her knees going a little weak. "I consider myself warned." He rolled up his sleeves as he spoke, revealing well-muscled forearms. He leaned over the trunk and said, "Here's the first problem. The toolkit has fallen back here. See? That's why you were having so much trouble getting the tire out." Once he removed the tool kit, he easily lifted the tire to the ground.

Lindsay squatted next to Adam and took on the role of operating theater nurse, handing him tools as needed. "So," she said, "what brings you to the hospital at this hour of the morning?"

"I'm visiting my mother. She had an operation a few days ago."

"Visiting hours don't start until eight," Lindsay said, cringing as she realized how pedantic she must've sounded.

"I know," Adam replied, loosening a wing nut on the flat tire. "I was going to get a cup of coffee first."

"Ah, yes. Our cafeteria does serve the finest horrible coffee in Mount Moriah. People who like ashtray-flavored coffee come from as far away as Greensboro. It's a Mecca."

"You're funny," he said. The way he said it sounded more like a scientific observation than a compliment or an expression of amusement.

"Sorry."

"Why are you apologizing for being funny?" Adam asked, an amused twinkle creeping into his eyes.

"Oh." She paused and thought for a moment. "Humor is kind of a thing I do when I'm nervous or upset or, you know, babbling incoherently to the man who is helping me change my tire."

She'd spent a lot of time during her chaplaincy training analyzing the way she automatically reacted to stressful, upsetting, or emotional circumstances with wisecracks. She also frequently found herself fighting the urge to say something—anything—in situations where silence would be a better response. Try as she might to cultivate the Zen persona she associated with being a perfect chaplain, more often than not, she found herself relating more to Bozo than to Buddha.

"Well, you don't have to apologize. A good sense of humor is the quality I seek out more than anything else in a woman. I can handle short, tall, curvy, skinny, but I can't stand boring women." He gestured to her engagement ring, which she had involuntarily begun to fidget with again. "But I see that you're already spoken for."

She looked down at her ring, a deep crimson blush rising in her cheeks. "So, your mother had an operation? What's her name?" Lindsay asked.

He turned back to his work. "Valerie. Why do you ask?"

"I just wondered if maybe I knew her. I'm a chaplain here. I visit with a lot of patients, and I thought I might have seen her."

"We're not religious."

It was the kind of thing people often said when they found out Lindsay's vocation. She had long ago stopped being bothered by it, but often found herself, as now, worrying that others might be bothered by thinking that she might be bothered.

"So, do you live around here?" she asked.

"No. In fact, I've been working in Germany and Slovakia for the past three years. I just flew over to make sure Mother gets settled all right back at home."

"Wow. All the way from Europe. That's awfully nice of you."

She stole a glance sideways at his face. Has a cool European job, loves his mother, can change a tire, drives an expensive car, and possesses *that face*. Surely this guy must be an axe murderer. Or, given her track record, secretly gay. As she stared at the finely-honed angle of his jaw and his plump, sensuous lips, she had to forcibly remind herself that she was betrothed. And that he was way out of her league.

"Least I can do," Adam said. "She's the only family I have." He rolled the flat tire towards her. "Just lean that against the trunk. I can put it away."

She took hold of the tire and began to roll it towards the back of the car. Adam noticed her stop suddenly.

"What's the matter?" he asked.

"Nothing," Lindsay shook her head. "Well, actually, something. Do you see this? I didn't really look at it before. I just assumed I ran over a nail or something, but look. It looks like it's been slashed." A neat, almost surgically-precise, three-inch gash ran along one side of the tire.

"Huh," he said, moving his fingertips over the cut. "That is weird. Who'd do that to a chaplain? Do you have a psycho ex-boyfriend or something?"

She smiled tightly, as the memory of Leander Swoopes's cruel eyes flashed in front of her. "Something like that."

Chapter 7

"Thanks for coming today. I know you probably had a rough time with having to come out in the middle of the night to pick Angel up," Lindsay said.

Lindsay had tried to fall asleep when she arrived back at her father's house after her shift that morning, but found that her brain refused to disengage. After tossing and turning for more than an hour, she got out of bed and called Dunette Oxendine, arranging to meet her at Simmy's rehab facility for an interview. Now, the three women sat around a small, round table in the facility's day room, sipping a beverage purported to be hot chocolate.

"I feel fresh as a daisy," Dunette said in her soothing, honey-drenched voice. "If there's one thing I'm used to, being a home health aide, it's getting up in the middle of the night."

"Is Angel feeling better? She seemed pretty upset last night," Lindsay said.

"Well, she looks like ten miles of bad road right now, but she'll perk up. She's seen more than her share of dying, but it never really gets easier, does it?"

The three women were quiet for a moment before Simmy broke the silence. "Enough about death. I'm proud of Lindsay for the work she does, but if you ask me, she's too gloomy for such a young person. Hell, even if she were as ancient as I am, she'd still be too damn gloomy. I forbid the mentioning of death when I'm around. Since I'm the reason for this whole operation, from now on I vote we stick to my approved topics: men, liquor, and men." She smiled affectionately at Lindsay and then turned her attention to Dunette. "So, you're from Pembroke, honey?"

"Are we allowed to talk about where we're from?" Lindsay teased.

"Yes," Simmy said with a chuckle. "I'll make a special allowance for getting acquainted talk. And we can also talk about other peoples' business, especially when the gossip is juicy."

"Well then, since I have your permission, yes, I'm originally from Lumberton, but I was living in Pembroke," Dunette said. "Moved up here to take the job with Boughtflower."

"What do you make of Mount Moriah so far?" Lindsay asked.

"To tell the truth, I was afraid it'd be one of them backwoods places full of white folks who got more tattoos than teeth," she laughed. "But it's all right. I can live with Angel to save on rent, and I been taking classes at the community college to try and get into a nursing program. Not much else to do here, but there wasn't much to do in Robeson County, either."

"Still," Simmy said, "it must've been hard to leave your family behind."

"Not much family left to leave. All the older folks are dead, and I don't have children. And to tell the truth, it was good for me to get away and make a fresh start." She sighed. "I'm always up front with the people I work for, so you might as well hear it now. I haven't always walked on the straight and narrow. When you do a background check on me, you'll see that I did time a few years ago. You see, I got involved with the wrong man and did some stupid things. We smuggled cigarettes between North Carolina and New York. We'd buy them here for cheap and then sell them to bootleggers in the city. I drove the van. When we got caught, I spent two years locked up at the Southern."

"My granddaughter—Lindsay's mama—is locked up there, too," Simmy said, sounding as delighted as if she'd just found out she and Dunette came from the same hometown.

Dunette raised her eyebrows. "Usually when I tell folks about that they look at me like I got the plague."

"Well, you're in good company," Lindsay said wryly.

"I'm sorry for that." Dunette said, laying her warm hand on top of Lindsay's. "That's hard on a child."

"Prison isn't easy on anyone," Lindsay replied.

"I made a lot of mistakes in my life, but I've learned a lot, too. I promise that if you hire me, I'll work hard and do right by you because I know I need to be grateful to those who are willing to overlook what I done in the past. I got good references from all those who were willing to take a chance on me. I've paid my debt to society, and now I just want a fresh start. I spent a long time feeling resentful and blaming my ex-husband for getting me mixed up in all that mess. But I realize now you can't blame other people for your choices."

"Don't be too hard on yourself, honey," Simmy said consolingly. "Half the women in that place are in there for getting mixed up with the wrong man. I know that's the case with Sarabelle anyway. Men—and one man in particular—led her astray."

"Do you really think Sarabelle doesn't deserve the blame for ending up where she is?" Lindsay said.

Normally she would've nodded in agreement, especially when discussing her mother in front of a stranger, but the lack of sleep seemed to have made her pricklier than usual. She'd grown up with her father constantly making excuses for her mother's shortcomings and bad behavior, and now that he was finally moving on, Lindsay felt like he'd passed his blinders over to Simmy.

"She had a hard life. Give her some slack. If her own family can't give that to her, who will?" Simmy countered.

"Because of her choices, I had a hard life, too," Lindsay said, more irritably than she intended. "You don't see me in prison, though."

Simmy stared at her silently. The old woman's face seemed to have caved in suddenly—hollow cheeks, wide eyes, slack mouth.

"I'm sorry, Simmy," Lindsay said quickly, casting her eyes down in shame. "I didn't mean to be so sharp."

Lindsay found, inexplicably, that she was almost on the verge of tears. Every time she thought she'd faced down all the demons of her childhood, they proved that they were simply lurking just below the surface. Her parents had been arrested when she was still a young child, and she'd grown up with her aloof great aunt in a loveless home on North Carolina's Outer Banks. Even after her parents' release, her mother's mercurial presence and frequent, painful absences, had been a constant source of sorrow for Lindsay.

During the process of training to become a chaplain, psychological wounds like this were dragged to the surface, examined, and laid out to bleach in the sunlight of self-awareness.

But Lindsay always felt that somehow she'd slipped through training by making the right noises. Like she had been able to hum along with the choir, but she had never learned to read the sheet music.

"It's probably a bit of both for some people," Dunette said, diplomatically. "Like some folks can eat Twinkies all day long and be okay, and other ones get diabetes if they do it. Some women just go toward that kind of man and then lose all their sense. I think you're right, that you do have to try to cut people some slack as much as you can, but you also can't ignore it when they do wrong. Lord knows it's hard to know when to forgive, and when to say enough's enough. Especially when it comes to family."

As usual, Simmy was able to brush away the unpleasant atmosphere without missing a beat. "Lindsay tells me you used to work for an older gentleman?"

"Yes, ma'am. Mr. Boughtflower."

"How long were you with him? Did you get to know him well?" Simmy asked.

"As well as you can know somebody who doesn't want to be known. Sometimes, I become good friends with the people I work for, but Mr. Boughtflower wasn't the being friends type. He liked to keep things professional."

"And his family? Do you know them well?" Lindsay said.

"I got to know his daughter, Margo. She was always nice to me."

"Did she and Mr. Boughtflower get along?" Lindsay asked. She was trying to get to the bottom of his strange comments during the night, but without directly asking a question like, "*So, did he ever mention stealing from somebody and then getting rid of their corpse?*"

Simmy looked slightly confused by Lindsay's line of questioning, but Dunette answered immediately, as if she expected a certain degree of nosiness from potential employers. "I don't want y'all to think I gossip about the people I work for," she said.

"Now, now, gossip is one of the acceptable topics," Simmy said.

Dunette smiled, but hesitated.

"Sorry, I didn't mean to pry," Lindsay said. "I spoke to Mr. Boughtflower yesterday and he said a few things about his family that made me curious about them."

"Well, since you're a minister and all, I expect you won't be blabbing all over town. It seemed to me that Margo caught the worst end of Boughtflower's temper. Not directly, mind you, but she was always trying to get in between her daddy and her husband. She seemed to take it as her lot in life, though, like she'd been born to suffer. She was the same with her husband and daughter. Spent all day at everybody's beck and call, and I never once heard a please nor a thank you from any of them."

They all sipped their drinks for a moment, grimacing at the chalkiness of the powdered hot chocolate mix.

"It's no wonder they offer this stuff for free," Lindsay said, sticking her tongue out. "I don't know why I always drink it, even though I know better."

Simmy laughed. "All the food in here is supposed to be low salt and low fat. I once asked one of the cafeteria workers how they can even make cocoa with no milk or chocolate in it. She just winked at me and said it was an old family recipe."

"Who's her family? The Witches of Salem?" Dunette said. When their laughter died down, Dunette asked. "Is there anything else y'all want to ask me?"

Lindsay looked at Simmy, who flashed a smile and gave a quick nod.

"Just one more question," Lindsay said. "Can you start next week?"

***

The way back to her father's house from the rehab center led straight past the home Lindsay's friend Anna and her new husband, Drew, had just moved into. Anna was out in front of the house, digging what looked like a long trench in the front yard.

Lindsay pulled her car into the driveway and hopped out. "Preparing for the Battle of the Somme?" she asked, gesturing to the ditch.

Anna forced the shovel into the ground where it was left standing straight up like a fence post. She wiped her hands on her jeans and walked over to Lindsay. "We have a groundhog."

"And your plan is what? To unearth it and beat it to death with your shovel?" Lindsay asked, frowning.

"I hadn't totally thought it through, but yeah, something like that. This whole homeownership thing is way harder than I thought. Planting a garden was supposed to be this wholesome thing, but there's nothing wholesome about how I feel right now. What the deer don't eat, they trample. What the deer don't eat or trample, the rabbits eat or trample. And now this damn groundhog digs up the yard we just paid $500 to aerate and reseed. I'm gonna put his little head on a spike as a warning to the others." She suddenly stopped talking and her expression transformed from anger to angst. "Oh crap! I haven't even congratulated you in person yet on your engagement!" She hugged Lindsay and began to sniffle. "I can't believe you're getting married and we haven't even celebrated yet. We were going to invite you two over for dinner. And it was your birthday, and I was so busy at work I forgot to call. I'm such a terrible friend."

"Um, Anna," Lindsay said, her brow furrowing. Anna was a top athlete, an ER doctor, and a serial perfectionist. Now, however, her usual calm, unflappable demeanor seemed decidedly flapped. "Are you still doing those fertility hormone shots?"

Anna wiped away a mixture of sweat and tears, smearing dirt across her cheek in the process. "I'm a hot mess, aren't I? I don't know how much longer I can do this. Drew's afraid to even come home. He's started calling me from the driveway to make sure it's safe to come inside."

Anna and Drew desperately wanted a baby, and because Anna had recently celebrated her forty-first birthday, she had started hormone injections in the hope it would boost her chances of conceiving.

"Why don't you come in?" Anna said. "You should have some champagne to celebrate your birthday and engagement. I'm not supposed to drink to help my chance of conceiving, not that it matters anyway since my ovaries are so ancient they should be in the Smithsonian."

"I'm sorry you're going through this, Anna," Lindsay said, squeezing her friend's arm.

"Don't get all chaplain-y on me. You'll make me start crying again," Anna replied, swatting her hand away.

"Fine," Lindsay said. "I'll get drunk and then we can come out here and beat up some innocent forest creatures together."

"Innocent?! After I planted twenty hydrangea bushes because the guy at the garden center told us 'deer don't eat hydrangeas'?"

"You're right. Let's get these furry bastards. You hear that, Groundhog?" Lindsay yelled toward the trench. She grabbed hold of the shovel and held it up like a maniacal villager wielding a pitchfork. "You better run or we're gonna put you six feet under ground." She placed her knuckle against her bottom lip thoughtfully. "Actually, he'd probably like that."

When they walked into the house, Lindsay saw Anna's teenage nephew, Owen, framed in the light of the fridge door. When Lindsay had first met him only a few months before, the seventeen-year-old had seemed stretched out, so tall and thin he looked like a rubber band about to snap. Back then, his tight halo of dreadlocks had reminded her of the feathers on the end of a long-handled duster. Over the past few months, however, he'd filled out into a muscular and handsome young man. As evidence of this transformation, whenever Lindsay had seen him out in public lately, he was trailed by a procession of moony-eyed, teenage girls and preening boys who wanted to be seen alongside him.

"Hey, Owen," she said. "I saw your car out front."

"Oh, hey, Lindsay," Owen replied. He turned to face her, balancing a bowl of fruit salad, a container of hummus, and a pitcher full of lemonade in his arms. He closed the fridge door with his knee as he set the food out on the counter. "We just stopped by on our way home from school."

Since Owen and his father, Mike, had relocated to Mount Moriah a few months previously, the boy had become a constant fixture in Anna and Drew's house. Almost every time Lindsay visited, Owen could be found draped over a sofa, or with his homework sprawled on the dining room table or, like today, rummaging in the kitchen for snacks.

"Okay if we take this stuff into the living room, Anna?" he asked.

"Sure, but you know where the Dust Buster is. Pita chips leave crumbs. Crumbs do not put me in a happy place."

"Who's 'we'?" Lindsay asked after Owen was out of earshot.

"Just the latest girl who is 'definitely not his girlfriend,' despite the fact that they spend every waking minute together. This one's a real piece of work. Owen's trying to play it cool, but it's obvious that she has him wrapped so tight around her finger, I'm surprised he isn't cutting off her circulation."

"Oh! Speaking of fingers, can you put on your doctor hat and look at mine? I meant to get one of the docs to look at it during my shift yesterday, but I never got the chance." Lindsay held out her hand for Anna to inspect. Her ring finger was so raw and blistered that it looked like it had been burned. It had now moved beyond merely itching to a constant, intense throbbing. "It got really swollen and now I can't budge my engagement ring."

Anna leaned over her friend's hand. "Jesus, Linds. This is one of the worst topical nickel reactions I've ever seen. How did you not notice that your finger looks like something that crawled out of a swamp in a horror movie? Why didn't you just take if off when this started?"

"It was kind of gradual. The ring was kind of tight to begin with, and my hands are always so dry and cracked from the constant hand washing and sanitizing at the hospital."

"This is really bad," Anna said, filling a basin with ice water and handing it to Lindsay. "Here. Soak." Anna left the room and returned a moment later with some dental floss and Vaseline. "Didn't you know you were allergic to nickel? It's a really common amalgam in gold jewelry."

"The only jewelry I ever wear is those silver hoop earrings my dad gave me for my graduation," Lindsay said.

Owen came back into the kitchen along with a stunningly beautiful girl that Lindsay immediately recognized as Jess, Otis Boughtflower's granddaughter.

"We're gonna head out, Anna," Owen said.

"Hi, Jess," Lindsay said. "Do you remember me? We met in the hospital chapel a few days ago."

Jess regarded her as if she were a long-lost bosom friend. "Of course!" She turned to Owen. "Reverend Lindsay was so sweet to me when I was upset about Grandpappy the other night."

"I heard your grandfather's doing a little better today," Lindsay said, not quite certain how to respond to Jess's over-the-top friendliness. "How are you doing with it all?"

Jess locked eyes with hers. For a moment, Jess's lower lip trembled, and Lindsay thought she might cry. But instead she broke into her radioactive smile. "How sweet of you to even worry about me. You're just the sweetest. Isn't she sweet, Owen?" She briefly rested her fingers on his arm when she spoke.

Owen nodded enthusiastically, unconsciously touching the place on his arm where her fingers had just been.

"Well, that settles it then. Lindsay is, in fact, *the sweetest*," Anna said. "She's so damn sweet, sometimes my pancreas feels inadequate in her presence."

Lindsay glared at her.

"What's going on with your hand?" Owen asked, gesturing to the bowl of ice water in which her fingers were submerged.

"I'm allergic to my engagement ring," Lindsay replied.

"Oh," Jess said, her amber eyes widening. "That's probably a sign." She flashed her sparkling white teeth at Lindsay, and then called over her shoulder. "Come on, Owen."

Jess breezed out of the room with Owen trailing behind her like an obedient dog.

"See what I mean about them?" Anna said. "Mike's convinced that she only hangs out with Owen to get rides in his car and piss off her father. Apparently he doesn't like her dating Owen. The guy's really old fashioned."

"Is her dad some kind of weird religious nut or something? Preventing seventeen and eighteen-year-olds from dating in this day and age seems beyond old fashioned," Lindsay said.

"Oh, did I say he was 'old fashioned'? I mispronounced that. I meant 'racist asshole.' From what I gather, the idea of Jess having a mixed-race boyfriend really gets to him."

"Maybe she's with Owen because she likes him. He's a great kid."

Anna frowned. "Hard to tell. You should see them together. It's all, 'Owen, I really wanted a Coke Zero. All they have is Diet Coke.'" Anna imitated Jess's imperious manner with perfect precision. "Before you know it, he's hit every grocery store in Alamance County to find what she wants. If that's how she treats someone she likes, I can't imagine how she treats her enemies."

"I definitely wouldn't want to be on her bad side."

"Looks like you don't have to worry then, because you're so darn sweet," Anna said with a smirk. "Okay, let's see that Cracker Jack ring of yours."

"You know what's weird? I helped Warren take his wedding ring off when we first met. His Vegas ring from Cynthia had gotten stuck on his finger. Maybe Jess was right that this is some kind of a sign."

Anna wound the floss around Lindsay's finger, compressing the swollen tissue just above the ring. "A sign of what? That you guys need to invest in hypoallergenic metal alloys? You can't seriously be taking relationship advice from that prissy paper doll."

"No, I mean maybe this is all too rushed," Lindsay said. "I threw up when he proposed. Did I tell you that? And now my skin is literally rejecting the ring. Maybe my subconscious is using my body to tell me this isn't right."

"Cast your mind back a few months. Remember when I was freaking out before my wedding, and you calmed me down and told me to quit trying to ruin a good thing? I'd give you that talk now, but it's probably easier if you just remember what you said and replace all the 'Annas' with 'Lindsays'."

"This is different. You were really stressed out with all the planning, and that whole fight you and Drew had was a big, weird misunderstanding. I haven't felt like myself ever since I said yes. I mean, Warren and Rob hate each other. Can I really have a best friend and a husband who can hardly be civil?"

"They're just jealous of each other. They'll get over it. They both want what's best for you."

"Well, I really don't think his mom likes me, either," Lindsay said.

"How can you say that? She raves over everything you do," Anna said.

"You can't hear it because you're not Southern. There's this thing Southern women do where they compliment you *too* much and you know they're lying. Like, if they say 'Cute haircut,' that's sincere. But if they're like, 'Did you get a new haircut? Honey, that is just so you! You'll have to tell me where you got that done,' you know they're faking."

Anna pressed her lips together. "I'll just have to take your word for that."

"And his sister is loony tunes," Lindsay continued. "What if that's genetic? I could be responsible for bringing another Tanner Satterwhite-White into the world."

"Wait," Anna said, pausing her ring-removal operation. "Warren's incredibly pale sister's name is Tanner Satterwhite-White?"

"Yeah, Gibb is Gibb White. She hyphenated," Lindsay said.

"You could always adopt."

"Anna, I'm serious," Lindsay said, frowning.

"Sorry. That's just really funny. Anyway, I think you're just having your normal commitment panic. I'd love to give you advice, but we both know that I'm really terrible at heartfelt advice. Sarcasm, I can do. And lately, I'm developing a new line in hormone-related screaming and crying. But heartfelt advice is not in my wheelhouse. You should probably talk to Geneva."

"Last I heard, Geneva was barfing her stomach inside out."

"Norovirus. I've probably seen a dozen cases in the Emergency Department this week," Anna said. "Well, I'll give you my best attempt at heartfelt advice then. Warren's a stand-up guy and he genuinely loves you. Not romance novel love, but the kind of real-deal ''til death do us part' thing. If a movie was made about him, some old-school dude like Clint Eastwood or John Wayne would probably play him."

"I just don't trust my instincts when it comes to men. I always mess up." Lindsay paused. "The ring hasn't moved at all, has it?"

Anna shook her head. "Now, I don't want you reading any cosmic signs into this, but you need to get this ring cut off ASAP. You're not getting enough circulation through the finger. I don't have the right tools, so you need to go to a jeweler or the hospital. Now, okay?"

Lindsay nodded.

Anna grabbed Lindsay's shoulders and looked her square in the face. "Linds, you could get nerve damage. Hell, you could lose the whole finger. Listen to me this time. Not like when you messed up your knee last year and then walked around on it for a week after I told you not to, and you ended up doing two months of physical therapy. Or when you tried to move your furniture by yourself last January when you had a bunch of broken ribs and reinjured them. Actually, screw it. I don't trust you. Get in the car. I'm driving you."

Chapter 8

"No side trips," Anna said. "That ring is coming off."

"John said it's an emergency," Lindsay replied.

Lindsay was sitting in the passenger's seat of Anna's car, for once having complied with Anna's medical advice. Even she had to admit that her finger had taken on an unhealthy resemblance to an uncooked sausage link. They had been on their way to get the ring removed when Lindsay received an urgent text message from Rob's boyfriend, John Tatum, who was acting as the general contractor on her home renovation project. John had written that the county building inspector stopped by earlier that morning to give the final sign-off, but now apparently there was a problem.

"My finger will survive a slight detour," Lindsay said. "John isn't the crying wolf type."

There was no disputing that if the normally imperturbable John Tatum was calling something an emergency, he wasn't likely to be overreacting. Anna sighed with resignation. "We can go there, but only because I know John will have something in his toolbox that can get this ring off."

They pulled up in front of Lindsay's small wood-sided house a few minutes later. John Tatum leaned against the tailgate of his F-250, which was parked in the driveway. He stood about five and a half feet tall and had a sturdy, compact build. Alongside his massive truck, he looked like a sailor about to climb aboard a galleon.

"What's up?" Lindsay said, climbing out of Anna's car. "You said something about forged inspection paperwork?"

John nodded and ran his hand over his trim, blond beard. "It's the damnedest thing. I was finishing up that last bit of trimwork in the new bathroom this morning when I heard somebody pull up. Came out and this man climbs out of his car. Introduces himself as the county inspector. Said Turner had retired and he was the new guy—Doer was how he introduced himself."

John paused and stroked his beard again. His tone was as even as ever; only the appearance of a single worry line between his eyebrows betrayed the slightest hint that anything was amiss.

"I don't get it. Did it not pass inspection?" Lindsay asked. This seemed impossible given how meticulous John's workmanship was. On at least one occasion, she'd seen him completely redo work that had seemed perfectly acceptable to her because it didn't meet his own exacting standards.

"Passed inspection all right. Mr. Doer was in and out of there in 15 minutes. Said it all looked hunky dory, and handed me the paperwork. Seemed a mite on the quick side to me, but I wasn't gonna argue with the man, especially if he was gonna be the new county building inspector."

Just then, a heavy-set man with a vivid white goatee and black-framed glasses stormed out of the house. He wore a thunderous expression on his face and brandished a sheaf of papers. "*Weaponless*? Is this some kind of a joke?"

"Weaponless?" Lindsay repeated the odd word. She looked at John, but he just shrugged his shoulders.

"Which one of you is the homeowner?" the man bellowed.

"I am," Lindsay replied. "I'm Reverend Lindsay Harding." She found that in volatile situations, especially volatile situations in which she was dressed like a slob and had a pulsating red swamp finger, it was best to play the "reverend" card immediately to establish some kind of credibility.

The man's expression softened slightly. "Any relation to Reverend Jonah Harding?" he asked.

"Yes, sir. Reverend Harding is my father."

"Why didn't you tell me she was a minister? And that Jonah Harding was her father? My sister goes to that church." The man glowered at John.

Anna put her hands up. "All right, people. Before this becomes a game of whose second cousin is married to whose Aunt Bessie, can we establish some basics? Like, for starters, what the hell is going on? And John, while Colonel Sanders here is filling us in, please get a thin metal file and some wire cutters and get Lindsay's ring off her borderline-gangrenous finger." She grabbed Lindsay's wrist and waved the offending hand. She then pivoted towards the older man, extending her hand with a tight-lipped smile. "I'm Dr. Anna Melrose. And you are?"

"Franklin Turner, county building inspector." He regarded Anna's hand as one might regard a cobra emerging from a wicker basket.

"It's a pleasure to meet you," Anna said, pumping his hand with what seemed to Lindsay to be unnecessary vigor.

The man's face turned an unnaturally-vivid shade of claret red, and he opened his mouth to say something. While Lindsay would admit privately that Turner's resemblance to KFC's Colonel Sanders was uncanny, it wasn't something she would've ever dreamed of saying within earshot of the man. Lindsay stepped between him and Anna. Anna's direct and dominant personality served her well in the Emergency Department, but Lindsay could see that a subtler approach would be needed if she didn't want to find her house slapped with a giant Condemned sticker. Affecting the best impression of a Southern Belle that could be managed given her present unwashed appearance, she said, "Mr. Turner, we'd be very grateful if you could fill us in."

Lindsay tried to make her expression as benign and unhurried as Anna's was aggressive and impatient. "Anna likes to get to the point of things. She's from New Jersey."

Turner nodded knowingly and addressed himself to Lindsay. "When I arrived to inspect your house a few minutes ago, Mr. Tatum informed me that the inspection had already taken place. He produced a set of documents that had clearly been forged."

By now, John had climbed down from the bed of his truck and produced the tools Anna requested. Anna immediately took the tools from him, grabbed Lindsay's hand, and began to work the tip of the file underneath her ring.

"And you accused John of forging the paperwork?" Anna asked, not lifting her eyes from her task.

"Well, that's about the shape of it," Turner said.

John put his hands on his hips and the wrinkle on his brow lengthened. It was the closest he was capable of coming to an expression of rage. "Turner, you've known me for years. What earthly reason would I have for doing that?"

"Hiding shoddy work. Not complying with the historic preservation codes. Who knows?" Turner replied testily.

"I don't do shoddy work," John replied through clenched teeth.

"We all know you'd never do that, John," Lindsay soothed. She winced as Anna moved the file further under her ring. "Mr. Turner, if you know John, you know he's telling the truth."

"You've got to see it from my perspective," Turner replied. "In 40 years of doing this, I've seen a lot of contractors cut corners. I've seen forged paperwork, people trying to spackle over a termite infestation, you name it. But never once have I had a contractor claim that an impostor showed up at a job site with a set of fake papers."

John shook his head. "I'm as flummoxed as you are. Doer had an answer for everything. I even pointed out that the paperwork looked different. He said he was implementing some changes to go digital and cut down on duplication. It seemed plausible."

"What were you saying when you came outside?" Lindsay asked. "Something about a weapon?"

Anna removed the wire cutters she'd temporarily stashed in her back pocket. In one deft movement, she snipped the back of Lindsay's engagement ring in half. She gently coaxed the two halves apart using the tip of the file until she could pull it off. The intense throbbing in Lindsay's finger eased almost immediately. She clutched her finger with her other hand and began to rub the circulation back into it.

Turner flipped through the paperwork, showing Lindsay the signatures on each page. They were all signed W. Doer, except for the final page, which was signed in a thick, clear script— Weaponless Doer. Lindsay studied it carefully and then held the page out for Anna and John to see.

"I didn't notice that," John said, his brow creasing.

"What did this 'Weaponless Doer' look like?" Anna asked.

John shook his head. "No question I'd know him again if I saw him. Hairline started about here," he said, indicating a point in the middle of his forehead. "And he was stooped over like a hunchback with a big paunch belly. You know those charts they show you in school where the chimpanzee is supposed to be evolving into a human? Well, I reckon he looked like the third one from the right."

"Could it have been a disguise?" Lindsay asked.

They all looked at her for a long moment, their faces exhibiting an array of surprised expressions.

John conceded, "Didn't think of it at the time, but I reckon it could've been."

The throbbing that had disappeared from Lindsay's finger seemed to have been transposed to her temples. Although she stood in full late spring sunshine, her whole body began to shiver.

Anna and John locked eyes, and John quickly added, "I know what you're thinking, Lindsay. I'd have recognized him. I swear it. There's no way he could've disguised himself that much. This guy was taller, different voice, different build. Hear me? The man I saw was not Leander Swoopes."

Chapter 9

"How can he be sure? He never even met Swoopes." Lindsay paced up and down the wide boards of her front porch, watching the last of the police cars pull away.

"We all saw the TV footage and mug shot a million times," Anna said. "Swoopes is very… distinctive. Besides, even if he's alive, which he probably isn't, why would he risk coming back here and posing as a friggin' county bureaucrat? It just doesn't make sense." Anna sat on the top step, her long legs stretched out before her. Dusk had fallen, and she slapped at the mosquitoes that seemed to materialize out of the shadows.

"What if he was scoping out my house? What if he comes back some night when it's just me and Simmy here?"

"It's gonna be okay, Linds. John's installed an alarm system. You said yourself it's like something out of a James Bond movie. Warren has arranged for an officer to drive by a few times a day to keep an eye on you. You'll be safe."

Despite Anna's reassurances, Lindsay remained on edge, unable to exorcise the anxiety that seemed to penetrate her body right down to the bone marrow. Lindsay's house had always been a safe place for her. When she bought it four years earlier, she'd felt like she was finally doing the kind of wholesome, sensible thing that responsible adults do, like flossing daily. Setting down roots by buying the house had been a huge step for Lindsay, who had a preternatural fear of commitment. Now, however, even her beloved little house couldn't conjure the sense of security it had before.

In times past, a combination of mistrust of authority and old-fashioned stubbornness would have kept her from calling the police about the bogus inspector's intrusion into her home. Her natural instinct had always been to take care of things herself, to keep things private, to pretend that everything was fine. Indeed, when her house had been broken into the previous summer, she was adamant that she could handle the situation without involving the authorities. Now, however, she had been the first one to suggest phoning the police.

Within minutes of the call, several units from both Mount Moriah's tiny force and the slightly larger force in New Albany had responded to the strange report of the sham inspector. Lindsay wasn't sure if the overwhelming show of force was due to the possible reemergence of one of North Carolina's most wanted felons or because she was Warren's fiancée. Frankly, she didn't care.

The responding officers, including Warren himself, had swept through the house looking for fingerprints or any physical evidence that could reveal the identity of Mr. Doer. They'd also brought in a K-9 unit, who had searched, fruitlessly, for explosives or other anomalies. After they finished, John had headed off to the station in New Albany, where he'd been met by a police sketch artist. Although every single person Lindsay encountered continued to assure her that the imposter couldn't possibly have been Leander Swoopes, it was clear from the all-hands-on-deck reaction that no one wanted to countenance even the remote possibility that *they* would be the person to allow a dangerous criminal to slip through their grasp once again.

Warren emerged from Lindsay's house, where he'd been speaking on the phone to his contacts at the State Bureau of Investigation. "Good news," he said. "Nobody's tampered with the alarm system. Once you enable it, it'll go off if anybody tries to open any window or door in your house, and we'll be notified immediately. You already know that the K-9s didn't turn up anything unusual around the property."

"What about the fingerprints you lifted?" Lindsay asked.

"They don't match Swoopes," Warren replied.

"Did they find a match?"

"They did. A con man named Terry Addison." He held up his tablet computer for her to see. "Do you know him?"

Lindsay studied Addison's mug shot. It showed a young man with long curly hair pulled back into a ponytail and a close-cropped goatee. Although she couldn't see his body, she could tell by his wide face and expansive upper body that he must've weighed at least 300 pounds. He glowered at the camera, as if he was daring the person taking the shot to photograph him.

"No," Lindsay said, shaking her head. "I've never seen him before."

"John didn't recognize him either. Mind you, this picture is more than a decade old, and we know for a fact that he must've lost some weight. John said he was heavy, but not as heavy as he looks here."

"What did he do?" Lindsay asked. "Is he violent?"

"He served time for felony fraud and theft in South Carolina about a dozen years ago. He was more than likely trying to make a quick buck, or maybe he was planning to scam you somehow. Anyway, since your laptop and other valuables are at your dad's house, he went away empty handed." Although Warren smiled as he relayed the news, Lindsay sensed a shadow of unease in his expression.

"What is it?" she asked.

He looked at her, seemingly weighing up the pros and cons of revealing what he knew. "Weaponless Doer," he said at last. "The SBI ran that name through their computer to check for known aliases."

"They shouldn't have bothered," Lindsay said.

"Why's that?" Anna said, rising to her feet.

"It's not an alias. It's an anagram," Lindsay said quietly.

"What?!" Anna and Warren said in unison.

"If you rearrange the letters, it spells Leander Swoopes," Lindsay explained.

"You'd already figured that out," Warren said, sounding half worried and half impressed. Although his words had been a statement rather than a question, Lindsay answered him anyway.

"It was such a weird combination of words. If you're going to come up with an alias, why not pick an actual name?"

"Holy crap," Anna said. "What kind of a sicko would do that, knowing what that psychopath put you through?"

"Why didn't you say something as soon as you figured it out?" Warren asked.

"I don't know." Lindsay gripped the porch railing and looked into the distance. "I guess I wasn't sure I could say it out loud. It scares me too much." She put her hands to the sides of her head and gripped the hair at her temples. "I want this all to not be happening."

Warren put his arms around her, and she leaned heavily against him trying to steady her whirling mind. "Just take me to my dad's house, okay? I just want to sleep."

Chapter 10

"How's your finger?" Warren asked.

"Fine," Lindsay said.

She stared out the windshield as the lights of Mount Moriah's familiar landmarks zipped past—the CITGO, the expressway underpass, the Wal-Mart with its sprawling parking lot.

"You know I don't care about the ring, right?" Warren said. "We'll get the diamond put in a different band if you want."

Lindsay made no reply. Warren had tried to start several conversations during their drive, but had been met each time with terse answers or silence. "We'll find whoever this guy was, okay?" he said.

"Like you found Leander Swoopes?" Lindsay snapped back.

"Letting him slip away was the worst mistake of my career. And worse than that, it almost caused me to lose you. Do you realize I think about that every day? What could've happened? What he almost did to you?"

"Sorry, I'm tired," Lindsay said. She put her hand on his arm. "I just don't want to talk about it."

Lindsay wanted to tell him that she didn't blame him, but something stopped her. How could she explain that the person she blamed was herself? It seemed impossible to form the words that would describe the well-trodden pathway inside her brain, formed after her parents were arrested all those years ago, that always led her to hold herself responsible whenever things went downhill. She had thought that all the introspective self-study she'd done during her chaplaincy training had redrawn that path. But here she was again, hearing the same sinister, insidious voice in her head, whispering that this was all her fault, telling her if she'd just called the police earlier, if she'd paid more attention, if she'd just killed Swoopes when she had the chance…

"I looked into that thing with Otis Boughtflower, by the way. The body and the money? He didn't have a criminal record of any kind—no arrests, no convictions. Not so much as a speeding ticket.

All the old timers I talked to said the Boughtflowers always kept themselves to themselves. And Otis has been a complete recluse since he sold the sock factory."

Lindsay just nodded. They pulled into the driveway, and Warren cut the engine.

"You don't need to come in. The light's on. I'll be fine," Lindsay said.

Warren put his hand on her leg. "Lindsay, please don't shut me out again. I'm in this with you, but I can't be there if you won't let me."

"I'm not asking you to," she said.

Her eyes stung with unshed tears. Adrenaline had carried her through the immediate aftermath of the New Year's attack, but in the weeks that followed, she had descended into depression and anxiety. It had taken all her energy to pull out of the tailspin that time, and she wasn't sure if she had enough gas in the tank to do it all over again. She'd taken almost a month off of work to recover—the longest she'd gone without working since she got her first babysitting job at the age of 14. During those weeks, she'd remained holed up in her bedroom, jumping at the slightest sound and then berating herself for being so terrified.

Never before had she felt so far away from the comfort of her faith. Even in her darkest times, she'd always thought of God as a pilot light deep within her soul—a perpetually burning spark of love and hope just waiting to be kindled. Sometimes, like when she saw a seemingly miraculous recovery in the hospital, or when she looked into a perfect Carolina blue sky, her faith would ignite, warming her right down to the tips of her toes. In those moments, she felt so close to the divine, her whole being lit up from within. But throughout that long, dark month, whenever she searched her soul, all she felt was an icy, hollow chill. Only with gentle encouragement from her father and Warren, and the less-than-gentle kicks in the rear from her friends Rob and Anna, had she finally been able to reclaim her life and rediscover that hopeful, little spark.

Warren stroked her cheek and smiled. "At least let me come in and tell Kipper about our day."

She smiled wanly and nodded. She loved that Warren wanted to go in and make sure the house was safe before leaving her. And even more, she loved that he knew better than to tell her that he wanted to go in and make sure the house was safe before leaving her. She would have automatically bristled at that kind of intrusive care-taking.

They walked in the back door together. Lindsay was surprised to hear the orchestral crescendo of a cheesy easy listening song.

"Lionel Richie?" Warren said, raising an inquisitive eyebrow. "I thought your dad only listened to hymns and gospel."

"He makes an exception for Dolly Parton and Lionel Richie," Lindsay replied. "He used to play this one sometimes when he was working on his motorcycle. I haven't heard it in forever."

"He's really rocking out." Warren had to raise his voice to be heard over Richie's silky tenor belting out, *Is it me you're looking for?*

They entered the kitchen, where they were welcomed by a barrage of licks from a jubilant Kipper. Lindsay threw her jacket over the back of a chair, and she and Warren walked into the living room. What greeted them there was a vision that instantly and indelibly burned itself into her brain.

Jonah lay on the sofa with a woman. Kissing. In fact, it was more than kissing. This was full-on, junior high-style making out. Even without seeing the woman's face, Lindsay immediately recognized the unmistakable Day-Glo orange bob. There could be no doubt that her father was lying on the couch, making out with Teresa Satterwhite, Warren's widowed mother. Jonah had one hand up the back of Teresa's shirt and the other planted squarely on her rear end.

"Dad?!" Lindsay screeched.

"What in the damn world?" Warren said slowly. He bowed his head and raised his hand to his brow, as if trying to shield his eyes from the glare of oncoming headlights.

At the sound of their voices, Teresa sprang up into a sitting position, catapulting Jonah onto the floor.

Jonah hit the carpet with a thud and let out a yelp of pain. "Ah!" He arched sideways, clutching his lower back.

They all rushed over to the spot on the floor where Jonah lay writhing in pain. Jonah had suffered from chronic lower back problems ever since he overexerted himself a few years previously on a school-building mission trip to Guatemala. When his herniated disc flared up, he was usually out of commission for days at a time.

"I'm so sorry, sugar! Are you all right?" Teresa knelt down next to him. "Is it your back again?"

"No, it's okay," Jonah said through clenched teeth. He rolled over and revealed the source of his agony—he'd landed smack on one of Kipper's massive rawhide bones. He pulled himself into a sitting position.

Teresa rose to her feet; her long, lithe movements made it appear as if she were rising out of a yoga pose. Even in her slightly disheveled state, her well-tailored clothes and perfectly-matched jewelry lent her an air of refinement.

"Well, I know this is just terribly embarrassing for all of us," Teresa said, patting her hair back into place. Lindsay felt an almost overwhelming urge to claw at the woman's face. She glanced at Warren, but his gaze seemed cemented to couch, as if he were still trying to process the events that had just occurred there.

"I suppose we owe you an explanation," Jonah said, blushing deeply.

"You think?" Lindsay said. She crossed her arms. "Actually, I don't want an explanation. It's your life. Do what you want."

She walked quickly down the hall into her bedroom, closed the door, and locked it. Now that the brief moment of concern for Jonah's back had washed over, the next emotion that rolled in was blind fury. She knew she should be happy for her father. He'd spent years faithfully married to Sarabelle, pining after her even as she repeatedly cheated on him and left for months, and even years, at a stretch. It was Lindsay herself who'd finally convinced him to give up on Sarabelle, file for divorce, and move on. And at last, he'd moved on…right on top of Warren's mother.

Lindsay flopped down on her bed and stared at the ceiling. During her rebellious teenage years, drama-queen displays of door slamming and locking had been an almost-daily ritual. Even though she'd managed to keep from shouting and slamming the door this time, she felt no different than she had all those years before.

She heard the murmur of voices, followed by a gentle knocking on the door.

"Linds?" Warren said.

She rolled toward the wall and pulled a pillow over her head. She didn't want to talk. She wanted to scream. While she was potentially being stalked by a psychopath, freaking out about her engagement, preparing to move back into her house with Simmy, and having her ring sawed off her bloated, scaly finger, her father had had his hands on Warren's mother's backside. Of all the women in Mount Moriah, why Warren's mother? A woman whose effortless perfection as a homemaker always made Lindsay feel grossly inadequate? Whose "Bless your heart" and "Well, aren't you a dear?" signaled that she'd never quite measure up?

She heard Warren try the doorknob. "Come on, Linds."

"Leave me alone."

He tried a few more times to talk her into coming out, his voice growing more frustrated with each entreaty. "You can't keep going into your shell like this, Lindsay. You're not the only person involved here. This isn't fair."

She wanted to speak to him, to find out what *he* was feeling. The man she loved, who'd stood by her over the last terrible months and helped her pull through, was on the other side of the door, and she couldn't bring herself to say even a single word to him. What was wrong with her? The huge weight of her emotions seemed to have squeezed all the air from her lungs and robbed her of the ability to move. She pressed the pillow down further over her face, almost wishing it would just finish the job and suffocate her. Why couldn't she get a grip? She was a minister, a spiritual guide for desperate people, an intelligent woman with a fiancé.

"Linds?" Warren called again. When he was once again met with silence, he said quietly, "How come you always have to push people away?" She heard him sigh. "I'm gonna drive Mama home. You can call me when you're ready to talk about this like adults."

She heard the muffled sounds of their departure and saw the flash of headlights as Warren backed his car out of the driveway. A few minutes passed, and the house fell silent. She wondered if

Jonah had gone out with them. Then she heard Kipper scratching at her door. He was what she needed right now—a sympathetic friend who, blessedly, lacked the power of speech. When she opened the door to let him in, however, her father was standing in the hallway, leaning against the wall. She rushed to close the door again, but he stuck his foot in to block her.

"We need to talk about this," Jonah said.

"I'm really not sure we do," Lindsay countered.

Jonah pushed the door further open. "We didn't want you to find out this way."

Lindsay remained standing in the doorway with her arms crossed, blocking him from coming into the room. "And how did you want us to find out? Maybe when we got invitations to your wedding in the mail?'"

"You're being unreasonable. Teresa is a good, Christian woman. We're happy. You should be happy for us."

"Please don't tell me how to feel right now," Lindsay said. "I get to feel shocked and betrayed and angry and, frankly, really grossed out. How long has this been going on, exactly?"

"Not long. A few months." Jonah rubbed his temples. "Teresa started attending my church with a friend of hers on and off last fall. Then she volunteered to chair the committee to organize the tent revival, so we started spending more time together. We didn't want to say anything until we knew whether or not it was serious. We were planning to tell you soon. I tried to tell you, but the time just didn't seem right."

"Well, you really have some sense of timing. This is just the crappy cherry on top of my crap sundae," Lindsay replied. When she eased him out of the doorway, he didn't resist. Having shut him out, she closed the door in his face and clicked the button to lock it.

Chapter 11

During the four days that had passed since Lindsay walked in on her father and Teresa Satterwhite, Lindsay hadn't spoken a single word to anyone. She'd realized almost immediately that she wasn't really angry about her father and Teresa's relationship. Freaked out, maybe, but not angry. Her real resentment stemmed from her feeling of utter hopelessness. She felt as if there was no chance that she'd ever be able to live a normal life. Seeing her father and Teresa together seemed to prove that while everyone else was happily getting on with their lives, her own life was forever tainted. *She* was tainted.

Since the discovery, she'd only left her room when she was sure her father had gone out. She hadn't been able to face him, or anyone else. She'd gotten other chaplains to pick up her shifts, and she filled her days with long naps and extended forays into the land of self-pity. She couldn't even bring herself to engage in her usual method of self-medication—long distance running. All she could do was stare at the walls and ask herself the same questions over and over—Why was she being targeted again? Was there something about her that marked her as easy prey? Other people got over traumatic experiences. Why couldn't she? She knew that her loved ones, especially Warren and her father, wanted desperately to protect her, but it seemed that neither earthly nor heavenly law could keep her safe from Leander Swoopes and the fear he had instilled in her.

For days, she overheard her father telling Simmy that she was still sick in bed and would call as soon as she felt better. Warren, too, had called and texted, but she couldn't bring herself to reach out to him.

Lindsay waited until the sound of Jonah's car faded out of her hearing and the house fell silent. She unlocked her door and padded down the hall into the kitchen, where a note from her father lay on the table:

Warren stopped by while you were sleeping.

There's some chicken pot pie in the fridge.

She removed the covered casserole dish from the refrigerator and plunked it down on the counter. A sudden, hard rap on the back door jolted her to attention. Through the glass door panes and sheer, gauzy curtains, she recognized the trim outline of her friend Rob. For a moment, she debated retreating to her bedroom to hide, but decided that a move like that would probably be too pathetic and childish, even in her current state. Still, she hesitated to open the door.

"Lindsay Harding, I see you in there," Rob snapped in his distinctive Taiwanese-inflected Southern accent.

She sighed, her limited defenses defeated, and opened the door.

Rob walked past her, took a seat at the kitchen table, and gestured for her to do the same.

"I didn't hear you pull up," Lindsay said.

"That's because I parked down the street and waited for your father to leave. I knew you'd have to come out to eat or use the bathroom at some point," Rob said.

"So you've been staking out the house?"

"Anna did a shift this morning, but she didn't manage to catch you out. You know there's a cop car out there, too?"

"Yeah, I noticed it when I took Kipper out."

"Good to know that you're not spending *all* your time lying around the house, watching reruns, and eating cold chicken pot pie," Rob said, gesturing to the dish.

"Look, I just need some time to myself. I haven't been feeling well," Lindsay said, staring at the table. "Maybe I'm coming down with what you and Geneva had."

"Since you're not projectile vomiting out of your ears, I highly doubt it. I just ate my first solid food since Sunday. It was a cracker, and I'm not 100% sure it's agreeing with me. I pulled myself off my deathbed to come over here and talk to you."

Lindsay raised her eyes to look at his face. His usually tan complexion was a sallow yellow, and his jet black hair hung limply across his forehead. The almond-shaped eyes that usually twinkled with mischief looked dull and lusterless behind his metal-framed glasses.

"You do look like death warmed over," Lindsay agreed. "Actually, not even warmed. More like microwaved on low for about 30 seconds."

"Well, by the look and smell of you, I'm not sure you're really in a position to judge. Have you changed your clothes today?"

"Me being a slob isn't exactly breaking news," Lindsay snapped. "Did you come over here to play fashion police?"

"No. I came over here to try to stop you from pressing the self-destruct button again."

"What do you mean?" Lindsay asked, avoiding his gaze.

"Look at you. Hiding in your dad's house like a refugee. Not returning my phone calls. I heard you've been getting people to cover your shifts this week so you don't have to come in. You used to do this kind of thing all the time, remember? After you didn't get into Yale for divinity school, after Tim broke off your engagement. I thought CPE helped you, and the crisis therapy you had after the thing with Swoopes. You've been doing so well for so long."

None of Rob's usual impishness was present in his tone. Instead, his words held concern and pity. In addition to being her friend and boss, Rob was also the chaplaincy program's Clinical Pastoral Education supervisor. Through CPE, Lindsay, like all professional chaplains, had been trained to draw insights from her interpersonal experiences and patient interactions to improve her ability to deliver care. And like most chaplains, she'd found the process of exhaustive introspection distinctly uncomfortable. Still, she had to admit that it had helped her to overcome her natural tendency to flee whenever she faced a setback. Prior to becoming a chaplain, any kind of uncertainty, unwelcome responsibility, or potential failure had caused her to run away, sometimes in dramatic fashion. After her former fiancé, Tim Farnsworth, had dumped her, for example, she'd quit her degree program and her job, broken her lease, run up a mountain of credit card debt and left the state where they'd been living. She realized now that she'd invented a new kind of escape—escaping within herself.

"What do you want me to do?" she asked peevishly, still not willing to engage in any kind of psychoanalysis. "Just pretend everything's fine?"

"I know everything isn't fine. John and Anna told me about the creepy guy coming to your house. Anyone would be freaked out by that."

"What if he comes back for me? He's still out there," Lindsay said, her voice sounding strained. She knew she didn't need to tell Rob she meant Leander Swoopes.

"Have you ever thought about the alternative?" Rob asked.

"What do you mean?"

"Well, you shot him, right? Five bullets from almost point-blank range. But you missed, and he survived the shooting. What if he hadn't? What if you'd blown his face open with bullets? Shredded his body to bloody ribbons?"

"Stop it," Lindsay demanded, shutting her eyes tightly. "What's wrong with you?"

"No, listen to me," Rob said, scooting his chair closer to hers. "What if you'd killed him? It was self-defense, right? Nobody would've blamed you. But would you feel relieved that he was dead?"

"Yes." She shook her head. "Maybe. Look, I don't know."

"Linds, I *do* know. I know you. If you'd ended his life, scumbag though he was, it would've wrecked you. You feel guilty for things that have nothing to do with you. You obsess about things that aren't your fault at all. Did you ever wonder if maybe God made all those bullets miss their mark for a reason? I know it's hard to live with uncertainty, knowing maybe Swoopes is out there somewhere. I've heard you tell patients all the time that uncertainty can be even harder than knowing a bad outcome. But did you ever stop to think how Swoopes was injured just bad enough so that you and Simmy and your mom could get away? How strange is that? I know this fear you feel is terrible, but maybe God spared you from something worse. The guilt of taking someone's life could've swallowed you."

There was a long silence, broken by the sound of Kipper slurping noisily from his water bowl.

At last, Lindsay said, "When did you get so smart?"

"I've always been this smart," Rob said. "You've just been distracted all this time by how sexy I am."

"That may be the grossest thing you've ever said."

"Speaking of things that are gross," Rob said, "I heard about the thing with your dad and Warren's mom."

"Who told you about that?" For a moment, Lindsay wondered if perhaps everyone in Mount Moriah had known about the relationship except for her.

"Warren. He called me," Rob replied.

"You and Warren talked on the phone?" Lindsay's mouth hung open in astonishment. She couldn't remember the two men passing a civil word between them, much less having a casual phone call.

"He was worried about you. That's what it's come to. Deputy Dogooder has climbed down off his high horse to talk to me." Rob smiled at her. "Please, Linds. I know you're scared, but the Lindsay we know can take on the world. She beats up the bad guys. She gets into car chases, and outsmarts criminals, and kicks them in the gonads. And there's no way that the Old Lindsay would have just forgotten about the whole weird thing with Otis Boughtflower confessing to killing someone."

Lindsay had been slumped over the table, but at the mention of Boughtflower's name, she perked up. "He didn't say he killed anyone. Just that he hid a body." She paused. "Wait. How do you know that?"

"You put it into your case notes, which I sign off on every week."

"Oh." She paused. "Wait. I thought you've been off work. Didn't you say you came here directly from your deathbed?"

"I've been in a few times to check on things. The work needs to get done because it's important. The work *you* do is important. *You* are important." Rob reached out and took hold of Lindsay's hand. "Please come back to us, Linds. Your friends need you. Your patients need you. And also, when you're depressed like this, it doesn't feel right to make fun of how weird your hair looks right now."

***

"What are you doing here, girl? I thought you were coming down with that stomach thing." Geneva Williams put her hands on her tiny hips. As usual, she was going through her rounds with her huge, white faux leather handbag slung over her shoulder. With her tight halo of grey curls, round glasses, and long pleated skirt, she looked very much like the mother of seven and grandmother of fifteen that she, in fact, was. She stood in the middle of the Geriatric Unit hallway, facing Lindsay, who had been scouring the hospital trying to find her.

"It was a false alarm," Lindsay said, with a sheepishness she hoped Geneva wouldn't detect. "Thanks for covering my shift. Since I'm feeling better, I thought I'd come in and see if you wanted to finish up early and go home."

Rob had sat at the kitchen table with Lindsay for more than an hour, letting her vent about the situation with her father and her upcoming move back into her own house with Simmy. She avoided the subjects of her engagement and the possibility of Leander Swoopes's return entirely. She thought Rob would press her to talk about these more troubling issues, but he allowed her to control the flow of the conversation. Even though she recognized this rapport-building tactic from the chaplaincy playbook, she didn't mind. She was grateful that, for once, Rob had decided to act more like her mentor and less like her annoying little brother. In the end, the conversation had convinced her that she needed to at least try to reengage with the world outside her childhood bedroom.

"Well, I'm not going to say no to that offer," Geneva replied. "My stomach still isn't right, truth be told, although you won't hear me moaning up and down the halls like Rob."

They walked over to the nurses' station together, where Angel stood talking on the phone. "What are you doing up here, anyway? I thought I was signed up to be covering mainly emergencies and the ICUs today?" Lindsay said.

"Angel paged me. She said one of her ornerier patients requested 'the tiny, curly-headed little chaplain'." She gestured to Otis Boughtflower's room. "She thought he meant me."

Angel, who'd been listening in on their conversation, hung up the phone and said, "I thought wrong. I didn't realize he was sweet on you, especially after he kicked you out of his room that first time." She laughed. "He's been asking about you ever since they brought him back up here from the ICU yesterday."

"So I guess he's doing better, since they discharged him back to the ward?" Lindsay said.

"Well, no," Angel said. "He filled out a DNR so that if he stops breathing again, they won't try to intubate him. Next time he goes down, that's it. There was really no point in keeping him in the ICU if he doesn't want anything done."

"I'm surprised they didn't try to send him home," Geneva said.

Angel sighed. "As long as he wants to stay, and his insurance keeps paying, they'll keep him. But I really think we're looking at a matter of days, if not hours."

Geneva clicked her tongue. "Well, I hope he's made his peace with his Maker. You know who he is, right?"

"Otis Boughtflower, the king of socks," Lindsay replied.

Geneva flattened her lips into a thin line.

"What is it?" Angel asked. She looked across the hall to make sure Boughtflower's door was closed before signaling that Geneva should go on with her story.

"There's something else," Geneva said, lowering her voice. "But you know I'm not one for idle gossip."

"It could be important, Geneva. The man clearly has something he needs to get off his chest," Lindsay said. "Whatever you know, if it's something that would help me reach out to him, please tell me."

Geneva's eyes darted to Boughtflower's closed door. "He was a Klansman."

Angel's eyes widened and her hands flew up to cover her mouth.

"Whoa. What?" Lindsay asked, looking equally shocked.

"You ever heard of the Battle of Hayes Pond?" Geneva asked.

Lindsay furrowed her brow. She'd majored in history in college, and continued to read books and articles about Southern history even after she graduated. However, even her near-encyclopedic knowledge of the region was found lacking. "That was the thing with the Lumbees and the KKK, right?" she said, looking at Angel for confirmation.

Now it was Angel's turn to click her tongue. "'Thing with the Lumbees'?! We still celebrate that 'thing' every year."

Lindsay had noticed, in the years she'd known Angel, how her membership in the Lumbee Tribe, a Native American group centered in southeastern North Carolina, had been a constant source of both pride and consternation. Many people outside the region knew next to nothing about the existence of the tribe. Those passing through might have had trouble telling the racially-mixed, mainly Christian, English-speaking people from their neighbors. But the Lumbees' close kinship ties, unique history, distinctive dialect, and deep connection to their land set them apart. Lindsay had sometimes witnessed Angel's frustration when she mentioned her background to patients, only to have them tell her she "looked too black to be Indian," or ask if her family lived in a teepee.

"Wait. It's coming back to me," Lindsay said, clicking her fingers. "The Klan was agitating in Robeson County because Indians were mixing with whites, right?"

"Mmhmm," Angel nodded. "They didn't like the fact that Lumbees can look white or black or tan or any shade in between. I even knew a Lumbee—my friend Sheila Locklear—who converted to Mexican."

"She *converted* to Mexican?" Lindsay asked.

"Yeah. She was light-skinned and had straight black hair like Dunette's, not kinky hair like yours or mine. Hers was nice. She married a Mexican guy and just decided to let everybody assume she was Mexican. It's not like she was ashamed to be a Lumbee. She still brings her kids to the Lumbee Homecoming celebration every year. But she said she just got tired of explaining what a Lumbee is. Once you set foot out of Robeson or Bladen County, ain't nobody ever heard of Lumbees. I'd never do that, but I understand where she's coming from. Even within the tribe, it can feel sometimes like there's a contest to be the truest 100% Lumbee person, like you've gotta explain yourself if you're more mixed, like I am. And when you've had somebody ask 'What are you?' for the hundredth time, I can understand how it could make you want to convert to Mexican."

"Next time some fool asks you what you are, you tell 'em you're a polite human being whose mama raised you not to ask stupid questions," Geneva said with a sniff.

Lindsay smiled thoughtfully. She'd had her own struggles with her lineage, but never before had it occurred to her to be relieved that these ambiguities were all contained inside her unambiguously white skin. There were a lot of rude, ignorant questions somebody could ask her about her family, but that particular one wasn't likely to be among them. For better or for worse, seen from the outside, she fit neatly into a category.

"Anyway," Angel said, "like I was saying. This was back in the 50's. The KKK said they were gonna have a big rally to scare the Lumbees back into their rightful place, but when they heard we were gonna come out in force, they got scared. Hardly any of those fools showed up, but more than 400 of our boys came out. This white preacher from South Carolina got up in front of the crowd and started his speech. Mongrel this and half-breed that," she said, practically spitting the words. "He'd hardly even started, though, when one of our boys, a sharpshooter who'd been in World War II, shot out the light next to the platform the preacher was standing on. Everything went dark, and the Klansmen all started to run. The preacher hid out in the woods for three days afterwards. That was the last time the Klan ever stirred up trouble for us." Angel smiled with satisfaction, as if she'd actually taken part in the events that occurred almost five decades before.

"So Boughtflower was involved in the Battle of Hayes Pond?" Lindsay asked, turning back to Geneva.

"He sure was. A photographer from *Life* magazine was there that night. Well, when the story came out, in one of the pictures you could see Boughtflower clear as day, standing like a dope with those fools. His name wasn't mentioned, but everybody around here knew who he was because of how prominent his family was. You used to see him driving all over the county in his fancy Cadillac Eldorado. But after that, no decent folks would go anywhere near him. Even the racists were embarrassed to be seen with him, considering how the Klansmen got their behinds handed to them."

"Did Dunette know?" Lindsay asked Angel. "I can't believe she'd work for Lumbee Enemy Number One."

"I don't think so," Angel said, shaking her head. "She never said a word to me about it, and she tells me everything. But even if she had known, it wouldn't've stopped her from working for him. She's always trying to bring out the good in people. And from what I've seen, he's just as mean to white people as he is to black. He's an equal opportunity son of a b..." she blushed. "Sorry, reverends."

Lindsay crossed her arms. "When it comes to Klansmen, I think even Jesus might speak a colorful word or two."

Chapter 12

After the women finished their conversation, Lindsay made her way alone across the hall to Otis Boughtflower's room. In her nearly five years of hospital chaplaincy, she'd seen the entire spectrum of human character on display. Everything from a selfless young man donating a kidney to a perfect stranger he'd met at the grocery store to an addict who didn't shed a single tear when her toddler almost died from overdosing on the drugs she left lying around the house. Facing down a Klansman, who had quite possibly confessed to also being a thief and a murderer, was in some ways just another day at the office. Still, as she raised her hand to knock on his door, she felt the same sense of lurking dread she'd felt during their last encounter.

"Mr. Boughtflower, do you mind if I come in?" Lindsay said, opening the door.

"I asked for you, didn't I?" Boughtflower's gruff voice called in return.

A tall, rail-thin woman stood near the windows, arranging flowers in a vase. She turned when Lindsay came in and flashed a timid little smile. As Lindsay extended her hand in greeting, the woman's eyes darted around the room, as if she was unsure whether the proffered hand was meant for her or someone else.

"Hello, I'm Lindsay, one of the chaplains here."

"Pleased to meet you." The woman briefly clasped Lindsay's hand, but then quickly withdrew hers and used it to tuck a stray tendril of thick, grey-streaked brown hair behind her ear.

"You must be Mr. Boughtflower's daughter," Lindsay guessed.

"That's right," Boughtflower answered for her. "That's Margo."

Lindsay heard the sound of the door opening again and turned around, expecting to see Angel or one of the other nurses coming in. Instead, a red-faced man with a corn-yellow mustache and matching hair came through the door. He walked with his barrel-shaped chest pushed slightly forward and his arms swinging slightly away from his body, in the manner of many former athletes who'd let themselves go to seed. He held a cell phone to his ear with his upraised shoulder. He smiled broadly and extended his meaty hand.

"Yancy Philpot." He jerked a thumb toward the bed. "The old man's my father-in-law."

"Hi, Mr. Philpot. I'm Lindsay Harding, one of the chaplains." Lindsay searched his face and his wife's for hints of the origins of their daughter's incredible beauty. She could see snatches of resemblance—eye color here, a strong chin there—but clearly in Jess's case, the whole was greater than the sum of its parts.

"Chaplain? Wonders never cease. I didn't expect a pretty young thing like you to be a chaplain!" He winked at her. "I bet that explains why the old man has suddenly decided to find religion." He laughed and slapped Boughtflower playfully on the shoulder. "Isn't that right, Otis?" He gave Boughtflower a wink, which was returned by an icy glare.

"Who I talk to, or what I do is none of your damn business," Boughtflower wheezed.

Yancy turned to Lindsay and, in a conspiratorial stage whisper, said, "Don't let him fool you, Chaplain. He's really just a big, ole' softie. Isn't that right, Otis?"

Boughtflower pressed his lips together and purple splotches blossomed on his face. He opened his mouth to speak, but instead he broke into a volley of phlegmy coughs. When he stopped coughing, Margo laid her hand gently on his arm.

"Daddy, Yancy's only teasing. Aren't you, Yancy?"

Yancy laughed. "He knows I am." Yancy gestured to Lindsay to join him in the corner furthest away from the bed. His phone was still balanced in the crook of his neck, giving him the appearance of a hunchback.

"It's hard on him being in here, you know?" he said in a low voice. "He's used to calling the shots. We've got to remember that he needs to feel like he's still in charge, even though I'm really the man of the family now." Suddenly, Yancy's attention turned to his phone, and his hand shot up to grab hold of it. "What's the idea of keeping me waiting for so long, Gary? How long does it take you to pull up this week's inventory?" He put his hand over the microphone on the handset and said, "Will y'all excuse me a minute? I swear, I leave 'em alone for half a day and the whole place falls apart. They're like children."

After he exited the room, Margo turned to Lindsay apologetically. "He's so busy with his work these days. I was worried when he took this big promotion that it would be too much."

"What kind of business is Mr. Philpot in?" Lindsay asked.

"Oh, it's all numbers and shipments. Way over my head. I was never good at that kind of thing. Thank goodness Jess didn't take after me," she smiled.

She walked over and straightened the blankets on her father's bed. "Daddy, did I tell you Jess is making straight A's this semester?"

The old man nodded. For once, he looked genuinely pleased about something. "You did a good job with that girl, Margo. She's your crowning glory."

"Oh, I can't take the credit," Margo said, blushing. "Heaven knows she doesn't get her brains from me."

"Well, she sure as hell didn't get 'em from Yancy," Boughtflower mumbled.

"Do you work?" Lindsay asked.

"No," Margo said, with a nervous giggle. "I didn't have the brains for college or anything. When I was little, I thought I might become a veterinarian until Daddy told me how competitive it is. He didn't want to see me embarrass myself. Since Jess started school, I've been volunteering at the animal shelter twice a week. Keeps me out of trouble, Yancy says. Anyone can walk a dog and clean out a litter box, you know?"

Yancy returned to the room and put his arm around his wife's shoulders. "Hopefully that'll hold 'em for a few minutes," he said, rolling his eyes theatrically.

Boughtflower shot a contemptuous glare at him.

"Do you want us to leave you alone with the chaplain, Daddy? So y'all can talk in private?" Margo asked.

Boughtflower nodded. "Y'all go get something to eat. There's some money in my wallet." He pointed to the wooden locker that stood at the side of his bed. The key was on a stretchy, spiral band, which coiled so tightly around his enormous wrist that Lindsay feared it would cut off the circulation to his hand.

The effort of removing the band and key from his wrist seemed too much for him, so Margo slid it off and unlocked the locker. She removed the wallet and held it up. "Is $20 okay, Daddy?"

"For dinner? Where are we supposed to go? McDonald's?" Yancy asked with a laugh.

"Could we take $60, Daddy? We'll take Jess, too."

Boughtflower frowned but nodded.

"Thank you, Daddy," Margo said, bending down to kiss her father's sweaty forehead.

"It was nice meeting you. Try not to flirt with him too much now. He's got a bad heart, you know," Yancy said, playfully elbowing Lindsay as he went past.

Although Lindsay appreciated Yancy's lighthearted friendliness, especially in contrast to the sourness of his father-in-law, there was something oily about his manner that made her uncomfortable. In fact, the whole scene—Margo's meekness, Boughtflower's irritability toward his son-in-law, Yancy's jokes, and especially the strange financial arrangements, all gave her the creeps.

When Margo and Yancy were gone, Lindsay turned toward the old man. "Is there something I can help you with?" she asked. "Would you like me to pray with you?"

He began to laugh, but it quickly turned into a choking fit. Lindsay moved toward the nurse call button, but he waved her violently away. Instead, she handed him a water cup from which he took small sips.

Lindsay sat quietly while Boughtflower recovered his breath. Evening was beginning to fall, and the sun glowed giant and red through the window. In the strange shadows the light cast, Boughtflower's huge form seemed to be draped across the bed like a deflated zeppelin. It was impossible to believe that a body so massive would soon be devoid of life.

When he spoke at last, his voice was quiet, a gravelly whisper. "You probably heard that this is the end for me."

Lindsay nodded.

"Well, there's a lot of things I've done that I'm not proud of. But the thing I'm gonna do now, I *am* proud of. I've made sure that not a single red cent of the Boughtflower money is passed on to any of them."

He closed his eyes and Lindsay half-wondered if he'd fallen asleep. Normally, she might have tiptoed out of the room in such circumstances to allow the patient to rest, but instead she prompted, "Do you mean you don't want your family to inherit your money? You said something before, about the money not being yours?"

His eyes flew open. "That's right. After he died... instead of sharing the money with all the people..." He paused and his attention seemed to drift for a moment, perhaps caught up in memories of the past.

"Right after who died? A relative of yours?" Lindsay asked.

He shook his head. "The Burnt Island people... We took it... Ran away with it... Everything that happened afterwards is because of that damned money. I tried to give it back... Let them be the ones to deal with it." He narrowed his eyes and his breathing became even more labored.

"Who should deal with it? The Burnt Island people?"

He nodded. "Need help... It needs to get back where it belongs." Boughtflower's breath was coming now in ragged gasps, and his lips took on an unhealthy, bluish tinge. "There's somebody else helping, too. Together, you'll make sure."

"Who else is helping? Together with who?" Lindsay asked.

Boughtflower gasped, his eyes bulging.

"Mr. Boughtflower, I'm going to ring for a nurse," Lindsay said, keeping her voice as calm and even as she could. She had stood alongside enough dying people to recognize the signs of an imminent departure. Even though she knew that Boughtflower had signed the paperwork to say he didn't want to be resuscitated if he stopped breathing again, she also knew that it wasn't her place to make medical decisions. And although she didn't want to say it out loud, she feared that if Margo didn't get back very soon, she was very likely to miss her father's last moments.

Boughtflower tried to speak again, but instead began to gasp and flail, his eyes growing wide. In a voice that sounded like air being squeezed from a bellows, he whispered, "Jess...tell her...I thought I'd have more time."

Chapter 13

Even though Lindsay had covered less than half of the hours of her normal shift, by the time she finished work just after 7:30 p.m., she was so emotionally drained she felt like she'd been working for several days straight. Boughtflower's words to her had turned out to be his last. He had gasped and choked, his ragged breathing becoming more and more irregular until it finally ceased altogether. The hospital staff hadn't been able to reach Margo and Yancy in time, so the brief deathbed vigil had fallen to Lindsay. Even now, hours after his body had been taken away by emissaries from the funeral home, she could almost feel the weight of Boughtflower's huge, heavy hand in her own. She could still see his eyes, which had stayed fixed on her until the very end. In fact, even after he'd drawn his last, gasping breath and his heartbeats had ceased, his eyes had continued burning into hers, as if he were trying to convey a final message. After the attending physician had called the time of death, she had been the one to reach over with a trembling hand and draw Boughtflower's eyes closed.

Lindsay handed over the on-call pager to the chaplain who was on night duty, gathered her things, and made her way slowly down the hall. She was in no hurry to return home. Although she'd tamed her inner turmoil enough to leave her father's house and get through part of a shift, she still wasn't sure if she was ready to face her father, Simmy, or Warren. She was caught in a vicious cycle— she was ashamed of her behavior in locking herself away from them, but the shame was now so pervasive, she felt like she needed to hide from them. She briefly toyed with the idea of returning to her own house, which John had informed her via Rob, was now clear for occupancy. But the prospect of sleeping there alone terrified her. Moving back in would have to wait until Simmy and Kipper could join her there this weekend.

She was so caught up in her own dark thoughts that she didn't hear her name being called at first. It wasn't until Adam Tyrell stood almost directly in front of her that she finally registered his words.

"Lindsay! I thought that was you, but when you didn't look up, I thought maybe you'd given me a fake name or something," he said. "I don't know if you remember me. I'm the guy from the parking lot. The tire?"

"Oh, yes. Of course, I remember," she stammered. "I was just daydreaming."

"Good dreams, I hope?"

She avoided the question, which seemed somehow too personal. "So, how's your mother doing?"

"Much better. They think she'll be able to go home the week after next."

"Must've been a pretty major operation if she's going to be here more than a week," Lindsay said.

"They had to remove part of her bowel. She has Crohn's disease." Adam paused, his cheeks coloring slightly. The expression on his handsome face held a disarming boyishness. "I bet you're sorry you asked. The details aren't pretty."

"I shouldn't have pried," Lindsay said. "It's just that people usually like to get up and out of here as fast as possible."

"Mother hates the hospital. She's spent way too much time with doctors and stuff over the years." Gesturing to Lindsay's jacket and backpack, he asked, "Are you on your way home?"

"Yep."

"I don't suppose you'd want to grab dinner? Don't get the wrong idea," he added quickly, putting his hands up in front of him. "I know you're taken. But you're the only person I know in Mount Moriah other than Mother." The corners of his full lips were turned upwards in a shy smile, and his face was tipped slightly forward so that he looked at her through his long, black eyelashes.

Lindsay almost couldn't bring herself to look at his face— afraid that the powerful attraction she felt toward him would pull her into his arms like a physical force. She couldn't remember ever having felt such an instant connection with someone—not with her first boyfriend, Tim, and certainly not with Warren, whom she'd known for more than a decade before they embarked on a relationship. Up to now, she thought that that kind of slow burn, comfortable attraction suited her, but now she began to wonder. What might it be like to throw propriety aside? To be with someone out of pure lust? The magnetic sensation she experienced was so palpable that she could almost feel what it would be like to have her body pressed against Adam's. Did she feel this way in reaction to getting engaged? Or was there something special about Adam? And of course there was the overriding question—how could a guy be *that* good looking?

"I'd love to, but I'd better not," she said, blushing at her own indecent thoughts.

"I hope you don't think I'm a creep or something. You just seem cool. I promise I have *zero interest* in stealing you away from your fiancé."

The last sentence was so emphatic that it hit Lindsay like a slap. Not only was it ridiculous to be mentally cheating on Warren with a guy she barely knew, it was doubly ridiculous to have thought for a moment that she was in the same league as Adam.

"Oh, no," she spluttered. "I wasn't implying… It's just that I'm tired. I'd love to go to dinner with you sometime as friends. Just not tonight."

"Great," Adam said, his face lighting up. "Are you free on Sunday night? Sunday's the worst day around here. Everything's closed and I usually don't have any work to keep me occupied."

"I'm working this Sunday night, 3 p.m. to 11 p.m."

"Well, what about the following Sunday?"

"Um, I think I work the eleven to seven shift that day," Lindsay said slowly.

"Perfect! I'll meet you right here next Sunday," he said, pointing to the ground where they stood. "You can pick the place, since Mount Moriah is your home turf."

"We'll probably have to go to New Albany, since the Mex-Itali and Bullards are both closed on Sundays. Everything else is just pizza or fast food. Since you've lived in Europe, how do you feel about somewhere really upscale and glamorous, like the Olive Garden?"

"Do they still have unlimited breadsticks?"

"Yes."

"Count me in. Here, take one of my cards so you can call me if anything changes. The one with the +1 is my U.S. number."

She turned it over and read it out loud, "Business Security Consultant? And you're based in Bratislava and Berlin? What are you, Jason Bourne?"

"Something like that," he said with a sly smile.

"Sounds like it might take awhile for me to get you to divulge all your secret identities and the names of the people you've assassinated," Lindsay said. "Good thing we'll have unlimited breadsticks."

***

"Do you have any more of those?" Owen asked, pointing the empty plate that had, until a few moments before, contained some of the leftover nutty buns from Lindsay's birthday. Her father had stored them in the freezer during her extended emotional crisis and sent them with her that afternoon as a housewarming present.

"Yeah, they're in the big Tupperware on the counter," Lindsay replied.

She was sitting at the paper-strewn kitchen table of her house the afternoon after her encounter with Adam alongside Mike Checkoway, Owen's father and Anna's brother-in-law. Owen had ostensibly come along to "hang out" with Kipper, but Lindsay suspected that the abundance of sweets she usually kept in stock might've influenced his decision as well.

Mike watched his son grab a nutty bun and a tennis ball and head out the back door with Kipper. "I know everybody thinks I don't feed him, but I do. I swear. He's like that plant from *Little Shop of Horrors* that just keeps getting bigger the more you feed it."

"It's all right," Lindsay said. "The more of those he eats, the fewer I'm going to have to jog off later today."

"In that case," Mike said, rising to grab another nutty bun for himself. "I'll do my part in saving you the extra mileage."

"Thanks so much for doing this," Lindsay said. "It's kind of exciting to be hiring an employee. I've never hired anyone to do anything before."

After years of practicing law in Chicago, Mike had moved to North Carolina a few months before and recently passed the bar exam there, allowing him to practice law in his adopted state. In Chicago, he had specialized in setting up charitable foundations for large corporate and private philanthropists. In Mount Moriah, however, he did a bit of every kind of lawyerly work, from wills and adoptions to, in Lindsay's case, an employment contract for Dunette Oxendine.

"Sure you have," Mike said, removing his reading glasses, his jewel-green eyes twinkling with mixture of curiosity and amusement. "What about a housecleaner?"

"Nope."

"That's impossible. Everybody's hired somebody at some point. What about when you've had work done on your house? Like, say, this huge renovation project," Mike said, gesturing to the expanded kitchen and the hallway leading to the new sitting room, bedroom, and bathroom that had been added to accommodate Simmy.

When it was built, Lindsay's house had been a one-room schoolhouse, but it had been renovated years before and turned into a small one-bedroom, one-bathroom dwelling. The new space that had been added for Simmy had almost doubled the square footage of the original structure, but John had made the changes with such sensitivity to the original design that it was difficult to tell where the old house ended and the new addition began.

"I've always done the small stuff myself, and John has helped with the bigger stuff," she shrugged.

"But you pay him, right? So you've hired people before."

"Nope. I couldn't afford him. He lets me just pay for the materials. I helped him and Rob rehab their house when I first moved here and I help out at the Tatum family Christmas tree farm a couple times a year. Besides, John owes me money for babysitting Rob all the time."

Mike chewed his nutty bun thoughtfully. In repose, his face looked somewhat fleshy—full lips, wide-set eyes, and a broad forehead. A wrinkle creased his forehead as he concentrated, and Lindsay could see the flecks of gray in the dark stubble on his chin. He was the opposite of chiseled and closer to 50 than 40, but he retained a definite allure, like a piece of well-built antique furniture that, given a good polish, would shine.

"Aha! I've got it. Owen said you hired him to walk Kipper when you're working." He smiled broadly, his large white teeth gleaming.

"But I'm paying him in doughnuts and brownies, so it doesn't count," Lindsay countered. "I declare myself the winner of this debate."

"On a technicality!" Mike protested.

Lindsay smiled. Her friendship with Mike had gotten off to a rocky start when he had drunkenly kissed her at Anna and Drew's wedding. Since then, however, the two had fallen into a camaraderie built around a shared love of American history, Mount Moriah's quirks, and trivial, good-natured arguments.

"Speaking of technicalities, how's the lawyering going? Are you staying busy?" Lindsay asked.

She knew that Mike was only happy when he could remain in constant motion. His wife, Jocelyn, had died of a neurological disease a few years earlier, and her careful financial planning had left Mike and his son with a very large amount of disposable income. Since then, the pair had crisscrossed the globe in what amounted to an extended, hyperactive holiday. At Owen's prompting, however, Mike had finally agreed to move to Mount Moriah to give his son a more stable upbringing and a chance to graduate from a regular high school. His friends had worried that the pace of life in the tiny town would be too slow for an adventure junkie like Mike, but so far he seemed to have managed to find ways to occupy his time.

Mike shrugged, running his hands carelessly through his salt-and-pepper hair. "It'll take a while. In the meantime, I'm researching scuba trips for me and Owen to do during his summer vacation. Oh, and did I tell you I bought a plane? It's a Piper PA-28. Two seater. I got my pilot's license a few weeks ago. It was actually pretty easy."

"You just up and bought a plane?" Lindsay asked. Even though she had by now become accustomed to Mike's sudden, capricious obsessions and hobbies, announcements like this still managed to surprise her.

"Yeah. When we moved here, I finally decided to sell our condo in Chicago. Prices in the South Loop had really skyrocketed since Jocelyn and I bought the place, and I guess penthouses with a lake view are pretty rare, so even after I gave a bunch of money to the charities I'm on the boards of, and bought the new house here, and furniture and stuff, there was so much money left over…"

"I know what that's like. Plane money just burning a hole in your pocket." Lindsay teased.

Even when Mike said things that might've sounded boastful if they'd come from a different source, he had an "aw shucks" quality that managed to come across as artless and unaffected, as if his own good fortune continually caught him by surprise.

"I didn't mean it like that. Houses here are just really cheap and planes really aren't as expensive as everybody thinks. It was a couple years old, so it cost less than a lot of cars. Oh, speaking of houses, I could use your advice on something. You know Morgan Partee, whose family owns Partee Auto World?"

Lindsay nodded.

"Well, Morgan and his wife have been looking for a house worthy of North Carolina Piedmont royalty, which, from what I've seen, is how they think of themselves. Anyway, they'd been searching for months and couldn't find anything in Alamance County sufficiently grand for them until a couple of weeks ago. Bingo. Perfect house. Their realtor, who helped me and Owen find our house, called me a couple days ago and asked me to do the closing for them. I guess Mr. Portofino, who she usually uses for closings, got arrested for indecently exposing himself from a highway overpass, so they were in a bit of a bind."

"No way. Portofino did the closing on my house. He's really, really hairy. And he has those weird teeth," Lindsay said, putting her index fingers up to her mouth and pointing them downward like tusks. "Are they charging him with a misdemeanor? Because in his case, that should really be a capital crime. People's actual eyeballs are at stake."

"I've never met the guy, so I'll have to trust you on that one," Mike said. "Anyway, what was I saying?"

"Sorry. You were doing the closing on the Partees' house…"

"Oh yeah," Mike said, picking up the thread of his story again. "So they'd been looking forever, and suddenly this luxurious mansion with acres and acres of land in New Albany comes on the market—pool, stables, six bedrooms. The house needs a lot of updating, but it was listed at just under $550,000, which is a really good price for that amount of land, so they pounced. Anyway, I show up for the closing, and who should be selling the house, but Owen's new girlfriend."

"Wait, Jess Philpot was selling the house?!"

"That's right."

"How does she own a mansion? She's a teenager!" Lindsay said.

"It's her grandfather's. He gave her power of attorney," Mike replied. "She can make any and all business decisions on his behalf."

"But doesn't POA only apply if he's incapacitated? He was totally with it." Lindsay sometimes helped her patients and their families navigate difficult end-of-life decisions, so she was familiar with advance directives and the other legal paperwork involved in ensuring that the person's final wishes were carried out.

"Durable power of attorney is the most common kind," Mike agreed, nodding. "That's what you're thinking of. It only kicks in under the specific provisions the grantor stipulates, like incapacity due to illness or death. But in Jess's case, the POA was what's called 'general.' Basically, in the eyes of the law, she *is* Otis Boughtflower."

"Why would he do that?" Lindsay wondered. "It's one thing to get your affairs in order, but it's pretty unusual to entrust hundreds of thousands of dollars in assets to a girl who's still in high school."

"I know, but that's not even the weirdest part. When Jess saw me, she freaked out. She took me aside and begged me not to tell her parents that her grandfather's house was being sold. She told me that as soon as he realized he was dying, he moved out of the house and into the hospital specifically so he could try to sell it before he died. He named her as his agent so she could complete the sale if he didn't live long enough to see it through."

"Weird," Lindsay said.

"The whole thing was bizarre, for sure, but perfectly legal. Apparently Boughtflower was trying to liquidate all his assets."

"I've seen Boughtflower in action with his daughter and her husband. He treated them like children when it comes to money, and yet he lets an eighteen-year-old handle a half-million-dollar real estate transaction? It just doesn't add up."

"Owen thinks the world of Jess, and, honestly, she's grown on me. She's a lot smarter than she lets on, and nicer, too, actually. But I don't understand it, either."

"So, did you go through with it?" Lindsay asked. "I would've been nervous to be a part of something that shady."

"I did think about backing out, but there was absolutely nothing wrong with the sale, the POA, or any of the other documents. I went through everything with a fine-toothed comb, and it was all in perfect order. The proceeds from the sale are all going into a trust, and the beneficiary of that trust won't be named until Boughtflower's will is unsealed."

"I suppose that'll be any day now. He died last night," Lindsay said.

"I didn't realize that," Mike said. "Well, I guess we'll find out who's getting the money pretty soon then. Jess says she doesn't know, but that her grandfather told her it's not her. Maybe he's leaving it all to his daughter and just wanted to save her the hassle of selling everything?"

"I don't think Margo's going to see a penny of that money," Lindsay said.

"Really? She seems all right from what I've seen. Not much going on personality-wise, but she's definitely devoted to her family as far as I can tell. Yancy, Jess's father, is a different story. I'm guessing this whole elaborate thing with giving the POA to Jess and keeping the will a secret is because Boughtflower doesn't want him to get his hands on the money. If Margo knew about it, she'd just tell her husband. She's nice, but spineless, and I bet Yancy would get the whole story out of her in five minutes flat. I don't know Yancy very well, and I'm all for giving people the benefit of the doubt, but that guy could use the benefit of somebody's fist in his face."

"Anna suggested as much. She said he's a racist?"

"Yeah. Nothing I can pinpoint, mind you. Just subtle stuff. Like telling Owen he should run track instead of going out for the tennis team. I might be over-thinking it because of having been in an interracial relationship. You wouldn't believe some of the stuff Owen's mom and I went through when we got together." He paused, a bittersweet smile playing across his handsome features. "You remind me of her, you know. A pain in the neck, but a cute one."

Lindsay rose and walked over to the sink, so Mike wouldn't see how unsettled the remark made her. Although she'd been as firm as she could in setting the boundaries of their relationship, it was obvious that the attractive widower still carried a brightly-burning torch for her. He constantly complimented her appearance and seemed to find her endlessly clever and fascinating. The comparison to his former wife, who Lindsay knew he thought of as the perfect woman, was the highest compliment he could pay. Worse still, she found she'd come to crave the constant verbal affirmation that Mike provided to her. His compliments, despite their occasional quirkiness, coupled with his unveiled adoration of her gave her self-esteem a regular jolt of positive energy, just as she'd been electrified by the sexual frisson she thought she'd felt between herself and Adam.

Were these feelings trying to tell her something was lacking between her and Warren? Warren showed his feelings through quiet action. He washed her car every Saturday. He brought her a gallon of milk if he noticed she was running low. He flushed her radiators in the autumn so they wouldn't clang. Is that what she wanted from love? Dependability, respect, and a steady supply of dairy products? Or did she want something more—an unending stream of compliments, fiery passion? Maybe all those things rolled into one?

"So," she said, shaking off the troubling thoughts and getting a glass of water from the sink, "you think Jess was just following her grandfather's instructions?"

"I have no reason to doubt her," he replied.

Lindsay turned back to face him.

"Lemme guess, you have a reason," Mike said, regarding her tell-tale frown with amusement.

"No, I don't have a reason. That's the problem. Something's off, but all I have is my Spidey sense, which is definitely tingling." She took a sip from her water glass. "I don't suppose Jess has ever mentioned anything about her family's money having been stolen? Or anything about a place called the Burnt Island?"

"Hmm… There's a village called Burntisland in Scotland. It's near Edinburgh. I remember going through there last summer when Owen and I were biking around the British Isles. What does that have to do with Boughtflower?"

"Just something he said right before he died. There's also a Burnt Island Lighthouse in Maine, and Burnt Island is a peninsula in Newfoundland. I Googled it. But the one I'm really wondering about is in North Carolina. Down near the Lumber River near Lumberton, there's a little road called Burnt Island, and I know for a fact that Boughtflower had been to that area at least once during his life."

"Was he doing business down there? Something to do with textiles?" Mike speculated.

"I guess you could say that. White sheets to be precise."

Mike looked puzzled, and opened his mouth to ask a question, but the sound of a hard knock on the front door interrupted their conversation.

Lindsay was surprised to see Warren's face framed in the small, glass rectangle on her front door. She still hadn't mustered the courage to return his calls, and he wore a scowl that let her know he'd noticed. She opened the door and let him in.

"So Mike's here?" Warren demanded, pointing to the car parked next to Lindsay's in the gravel drive.

"Uh, yeah. With his son," she hastily added. "Mike's helping me with an employment contract for Dunette."

"Who's Dunette?" he asked.

"Dunette's the home health aide I'm hiring to help out with Simmy."

With a sinking feeling, Lindsay realized that she hadn't yet told Warren about her new employee, nor that she was set to start working the following day when Simmy and Lindsay officially moved back into her house.

"When were you gonna tell me you'd moved back in? Or were you just going to wait until I found out from the officers I've had checking up on you every day to make sure you're safe?"

Lindsay touched his arm. "Sorry, okay? I messed up. I should've called you sooner," she said.

"I called *Rob*. I was so worried about you that I asked *Rob* to make sure you were okay," Warren said, his voice rising in volume.

"Don't say his name like that," Lindsay said.

Mike emerged from the kitchen sheepishly clutching his briefcase. "Hey, Warren. How are you?" Warren didn't return the greeting; he just glowered at Mike as he passed. "Lindsay, I left the contract on the table. I'll just go out back and grab Owen, and we'll head out. Call me if you have any questions."

"Thanks a bunch. That was really nice of you," Lindsay called after him as he made a quick exit out the back door. When he was out of earshot, she turned to Warren. "I know you're mad at me, and you have every right to be, but there's no reason to be mean to Mike. He was just helping me."

He laughed bitterly. "Surprise. Single guys like to do favors for pretty women."

"It's not like that with him," Lindsay countered, but even as she said it, she doubted the truth of the statement.

"You know what? You're right. There's no reason to be mad at Mike. You're the one who's spent almost a week ignoring my calls. I'm supposed to believe that you're terrified of Swoopes, that you're deep in the throws of depression, but I come to find out everybody's just hanging out at Lindsay's having a good old time. You can't pick up the damn phone to call me, but you can pull yourself together enough to call Mike to help you put together an employment contract for someone you apparently saw fit to hire without even mentioning it to me?" By now, Warren was full-on shouting.

"I can make decisions on my own, you know," Lindsay snapped. Even though she was well-schooled in techniques to diffuse hostile situations, somehow, when it came to her personal relationships, she always seemed to fall back into old patterns of self-protection and stubborn refusal to yield ground.

"Like deciding to go back to work? And have a heart-to-heart with Rob? I bet you've returned Anna and Simmy's phone calls, too. From what I can see, my supposed fiancée has decided to move on with every aspect of her life that doesn't include me."

"I was going to call you. Tonight. Things have just been really weird and confusing ever since we got engaged. I'm not good at all of this, okay?"

"You're not the only one who has doubts, you know. You don't have a monopoly on that."

"Are you saying you're not sure we should get married?" Lindsay asked. She was ashamed to admit that she had never seriously considered that Warren could experience the same kinds of uncertainties and insecurities that she did. He always seemed to proceed with such an abundance of caution and care that it seemed impossible he could doubt his decisions.

"No, I'm not saying that. I'm saying it's not like I have a crystal ball that guarantees everything's gonna be okay. I thought long and hard before I asked you to be my wife. I think we make a good team, and I've never cared about anyone's opinions as much as I care about yours. And I would do anything to keep you safe. But I can't do any of that if you keep shutting me out like this. At first I thought you just needed time away from everything. It hurt, but I could handle that because I thought I understood you. But I can't handle it if the only thing you need time away from is us. Or me. How can we build a future on that? That's not a basis for a marriage. That's me driving around town until I find you holed up in your house with some other guy."

"We weren't holed up here, Warren," Lindsay said desperately. Now that her initial anger had faded, the emotion that took its place was fear—fear that she might have pushed Warren further than she meant to. "I don't know how to explain it. I was just in a weird place mentally, and the longer it went on, the harder it became to talk to you."

"Stop," Warren said quietly. "You know what? I'm done."

"Are you dumping me?" Lindsay asked.

"I love you, and as much as it kills me, there's probably nothing you could ever do to me that would change that. But it finally dawned on me that if you loved me, you'd run towards me when things get bad instead of running away."

"I'm sorry I hurt you. Please, let's talk about this," Lindsay pleaded. Tears were now streaming freely down her cheeks, in contrast to Warren's cheeks, which were bone dry.

The affection seemed to have drained from his brown eyes. In that moment, Lindsay realized that she'd brought about the very thing that was at the root of her fear of commitment. She had been afraid that there was something broken deep inside her, something that made her deserve all the bad things that had happened in her life—her parents' abandonment, her aunt's coldness, the unattainable standards her father had set for her, her first fiancé's betrayal, her mother's deceptions, her victimization by Leander Swoopes—all of it. She'd thought she was damaged goods, so she'd nurtured a dark space where her flaws had been magnified. Her inability to trust her instincts had left her feeling that committing to Warren might be the wrong choice, and now she'd lost her chance at a life with him. She'd been so terrified of trusting him with her whole heart that she'd locked him out of it permanently. The weight of her failures ached so much she thought she was going to stop breathing.

"*Now* you want to talk?" Warren answered with another bitter laugh. He shook his head. "There's nothing left to say. Good luck. Hope you find somebody who can make you happy."

Chapter 14

"When did you get home, honey?" Simmy asked Lindsay, as she and Dunette walked into the kitchen of Lindsay's house. The two women had just returned from Simmy's weekly physical therapy appointment in Greensboro to find Lindsay sitting at the kitchen table paging listlessly through a book, with Kipper stretched out at her feet.

"Just a few minutes ago. It was really quiet at the hospital today, so I was able to leave early," Lindsay replied, forcing a smile.

In truth, her shift at the hospital had been quiet. So quiet in fact that she'd been left with too much time to wallow in her own misery. Rob had stopped into the chaplains' office during her shift to find her crying uncontrollably. It had been a week to the day since Warren dumped Lindsay, and each day it seemed to become more difficult to put on a brave face at work. Rob had done what he could to improve her spirits, but decided it would be best if he called in one of the pool chaplains and sent her home early.

Lindsay, Kipper, and Simmy had moved back into Lindsay's house the day after her fight with Warren, and although in some ways the added chaos and lifestyle adjustments couldn't have been timed any worse, it was an unexpected blessing to have the perpetually forward-looking Simmy in her home. It didn't hurt that Dunette—warm, reassuring Dunette—was also an almost daily presence. So far, Lindsay had been able to keep herself together in front of them in part because she didn't want her great grandmother's arduous rehabilitation and the transition to her new surroundings to be made even more difficult by her despondency. But Lindsay had to admit that it was also pretty tough to remain glum around a woman who'd spent the morning doing outlandish, self-styled yoga poses and giving a glitter manicure to Kipper while belting out Ella Fitzgerald songs at full volume.

"How was aqua therapy?" Lindsay asked.

"Wet," Simmy said, hanging her pink metal cane over the back of a chair and using her fists to knead circles on her hips. "And that new physical therapist is a born sadist. Like Stalin in swim shorts. But on the plus side, Dunette finally took me to the liquor store. We now have what it takes to make a house a home: a fully-stocked bar." She gestured toward the paper bags Dunette had set on the countertop. "It was shameful how little alcohol you had in the house before. I know you're your father's daughter, but I'd hoped that you'd at least get some of my good traits."

"Like your iron liver?" Dunette said with a smirk.

Simmy's alcohol intake had been severely curtailed during her months in the rehab facility, and she'd made it clear that she intended to make up for lost time.

"It's my philosophy that life goes along a little easier when it's properly lubricated," Simmy replied, removing the largest bottle of Maker's Mark Lindsay had ever seen from one the paper bags. "You could join us, you know, instead of standing over there clucking like an angry hen," Simmy said, lifting the bourbon bottle by the neck and giving its contents a little shake.

"You know I don't drink on the job. And even if I did, I have church in the morning, and some of us don't think we should be showing up to the Lord's House drunker than Cooter Brown," Dunette said, folding her arms over her ample chest. She cast a sharp eye at Lindsay. "When I took a job working for a minister to look after an old lady, I didn't know there'd be so much hard drinking."

Lindsay threw up her hands and shrugged.

"Can I remind you," Dunette continued, "that Simmy's doctor said she's supposed to be eating a healthy, balanced diet to support her recovery?"

"My diet is as balanced as they come. Whatever food I eat, I balance it out with an equal amount of liquor," Simmy quipped. "I reckon bourbon is gonna be one of those things like cholesterol. First they say it's bad for you, but later they find out we should've all been guzzling it by the gallon this whole time. I'm just ahead of the curve." She raised her glass. "To Cooter Brown and good Christians!"

Dunette tried to look stern, but it was impossible not to laugh at the brimming *joie de vivre* of the tiny woman, with her perfectly bobbed wig, her neon pink lipstick, and her gypsy-style dress of diaphanous, batik-patterned silk. Lindsay smiled, too, glad to see more and more of the old Simmy beginning to shine through. Although Lindsay didn't support her great grandmother's excessive drinking, her constant adoption of the latest pseudo-scientific health fads, or the way she left a trail of messiness and discombobulation everywhere she went, she was secretly relieved to see more and more of the older woman's vim returning. Simmy still had great difficulty maneuvering, but having Dunette around had restored much of her internal spark and confidence. Lindsay couldn't help but notice with a twinge of painful nostalgia that the banter between the two women mirrored the kind of Odd Couple back-and-forth that the free-spirited Simmy and Lindsay's stern Aunt Harding used to engage in.

"What were you reading, honey?" Simmy asked, picking up a book from the table in front of Lindsay.

"A history of Lumbee Indians, written by a Lumbee woman who's a professor at UNC," Lindsay said. "I realized when I was talking to Angel and Geneva the other day that I don't know very much about them, so I ordered this and a couple other Lumbee history books on Amazon."

"You want Lumbee history? You should come home with me sometime," Dunette laughed. "Just go into any barbecue joint where the old Lums hang out and they'll tell you about Henry Berry Lowrie like he was their daddy."

"You know, a lot of my classes focused on Southern history in college, and I'd never even heard of Henry Berry. I was just reading the chapter about him," Lindsay said.

"Any sex in this?" Simmy asked, looking the book over dubiously.

"Well, there's a romance that's even better than Robin Hood and Maid Marion," Dunette said, settling into a chair to tell the story. "Toward the end of the Civil War, the Home Guard boys got a little too big for their britches and started harassing the Indians, especially ones like the Lowries who had a bit of land and money put by. So Henry Berry and some others started fighting back.

They laid out in the swamps around Scuffletown so they could raid some of the rich folks' farms and then distribute what they stole to the poor people."

"That's robbers, not a romance," Simmy interjected.

"Hold your horses. I'm getting to that part," Dunette said. "Henry fell in love with Rhoda Strong, the most beautiful girl in the whole county," she continued. "Even the newspapers wrote about how pretty she was, called her the Queen of Scuffletown. The two of them met in secret for months. Finally, they got married, and his family threw a big enfare, that's a big reception party for them. But somebody had tipped off the Home Guard that Henry Berry had come out of hiding in the swamp, and they rode in and arrested him at his own wedding reception."

"So they didn't even get a wedding night?" Simmy said. "That's why I don't read books unless they have a man without a shirt on the cover."

"That's not the end of the story," Dunette said. "A few days afterwards, Rhoda Strong came to the prison with a cake for her husband. Later that night, the prison guard found a half-eaten cake, and an empty cell with all the iron bars filed through. Henry Berry lived as an outlaw around Scuffletown for the next ten years, but he snuck meetings with Rhoda whenever he could."

"Well, I guess that's better than nothing," Simmy said.

"Speaking of the Lowrie Gang, have you ever heard of a place called Burnt Island?" Lindsay asked.

Dunette furrowed her brow in concentration. "There's a Burnt Island Road out in the county. But there's nothing out there. Maybe a house or two, but I've never been back in there. I only know about it because I grew up out there and the school bus would go past. Why do you ask?"

"Burnt Island Road just dead-ends into forest and swamp. But I'm sure that has to be the Burnt Island Boughtflower mentioned. He also mentioned a man that died. It fits too perfectly to just be a coincidence. One of the Lowrie Gang's hideouts was Burnt Island Swamp, but there's nothing really left of that place. The area's all been drained, and the rivers and creeks keep moving, so there's nothing left of what was there in Lowrie's time. And we know

Boughtflower was there or at least close to there, during the Battle of Hayes Pond."

The front doorbell rang, and Lindsay pushed her books aside and rose to answer it. In what had become an involuntary ritual each time the phone rang or the doorbell sounded, she closed her eyes and willed the person to be Warren. She'd had no communication from him at all since the previous Saturday, despite her repeated attempts to contact him. He'd turned the tables on her, and now she saw how it felt to have the object of your affection suddenly drop out of reach.

Kipper raced ahead of Lindsay and stood in front of the door, emitting a series of ferocious barks.

"Kipper, heel," Lindsay commanded. The dog took a step backwards but retained his laser-beam focus on the door.

The face that appeared in the glass pane of the front door was one she never could've anticipated—the small window framed the round, ruddy visage of Otis Boughtflower's son-in-law, Yancy.

Lindsay unlocked and opened the main door, but left the screen door closed to keep Kipper from lunging at the visitor.

Before she could utter a word of greeting, Yancy's mouth fell open.

"You?!" he said.

She met his baffled expression with one of her own. "Mr. Philpot. How can I help you?"

"What are *you* doing here?" he sputtered.

"I live here," she said slowly. "You're at my house."

His momentary confusion transformed into an expression of rage. "I should've known you were in on it. No way would that old bastard have voluntarily talked to a chaplain. If you even are a chaplain…"

"I can assure you that I'm a chaplain. I'm not catching your drift, though," Lindsay said. "Why are you so surprised that I live in my own house?"

"She's here, isn't she?" he demanded.

Kipper growled. Clearly he didn't like Yancy's tone any more than Lindsay did.

"It's all right, Kipper," Lindsay soothed. Then, turning back to Philpot, she asked, "who's here?"

"That Oxendine woman." He was peering around Lindsay, keeping one hand on the outside handle of the screen door.

"Do you need to speak to her?" Lindsay began, but stopped herself. Yancy looked nothing like the jovial, past-his-prime athlete she'd met at the hospital the previous week. Instead, he filled the doorframe like a shadow, intent on some dark purpose. "Wait, did you follow her here?"

By this time, both Dunette and Simmy had emerged from the kitchen and were walking down the short hallway that led to the front door.

"Yancy?" Dunette said, her forehead furrowed with confusion. "That you?"

"I'll wring your neck, you conniving little…" Yancy tore open the screen door, but before he could enter the house, Kipper advanced toward him with a menacing growl.

"You call that dog back," he demanded.

"Not until you explain yourself, bub," Simmy snapped. "How dare you barge into my great granddaughter's house making threats? You have five seconds to start behaving yourself or you're gonna meet the pointy end of a 90-pound Doberman."

"I don't need to explain myself to you or anyone else," Yancy said. Although his voice was full of bluster, he stepped back and removed his hand from the door. "Y'all just better watch yourselves. Ain't no way I'm gonna let this stand. You hear me?" He stabbed his finger toward Lindsay and Dunette. "Ain't no way I'm letting some little midget minister wannabe and that fakety-fake injun steal from me!"

With that, Yancy turned on his heels. The day before, Dunette had placed three small clay pots planted with geraniums, snapdragons, and blue salvia on the steps leading up to the porch. Yancy kicked each one of these in turn, sending pottery fragments hurtling across the yard and smashing into the line of pine trees at the edge of the property.

The three women stood in shocked silence, while Kipper continued to bark and lunge at the closed screen door. Once Yancy drove away, the dog moved to the front window. He put his paws up on the sill and glared at the spot where the car had been.

"What in the world was that man jabbering on about?" Simmy asked.

"I have no idea," Lindsay replied. "You did a great job handling him, though. I don't know who was scarier, you or Kipper." She turned to Dunette. "Do you have any idea why he wanted to talk to you?"

"I don't know what he was talking about. I've never stolen anything in my life," Dunette said, shaking her head. "That's the way it goes. If something goes missing, people always blame the hired help. But I never took anything from Otis Boughtflower other than my paycheck."

"How well do you know Yancy?" Lindsay asked.

"Hardly at all. I just don't understand. He was always fine to me when I worked for the old man. A bit too big for his britches maybe, but nothing like that."

While they were still all standing in front of the open screen, a black sedan pulled into the driveway. A well-groomed man in grey dress slacks and a button-down shirt emerged and approached the front door. Again, Kipper had to be commanded not to attack.

"Dunette Oxendine?" the man asked. When Dunette nodded, he continued, "I'm a process server who's been commissioned to deliver a document to you on behalf of the Alamance County Court. Your cousin told me I could find you here. I need you to sign for this personally." He produced a large envelope marked, *from the law offices of Marshall Pickett, LLC,* and held it out to her. "Please sign here to confirm receipt," he said, indicating a form on a clipboard.

Dunette glanced at Lindsay and Simmy briefly and then signed the paperwork.

The man headed off with only a brief word of parting, and again the women were left in shocked silence. A crow descended from the sky and perched on the railing of the porch. Its beady black eyes moved across the front of the house. It cawed three times and then took to the sky again.

Dunette gripped Lindsay's arm. "That crow was a toten."

"What's a toten?" Lindsay asked.

"That's what we call a bad omen," Dunette whispered, glancing anxiously down at the envelope in her hands.

They returned to the kitchen where Dunette began to page through the documents she'd been handed, while Simmy poured them all generous glasses of Maker's Mark over ice.

"What in the world?" Dunette whispered as she read. When she finished, she pushed the papers across the table to them. "The first one's a letter from Boughtflower's lawyer. It says he's leaving everything—all his money, the proceeds from any property he has, stocks, bonds—to me to distribute for the benefit of 'my people.'"

"What?" Simmy and Lindsay said in unison. Even Kipper looked at Dunette with a quizzical expression.

"That's what it says. I get everything. The only other beneficiary named here is Jess."

"What does she get?" Lindsay asked, scanning through the document.

"An astronomy guide and a key," Dunette replied.

"A key?" Simmy said. "Maybe he left her his house?"

"Can't be. Mike told me he sold his house to Morgan Partee and his wife last week," Lindsay said.

"What then?" Simmy asked.

"It doesn't say." Lindsay found the passage and read it aloud. "To my beloved granddaughter, Jessica Boughtflower Philpot, I leave a key, which my lawyer has placed in a safe deposit box for you to claim. May it remind you that you are a young woman who has the ability to unlock anything. I also leave my cherished star chart. May it remind you to reach for your highest potential. I'm counting on you to make us all proud."

"It's hard to picture Boughtflower being sentimental. He didn't really strike me as the poetic type," Lindsay observed.

"Well, people do surprising things when it comes to family," Simmy replied. She and Lindsay exchanged a meaningful glance, remembering their shared history. "Anyway, that explains why the son-in-law came thundering over here. He must've just found out about this and gone out looking for you."

Dunette didn't appear to be listening. With a shaking hand, she grabbed the glass Simmy had poured and took a long swig of bourbon. She coughed a bit and then said, "I'm gonna send it back."

"Send what back, honey?" Simmy asked.

"The money and whatnot. I don't want that man's money. Why would he do this to me?"

"Don't be a ninny. Of course you should keep the money. From what you've said, he must've been loaded. You'll be set for life," Simmy said.

"You saw Yancy," Dunette replied, the color draining from her face. "Money makes people act like that. The more money you have, the more trouble it brings."

"But doesn't Yancy have his own money?" Lindsay asked. "I thought he had some high-level executive job."

"Yancy?! Oh please. He's a produce manager down at the Kroger in Burlington, and I think he only got that job as a favor to Boughtflower. I wouldn't let that fool put gas in my car, much less run some kind of fancy business." Dunette took another sip of her drink. "Why would he leave all that money to me? And who does he mean when he says 'my people'? I don't really have any close relatives."

"What about your cousin?" Simmy said.

"Angel's not even my real cousin. We just call each other that. My mama was sick with cancer for years and years, so Angel's grandmama always took care of me like I was one of her own. Pretty much anybody who's Lum is some kind of cousin or relation of mine. If he means family, though, my mother was an only child, and both my daddy's brothers died before they had children."

"Could he mean the Lumbees?" Lindsay guessed. "He felt terribly guilty about something. Maybe what he said about the Burnt Island people has something to do with it? Maybe he wronged the Lumbees who used to live there? Or maybe it was his involvement in Hayes Pond. I don't know if you knew this, but he was one of the Klansmen who came to that rally."

"Angel told me about that the other day, after you and Geneva and her talked," Dunette said. "But I didn't know about him being involved before that. He never mentioned it to me."

"Maybe he was trying to make up for what happened," Lindsay said. "Was anybody hurt during the rally? Was any money stolen? He said his money was all ill-gotten."

"Nobody got hurt except a couple of those Klan fools who got roughed up. And I never heard about money getting stolen. Besides, the South is full of old Klansmen, and you don't see them lining up to hand out checks just because they feel bad."

"I guess that wouldn't make much sense anyway," Lindsay agreed. "The Boughtflower family was already rich way before that happened. They built that factory before the turn of the century. There has to be a connection."

"Maybe he just didn't want to leave his money to his family. We know he didn't like that son-in-law, but maybe he didn't like any of them," Simmy speculated.

"He and Margo seemed to get along, and Jess was the apple of his eye," Dunette said. "No doubt about that. It was Jess, Jess, Jess, all the time. 'Jess is so pretty that the flowers write poems about *her*. Jess is so smart she drove her parents home from the hospital on the day she was born'. That admiration was the one thing that whole family had in common, including Jess herself. No way was he faking that. There's something wrong with this money, I can feel it."

Lindsay couldn't argue. There was definitely something fishy about Boughtflower's fortune. She recalled Boughtflower's dying words about wanting to return the money. *Let them deal with it*, he'd said.

"Well," Simmy interjected, "we don't really know what kind of relationship he had with them. Maybe when you came along, he just thought you were a nice person and deserved a bit of good luck. Did he ever ask you questions about yourself, like he was trying to find out if you were worthy of his gift?"

Dunette paused. "He did seem very curious about me, come to think of it, which was unusual because he wasn't big on chitchat. He asked me a lot about where I was from. I thought that was strange considering how he hired me. If he had any doubts about me, why would he have asked for me especially?"

"What do you mean 'asked for you especially'?" Lindsay asked.

"Didn't I tell you? I got a phone call out of the blue from Boughtflower's secretary about a year ago saying that I'd been recommended, and he wanted to hire me. I didn't know him from

Adam. I thought it was strange, with him living so far away from Lumberton, so I kind of put her off. But she was persistent. She said he wanted me especially because he'd heard that I was good and did flexible hours, and he didn't let just anybody into his house. I was flattered, I'll have to admit, but part of me didn't believe it. Lord knows I'm a hard worker, and I got good references, but with my criminal record, I didn't understand why anybody would go out of their way to hire me.

"Anyway," she continued, "I told him that I had agreed to start work for a woman who'd just gotten out of the hospital, and I couldn't leave until she was better. He said he'd hire a different nurse for that woman and he'd pay me 25% more than whatever I'd agreed with her. I thought about it for a few days, and then decided to go for it. Since I could live with Angel, it would be much better for me financially, and because of the hours I'd have more time to study for my nursing classes. It was also a way to got out of Robeson County and start fresh."

"Boughtflower has a secretary? Maybe she can shed some light on this whole thing," Lindsay said.

"I don't know where she is," Dunette said. "She was from Ireland and she went back there."

"Did she ever say anything that would help us track her down?" Lindsay asked. "Like mention her home town?"

"All I remember is that her name was Ellen, and she was Irish. I only talked to her a couple times on the phone. She left before I even got there, so I never met her. None of them ever talked about her either. She was like a ghost."

Chapter 15

Lindsay woke up unusually early the next morning still mulling over the revelations about Boughtflower's will. Why had he sought out Dunette? Had he already planned to leave his fortune to her, or was he simply looking for a caring and attentive nurse to shepherd him through his final days? Why had he entrusted Jess with his affairs, knowing that she had complete control of all his finances, only to disinherit her in his will? Why had he apparently strung the Philpots along financially right up until the end, instead of warning them that they would receive nothing in his will? Was Boughtflower's secretary the "somebody else" he'd told Lindsay was helping to ensure that his wishes were carried out? If so, where was she? And, of course, there was still the lingering question of his confession about hiding a body and stealing money from the inhabitants of the Burnt Island.

She'd called Mike the previous night to see if he could shed any light on the legal ramifications of the bequest. He'd spoken with Dunette briefly and offered to pay a visit to the Law Offices of Marshall Pickett, LLC on her behalf first thing Monday morning to see if he could discover the reason for the strange distribution of Boughtflower's assets. Because it was Sunday, getting more answers would have to wait at least a day.

In her stocking feet, Lindsay padded quietly through the house. The sun shone brightly through the windows, and for the first time since her fight with Warren, she felt strangely contented. Kipper's glitter-painted nails click-clicked on the floor as he walked alongside her down the hallway toward the kitchen. Simmy's buzzsaw snoring could be heard through her closed bedroom door. Lindsay realized that, for the first time in four months, several days in a row had passed since she'd last given any thought to Leander Swoopes. The raw anxiety that had plagued her seemed to have been dulled slightly, although she wasn't entirely sure why. By all external measures, her life hadn't improved. She'd had an emotional breakdown at work and been sent home by her boss. The police were no further in their attempts to discover the identity of

W. Doer. Her heart still contracted into a painful, tight ball every time she thought about losing Warren. And yet, something inside of her had definitively shifted.

She made herself a cup of coffee and paged through the Sunday *News & Observer*. The paper contained an almost comically brief obituary of "the beloved patriarch" Otis Boughtflower, stating that the former owner of Boughtflower Textiles "died peacefully" and was "resting in the arms of Our Lord." It went on to describe how he had been survived by "his loving daughter, Margo, her husband Yancy, and his beloved granddaughter Jessica." Only the almost inhuman corpulence captured in the memorial picture marked Boughtflower out from the twenty or thirty other people eulogized in the paper. Lindsay thought for a moment what a truly honest obituary for Boughtflower might look like. Something like, *Otis Boughtflower, closet racist, glutton, and misanthrope, died painfully, gasping for air and fearing eternal damnation. His grumpiness, anger, and bizarre secrecy about his past, possibly involving murder and robbery, will be remembered by those few who he allowed to know him. He is survived by a confused and angry family, who feel they've been jilted out of a fortune that should have been theirs.* No doubt, frank obituaries would improve readership.

The sun streaming in through the kitchen windows already felt warm. The rising heat of early May in North Carolina's Piedmont would be counted in many regions of the country as summer weather, but here the high 70s and low 80s of May were merely a precursor to the real heat and humidity still to come. Lindsay considered how to fill the three hours that remained until the start of her 11 a.m. to 7 p.m. shift.

During the time she'd lived with her father, the question of what to do on a Sunday morning had never once arisen. In fact, the entire week had been structured by church activities. Sunday morning, two services. Sunday night Bible study. Wednesday evening, the Awana children's ministry met. Saturday nights were for potlucks. Since moving back to Mount Moriah and beginning her chaplain job, however, she'd been an infrequent churchgoer. One obstacle was her work schedule; the frequent night shifts threw her weekend sleep schedule into disarray. The main problem, though, was her father. The church he'd founded had grown into one of the largest congregations in the region, but frankly, she didn't like it. People would spontaneously arise to share their testimony with the congregation, and the praise band's leader seemed to favor songs with titles like, "Truckin' Home to Jesus" and "Whole Lotta Holy." There was altogether too much hallelujah handclapping and glory-be hand raising for Lindsay's taste. For someone who'd spent so much of her life in church, she had an odd aversion to worshiping in a large group. For her, God was most readily seen and felt in personal reflections and one-to-one interactions. Worst of all, though, at Jonah's church the straight-backed wooden pews made you feel like you were atoning for a lifetime's worth of sin in the space of an hour and fifteen minutes. But in a place as knit-together as Mount Moriah, it was nearly impossible for her to try out another church's Sunday service without setting tongues wagging.

Today, though, she decided to throw on a dress and head over to the large, red brick building on the edge of town that housed Jonah's church. As usual, when it came to dealings with her father, guilt was her major motivating factor. Despite the fact that she'd behaved like a sullen teenager after finding out about his relationship with Teresa Satterwhite, Jonah had uncomplainingly helped Lindsay and Simmy move into her house. He even put contact paper down in her new kitchen cabinets and mowed the overgrown lawn. She hadn't managed to apologize to him or thank him properly, and she knew that an appearance at the 9 a.m. service would go a long way towards making amends.

Because she'd arrived at the service a few minutes late, there were almost no seats left. Lindsay was surprised at how much the already-large congregation had grown even since her last visit. Although it hadn't yet been made public, she knew that Jonah had recently been invited to give the sermon the summer after next at the big annual "Singing on the Mountain" gospel event at Grandfather Mountain, a huge honor that would no doubt add to his prestige and make it more likely that his church would soon need a bigger sanctuary.

Lindsay was ushered into a pew near the back and seated next to Courtland Bugbee Jr., a surly and chronically sweaty thirty-something man. By dint of their both being single, straight, and human, over the years Courtland Jr. had frequently been mentioned by various middle-aged churchgoing women as a potential romantic partner for Lindsay. He smiled at her in his strange, leering way when she sat down beside him, and she shuddered involuntarily when her warm hand touched his clammy one while reaching for the same hymnal. He smiled again and scooted closer, until she found herself sandwiched between his meaty, khaki-clad thigh and the wooden arm of the pew.

During the sermon on the parable of the Prodigal Son, she tried to catch Jonah's eye. It was no easy task. He had a charismatic, animated style of preaching, which often meant that he spoke with his eyes shut, waving his arms around as if he were being attacked by a swarm of wasps. At last, he noticed her and smiled warmly in her direction. She hadn't told him she'd be there, but she half-wondered if he'd chosen the subject matter specifically because of her visit. As she glanced over the gathered congregants, their faces turned to her father with rapt attention, she caught sight of Teresa Satterwhite's glowing, orange hair, which blazed like a traffic cone in a row near the front. Lindsay's heart fluttered as she scanned the pew next to Teresa for Warren, but of course he wasn't there.

The service passed swiftly, despite Courtland's encroachments on her personal space, and after the final hymn, Lindsay rose to leave. There was no point in staying to try to speak with Jonah. She knew from many, many hours of waiting after Sunday services when she was younger that her father would be surrounded by a mob of parishioners for the foreseeable future. The key was to leave before she could be accosted by any of the church's resident busybodies. She moved quickly through the crush of people, stopping for quick greetings with some of the families she'd known for years. She made the appropriate ooh-ing and aah-ing noises over the babies that'd been born since her last visit, and paid the necessary homage to the deacons, all the while skillfully dodging the cadre of older women who made it a hobby to ask intimate questions about her personal life and give her "helpful" tips about makeup and hair care. The scrutiny had become ten times as intense after all of the publicity surrounding her run-in with Swoopes. It was as if all the women's suspicions about her being not quite normal had been confirmed.

She had almost reached the narthex of the church when she felt a hand take hold of her elbow. "Well, Miss Lindsay, look at you! It's been an age and a half."

Lindsay turned to face the squat, flat-faced form of Coletta Bugbee. The woman was an amazing baker of Nutty Buns, but she was also the undisputed queen of the church's gossipmongers and know-it-alls.

"Hello, Mrs. Bugbee. How are you?" Lindsay said, silently cursing the adorable newborn baby who'd distracted her attention from her busybody evasion mission.

"I'm just fine, honey. Just fine. But how are *you*? We were all so sorry to hear that you and that nice Warren Satterwhite have parted ways. That's such a shame. We'd all been thinking we were gonna get to have a double wedding. Father and daughter with mother and son—wouldn't that have just beat all?" Mrs. Bugbee's shoulders rose in what might have been a nonchalant shrugging motion, but since the woman almost entirely lacked a neck, it was difficult to tell what emotion or concept she intended to convey. "Well, I guess it was too good to be true," she continued.

Lindsay tried to form words, but her thoughts were drowned in a sea of hurt and anger. She'd felt uplifted and optimistic that morning, but those positive feelings had evaporated in an instant. Apparently the entire church knew about her father's relationship with Teresa Satterwhite, and about her broken engagement with Warren.

"I couldn't help but notice that you were sitting with my Courtland," Mrs. Bugbee continued quickly.

"Yes, ma'am," Lindsay said.

"It is just a bafflement to me that he can't find a good woman to settle down with." Lindsay waited for the usual full-court press attempt to get her and Courtland Jr. to interact. Instead, Mrs. Bugbee made the same philosophical up-and-down motion with her shoulders. "There's bound to be somebody out there for you, too, honey. But, you'll have to be careful. That's two broken engagements now by my count. You were engaged to that Northern boy, too, right? I remember getting a wedding invitation a few years back. Anyway, mind what I say. You don't want to get a reputation."

"A reputation?" Lindsay repeated the words coldly.

"Well, you know what I mean, honey," Mrs. Bugbee said with a tittering little laugh. "Nice, single men like Warren Satterwhite and my Courtland Jr. don't grow on trees, you know. And time is ticking away. It's different for women," she continued, placing a consoling hand on Lindsay's forearm. "You think you have all the time in the world…"

Lindsay felt an arm encircle her waist and caught a whiff of a subtle, flowery perfume she recognized.

"I just know how much Lindsay appreciates your concern, Coletta. But I'm sure the only thing she has a reputation for is being a lovely, intelligent young woman who would be a credit to any man."

Lindsay's eyes widened in shock when she realized that her savior—the person so expertly steering her away from Mrs. Bugbee and out the front door of the church—was none other than Teresa Satterwhite.

"Do you think it's stuffy in here, sugar?" Teresa continued, addressing Lindsay. "Because I sure do. Positively claustrophobic! Let's get some fresh air." She was originally from Richmond, and her Southern accent dripped like honey when compared with the twang that peppered the speech of most native Mount Moriahans.

Once they were outside, Lindsay turned to Teresa. "Thank you, Mrs. Satterwhite," she said.

"Please, call me Teresa. We're practically family."

Lindsay studied Teresa's face for some indication of what she meant by "practically family," but all she saw was the same mask of flawless makeup and perfect composure that Teresa perpetually wore. Was Teresa still counting her as a daughter-in-law-to-be? Or had she taken on the role of stepmother-in-waiting?

"I'm so glad you decided to come today. Your daddy must be so happy to see you here, and besides that, it'll give the old biddies something to talk about all week," Teresa said with a conspiratorial wink. "Take some of the focus off me and your daddy's romance."

"I should really come more often. I know how much it means to him. Besides, I felt like I owed him one after how I behaved the other night," Lindsay said. "I'm sorry, by the way. I wasn't at my best."

Teresa raised her eyes heavenward. "None of us were. That was the most embarrassing thing that's happened to me since my skirt blew over my head at the Junior Assembly Cotillion when I was 12."

Lindsay smiled. This was one of the only one-to-one conversations she'd ever had with Warren's mother, and she had to admit that she was finding Teresa far less stiff and judgmental than she'd expected. Usually when they were together, Teresa was so busy doting on her son, and Warren was so busy basking in the glow of his mother's affection, that it was hard for Lindsay and Teresa to interact with each other.

"I meant what I said to Mrs. Bugbee," Teresa continued. "Your relationship with Warren is nobody else's business, and I will not allow Coletta Bugbee to fan the flames with that kind of gossip. And how dare she say you're not good enough for Courtland Jr.? As if that lumpy little son of hers is in the same league as my Warren."

So that's what this was about, Lindsay thought. Teresa had to ensure that Lindsay's reputation was preserved in order to uphold her son's reputation. If Lindsay was thought to be a bad prospect, then by extension Warren would be tarnished for having been engaged to her. Lindsay tried to conceal her annoyance. Teresa was circling the wagons to protect her darling son, but in this instance, at least Lindsay would benefit from being inside the circle.

"Anyhow, these things have a way of working out for the best," Teresa replied, patting Lindsay's hand. "Just look at me and your daddy. We both thought we'd had our one chance at love. After Warren Sr. died, I couldn't see how I'd ever find somebody who could hold a candle to him. And I bet your daddy felt the same way about his former wife. But here we are." While they'd been talking, Jonah had emerged from the church and was standing on the lawn speaking with two of the deacons. Teresa looked across the lawn at him with open admiration.

As she regarded them, Lindsay felt a tug-of-war inside her mind. The part of her brain that had done extensive Clinical

Pastoral Education training reminded her that anger, hurt, and jealousy were normal reactions when children, even adult children, were coping with a parent's new relationship. The other part of her brain told the CPE part that it could go to hell. There was no way she was letting this tangerine-haired Southern belle, this picture-perfect priss of a woman whose oh-so-perfect son had dumped Lindsay in her hour of need, wheedle her way into Jonah's life.

She withdrew her hand from Teresa's as if it had been burned. "Well, I better be getting to work. I'm sure I'll see you around."

Without a backward glance, she swept across the parking lot, firmly in the thrall of some very unchristian thoughts.

Chapter 16

Lindsay walked through the front lobby of the hospital at the end of her shift that evening feeling almost buoyant. Despite the emotionally turbulent start to the day, she'd managed to make it through her entire shift with her equanimity intact. It helped that, for once, her shift had been filled with a steady stream of glad tidings—babies safely delivered, cancer treatments proving effective, and patients' small prayers being answered. A whole shift without a tear being shed by her, the hospital's staff, or the patients had become a rare thing, and she was grateful for it.

"I thought you'd stood me up."

As usual, Lindsay had been lost in her own thoughts and hadn't noticed Adam Tyrell leaning up against a wall near the hospital's front entrance. Right near the spot where they'd agreed to meet. For dinner. That night.

"Adam! Hi."

"Did you forget? I should've called to remind you," he said.

Adam wore a cornflower blue button-down shirt with an almost imperceptible flower pattern. It was the kind of trendy item of clothing that would leave most men in Mount Moriah scratching their heads in wonderment, but Adam wore it with a natural sophistication.

"Oh, no. I mean, yes," Lindsay sputtered.

"Don't worry about it," he said, the corners of his sensuous lips turning down in disappointment, "if you're tired or whatever."

She thought for a brief moment about calling the dinner off. She was tired, and it had been a terrible, terrible week. She'd agreed to it only reluctantly at the outset, and that seemed like a lifetime ago, before she'd passed through her emotional crisis, when she was still engaged to Warren. Without the safe berth of that established commitment, she felt lost. When she was in a relationship, a dinner with a single man seemed less dangerous. Nothing could happen; she was spoken for. But going out with a single man as a single woman, even if he didn't know she was single, would be casting herself out into a stormy sea. Looking at

Adam's shy, attractive face as he ran his hand through his wavy, black hair, however, she decided that dinner with this single man might be just what she needed to perk up her spirits.

"I'm sorry. I did forget. But I'm here now, and I haven't eaten."

"Great! My car's out front, if you want me to drive."

"I'll drive," she said hastily. The Lindsay of last year might have gotten into a handsome stranger's car, but the post-Leander Swoopes Lindsay wasn't taking any chances. "Actually, do you mind if I just make a quick phone call before we go? I need to let some people know where I'll be and who I'll be with."

"No problem. I'll just page through this…selection of literature about sexually transmitted diseases," he said, frowning at the brochure stand mounted against the lobby wall, which was packed with informational flyers.

Lindsay returned his smile and stepped into a quiet alcove. She called Simmy to make sure she'd be okay on her own. Although she knew that Dunette had stopped by earlier to help her with her physical therapy exercises and make her dinner, she didn't like leaving the older woman by herself for nearly an entire day.

"Don't be silly," Simmy said, after Lindsay related the situation to her. "I'll be fine. I can't wait to hear how it goes. Or better yet, bring him back here after your date and then I can ask him myself over breakfast tomorrow morning."

"It's not a date, and he's definitely not going to be spending the night."

"You can't go into it with that attitude, honey. Rebound sex is the best kind of sex. Well, after make-up sex, that is."

"Goodnight, Simmy. I'll be home by 10."

"I'll put some condoms in your nightstand drawer, just in case."

"Why do you even have condoms?" Lindsay began. "You know what, never mind. I'll see you by 10."

On the drive to the Olive Garden, Adam put Lindsay at ease almost immediately, telling stories about his difficult early life and asking her questions about her own strange childhood on the Outer Banks. He hadn't seemed to mind that he had to move a mountain of junk mail, candy wrappers, and coffee cups in order to sit down in her car. She hoped he didn't notice that—thanks to her mother's car "borrowing" shenanigans a few months before—she had to start her car by finessing a thin piece of metal that looked like the end of a screwdriver into the ignition.

The conversation continued after they'd been seated at a booth in the back corner of the busy restaurant and ordered a bottle of wine to share.

"It's unusual to meet someone who had such a crappy childhood and turned out okay," Adam said in response to her story about helping to water her parents' marijuana plants as a child.

"What about you? You seem to be doing all right. And it sounds like you and your mom had a pretty rough time of it. Her illness, losing her job, bankruptcy, moving from place to place. Did your father ever help out at all?" Lindsay asked.

"He really wasn't in our lives," he said.

"I'm sorry. That must've been hard."

"It was. But it toughens you up, you know? Teaches you how to run your life, instead of letting it run you. Some of the people I work for are wildly successful. Private islands, mansions, servants. They have everything, but they wouldn't be able to survive a day without all their comforts. Growing up like I did lets me know I can make it no matter what."

"I feel that way, too, sometimes. Other times, I feel like my whole soul is just covered in scars, you know?"

"Scars are thicker than regular skin. Remember that," Adam said. His rich, cinnamon-colored eyes locked eyes with hers.

Lindsay's whole spine tingled under his penetrating gaze. She could feel the color rising in her cheeks. "She must be proud of you. Your mother," she said.

"I do what I can for her, you know? I want her to have all the things we couldn't have when I was young. I just want to be a good son." He took a sip of wine. "So your parents were both in jail? That's pretty wild," he said.

"Tell me about it," Lindsay said wryly.

"What are they doing now?"

"Well, my dad's a preacher and my mom's…back in jail."

"Does this have something to do with that guy? The kidnapping?" Adam said, taking a casual sip of his wine.

Lindsay's mouth fell open in shock. It was as if she'd just flipped the channel inside her head. She'd been watching a lighthearted romantic comedy, and now she suddenly found herself back in the horror movie that had played out a few months before. When she didn't reply to his question, Adam continued.

"That must've come out of nowhere," he said. "You're probably going to think I'm some kind of psycho, but I Googled you. There were news stories from earlier this year about how you and your mother and another lady were held hostage by an escaped convict."

"Yes, that's true," Lindsay said quietly.

"Do you still talk to your mother?" he asked.

"Sometimes. Our relationship is probably better now than it was when she was on the outside."

"So you've managed to forgive her? For all the stuff she's done?"

"Can we talk about something else?" Lindsay said sharply.

"I'm sorry," Adam replied, the color rising in his cheeks. "I should've known that would be a sore subject. Mother says this is why I don't have a girlfriend, or, well, friends. I just say things without thinking. She's always saying how I'm 'on the spectrum.' A few years ago, she actually made me a list of safe topics to discuss when I first meet people. You know, the weather and hobbies and stuff."

Lindsay smiled tightly and took another sip of her wine. "It's okay. I'd be curious, too, if I'd read a news story like that about you." She paused. "Actually, I Googled you, too."

"This is the modern age," Adam said with a smile.

"Anyway, hardly anything came up. Just your website, which sounded pretty vague. What exactly does a Business Security Consultant do?"

"I mainly work for high net worth individuals to do contingency and disaster planning. Making sure they have appropriate strategies and countermeasures in place."

"What does that *mean*?"

"Well, like coming up with plans for what they'd do if their personal data was severely compromised, or if one of their family members was held hostage."

"Oh."

Adam cringed. "Sorry, I didn't mean to bring the kidnapping thing up again."

"Well, it's a shame you weren't there when that happened to me. It would've been good to have a professional contingency and disaster planner," she replied, as usual trying to use humor to ease the tension.

"It sounds like you made your own plan. Not everybody could've escaped like that, you know. Most people just crumble. Like your mother. It sounded like she played right into that lunatic's hands."

Lindsay picked up her menu. At first she'd been a little baffled that such an impossibly handsome man could be single and seemingly friendless, but she was beginning to understand why that might be the case. Each time he attempted to delve into her past, the magnetic appeal of his looks began to wane. His looks were almost too perfect, she thought, like he'd been sculpted as someone else's idea of a perfect man. Were all the normal guys taken? As soon as the question popped into her brain, she banished it. This most definitely was not a date, and she was most definitely not looking for a boyfriend.

"It's not a very pleasant topic of conversation for me," she said. She held the menu in front of her and began surveying it. "So, what looks good to you?"

"Sorry," he said again, seeming finally to get the signal that he'd strayed too far into unsafe territory. "I meant it as a compliment. Clearly, you're somebody who's able to keep their wits about them when things get tough. I admire that."

When she remained silent, he continued. "I'm really much better with computers. It gives me more time to think of what I'm going to say. I've done online dating a few times, and that part of it always goes pretty well."

Lindsay glanced up at him. She could imagine that his profile picture would attract a lot of interest. His face was almost too perfect. Angled jaw, sensuous lips, and that unbelievable, penetrating gaze. Warren was handsome in a wholesome, freckly kind of way. But his frame bordered on gangly and in certain lights, his skin looked sickly pale. Even Mike, she thought, who shared his younger brother Drew's arresting green eyes and perfect white teeth, had his attractions. But he tended to look unkempt, and his midsection bore the telltale thickening of middle age. Adam, though? It was like a sculptor had chiseled him out of some rare and precious stone.

The waitress came by to take their orders, and an awkward silence descended. Adam drummed his fingers on the table. "So, do you play any sports?" he asked.

"Are we back on the list of safe topics then?" Lindsay said.

"Absolutely. I'm going to stick to weather and hobbies from now on," he said, with a sheepish half-smile. "So do you? Play sports?"

"Not really," she replied.

"Not even in school?"

"Nope. Whenever we had to play games, I just tried to keep as still as possible. No one wanted me on their team because I'm such a pipsqueak, and I could never manage to hit the ball, or catch it, or throw it, or, you know, whatever you were supposed to do with it."

"You don't seem like a pipsqueak. I mean, I guess you're small, but I wouldn't say it that way. You're, uh…concentrated."

"Oh, no," Lindsay said.

"Sorry, did I say something wrong? Again, I meant it as a compliment. Because pipsqueak sounds insulting," Adam said.

"No, no, it's not that. I just noticed a family at that table over there in front of the windows that I really don't want to see right now," she explained.

Without even looking, Adam said, "You mean the pudgy guy, the horsey woman, and the supermodel daughter?"

"How did you do that without turning around?" she asked.

"I noticed them when we came in. I always try to scan a room when I come into it and memorize details about people. It's one of my parlor tricks."

"I guess they're pretty noticeable. Jess is so stunning. And, Yancy. What's with his mustache? Is he trying to look like one of the perps on *To Catch a Predator*?"

Adam laughed out loud. "You really are funny."

"Sarcasm is *my* parlor trick, I guess," Lindsay replied flatly, not taking her eyes off the Philpots.

"Who are they?" Adam asked.

"It's a long story, but Mr. Philpot seems to have gotten it into his head that my great grandmother's nurse and I are conspiring to steal away his wife's family fortune."

"Are you?" he asked, his lips curling into a smile.

She frowned. "Last summer, I had an FBI agent trying to implicate me in a murder, and now this. Do I have a suspicious face or something? In between working double shifts at the hospital, visiting my mother in prison, walking my dog, and taking care of my elderly great grandmother, when exactly do people think I find the time to be a criminal mastermind?"

"Well, whoever said small towns are dull definitely didn't live in the same town as you," Adam said.

"Oh, shoot. He saw me," Lindsay said, trying, too late, to duck behind her menu.

Yancy Philpot had indeed locked eyes with hers. His eyes bulged in rage, and red splotches burst out on his cheeks. He tossed his napkin on the table, rose, and began walking quickly in her direction.

He walked right up to their table and leaned over it, putting his meaty palms flat on the surface. "You've got a lot of nerve showing your face in public," he growled.

"Mr. Philpot," Lindsay said, trying to keep her voice calm and steady despite her racing heart, "your father-in-law's decisions were as much of a mystery to Dunette and me as they seem to have been to your family. Please sit back down and enjoy your dinner. Nothing is going to be solved at the New Albany Olive Garden on a Sunday night."

"That money was supposed to come to us," Yancy continued, leaning over until she could almost feel the anger rising off of him like heat. "I put up with that old bastard's insults for thirty years, and *you*," he punctuated the word by slamming his fist down on their table, "think you can come in at the eleventh hour and take it all away?"

By now, people at nearby tables had turned their attention towards the fracas and were listening with rapt attention. Jess and Margo made their way quickly towards them. Adam rose to his feet. His expression remained as blank as a freshly-painted wall, but the mere act of his standing caused Yancy to back off a little. Although Adam was a well-built man, looking at his lithe body alongside Yancy's ex-football-player physique, his action seemed either extraordinarily brave or astonishingly foolhardy. Lindsay, too, rose to her feet. She hated drawing additional attention to their conversation, but it felt ridiculous to remain sitting while Yancy hung over her like a thundercloud about to burst.

"Please, Yancy," Margo said, taking hold of her husband's arm and trying to pull him backwards.

"People are staring." Jess said flatly, her arms crossed tightly over her chest.

"She stole your inheritance," he said, shaking himself free of Margo's grasp.

Jess stepped towards Lindsay and Adam, narrowing her amber eyes into a cat-like glare. She then turned to her parents and said. "This is completely stupid. I can't wait to get out of this godforsaken town. I'll be out in the car."

"Should we go, Lindsay?" Adam said. His voice had a pleasant neutrality, as if he attached no particular significance to the question or its answer.

"No," Margo said, stepping between Lindsay and her husband. "You don't need to leave. Just enjoy your food." She looked imploringly at Yancy. He took stock of her and of the general hush that had settled over the room, and at last he yielded.

"This isn't the end of this, *Reverend*," he said before stomping out of the restaurant.

Margo stood next to their table, clutching her hands to her heart. "Oh, dear," she murmured, to no one in particular. "We haven't paid. We can't leave without paying." She patted her pockets absently and her head whipped back and forth, scanning the restaurant like a meerkat. "I don't have my purse."

"I'll take care of it," Adam said. "It's on me."

Lindsay smiled gratefully at him. By now their fellow diners had resumed their meals, although their conversations had no doubt shifted to the topic of what Jonah Harding's eccentric daughter had done to get herself into hot water this time.

Margo turned to Adam, wide-eyed, as if he'd just materialized out of the wallpaper. "Oh, I couldn't ask you to do that. I'll get Yancy."

"Let's leave him to cool off for a few minutes," Lindsay suggested.

"It's my pleasure, really," Adam said, flashing his 1,000-watt smile. He walked off to find the Philpots' server, leaving Lindsay and Margo standing awkwardly beside their table. Margo held the top of the booth for support, looking as though she might fall if she released her grip.

"Are you okay?" Lindsay asked. "Why don't you sit down?"

Margo sank gratefully into the seat Lindsay offered to her. She looked drained and defeated. "I'm so sorry about Yancy. I don't know what to say."

"It's okay," Lindsay said. "Death brings out both the best and worst in people." She paused. "You don't seem to share your husband's anger, though. I'd have thought you'd have even more reason than Yancy to be upset."

Margo shrugged. "I suppose this was just one more of my father's nasty surprises."

"What do you mean?" Lindsay said, taken aback by the other woman's candor.

"I didn't grow up with him. I only met him when I was about Jess's age. I lived with my mother when I was a child. I suppose I don't feel like I ever really knew his mind."

"So you don't have any idea why he would've left his money to Dunette? She said he sought her out in particular. She never knew why. She was more surprised than anybody when she found out about the inheritance."

Margo's large eyes searched Lindsay's face. "He sought her out? That just can't be right. She's a Lumbee, right? That's what Yancy said."

Lindsay nodded.

"Well, that just doesn't make any sense. I thought Yancy must've got that wrong. My father hated Lumbee people, I'm sorry to say. I know that sounds awful, but it's so. That's one thing I did know about him. He blamed them for ruining his life."

"Ruining his life?" Lindsay repeated. The words seemed to bounce around in her skull. She wished that she hadn't had a glass of wine before eating—it had gone straight to her head.

"Yes. He and my mother were down in Maxton to make some kind of charitable donation to the Lumbee tribe. She was pregnant with me at the time. Anyway, there happened to be a protest of some sort going on, and my mother and father got separated in the crowd. The Lumbee men told her my daddy had turned tail and run away, and left his pregnant wife all alone. After that, my mother couldn't forgive my father. A few months later, she left him and never came back. My father couldn't let go of what happened. After all he was only trying to do something good. I never heard a word about any of that from my mother, mind you. She never talked about him or any of it. I didn't really even know who my father was until after she died."

"Did he tell you that story?" Lindsay asked.

"Yes. Why?"

"And you've never looked into it? It was a Klan rally, Margo. It's pretty well known. I mean, it seems strange that he just happened to get caught up in the middle of a Klan rally. And did he ever explain why he wanted to give the tribe a donation? Was it money, or what?" Lindsay asked.

Despite the seriousness of Margo's revelations, Lindsay felt strangely giddy. In fact, could only barely suppress the urge to giggle. Her head was starting to spin and she could hear herself slurring her words.

"What do you mean?" Margo asked, her cheeks beginning to color.

"It's just, people's memories can be…" she searched for the word, "faulty."

"For your information, I trust what my father told me, whatever his flaws were. And I'm sure whatever he did, he did because he thought it was right. He only wants what's best for me and Jess. You really should be careful what you say about people's daddies," Margo said.

It was the first time Lindsay had ever heard Margo's words be anything but soft and cloying. "I didn't mean to upset you," Lindsay said. "I really am sorry for your loss."

"I'm sorry I was sharp with you," Margo said, her anger seeming to dissipate almost as quickly as it had risen. "His passing has been difficult for all of us. Especially Jess. He just adored her. For a long time, I didn't think I could have children, so she is especially dear to us all."

"I have a friend who's going through that now. It's hard," Lindsay said. Although she was able to hold up her end of the conversation, she was experiencing the odd sensation that she had no connection to the words rushing out of her mouth. They just emerged, like water from a spigot.

"Yancy and I married while I was still in high school because I was expecting, but then I lost the baby. We lost five little ones after that. It was a terrible, terrible time. My daddy took it harder than we did, I think. He was so beside himself he couldn't work. He sold his company. Everything he'd worked for. And wouldn't you know it? I got pregnant with Jess right after that. She's been such a blessing to our family. He was always superstitious about the timing of that afterwards. Said selling the company lifted a curse that had been on us."

"A curse?" Lindsay repeated the words.

Adam came back into Lindsay's line of vision. "Sorry that took so long. Credit card machine problems. Anyway, you're all set."

Margo rose to leave. "Thank you." Turning to Lindsay she said. "I'm sorry again for snapping at you. Please tell Dunette I don't blame her, but Yancy said we can't let her take that money. Jess needs money for college, and Yancy says it's not right that a stranger should get it. He thinks maybe my daddy was confused near the end and someone took advantage of that. We have no choice but to fight this."

Lindsay wanted to ask her more questions, but her brain couldn't form the words. It was as if suddenly her skull had filled up with molasses. She watched Margo walk across the room and then said to Adam. "I don't feel very well. I think I need to go home." Again, the urge to laugh arose from her chest like champagne bubbles. "You're really hot. You know that?" she said, giggling like a middle-schooler.

"Are you okay?" Adam asked, his brow creasing with concern. "Did she say something to you?"

"No, I feel..." her words trailed off as she began to slouch in her seat.

"Whoa, I think you overestimated your tolerance," Adam said, seeing her empty glass and her inebriated condition. He put some cash on the table for their wine and said, "Let's get you out of here."

Lindsay found herself almost unable to stand under her own power. Her surroundings were now coming through in broken flashes. Adam hooking his arm around her waist. The fresh, sea salt smell of his skin. The eyes of the restaurant patrons on her as she stumbled out the door. Sitting in the passenger's seat of her Honda. Adam fishing through her purse for the keys.

The car was moving and she saw lights flashing by. "Sorry, I shouldn't have taken you out when you were so tired," Adam was saying. "I'll just drop you at your house. I can get a cab home."

Suddenly the car juddered to a halt. She saw him try the Honda key, and she watched it fall straight out of the ignition and onto the floor of the car. She tried to tell him that the key didn't usually work. When it fell out like that, you had to jimmy the ignition switch with the small metal rod attached to the keychain. But the words came out as if her mouth were filled with marbles.

"Lindsay? Are you okay?" Adam asked, seeming to suddenly realize that her condition was more than just fatigue and tipsiness. He leaned over her, looking into her eyes, and she could feel his warm breath on her face. Sweet and perfumed with wine.

Chapter 17

When Lindsay regained awareness, she was lying alone in a hospital bed. She immediately recognized the spot as the area next to the main ER where patients waited to be seen by a doctor, or to be discharged or admitted. A curtain was drawn around her, but she could hear the sound of voices and hospital machines. Her head pounded; it felt simultaneously weightless and heavier than lead. She rolled onto her side and pressed the nurse call button.

Lindsay heard the squish-squish of soft-soled shoes on linoleum and a few seconds later Anna's face appeared around the curtain. "Jesus, Linds. You scared the crap out of everybody," she said.

"What happened?" Lindsay murmured. Her own quiet voice sounded almost deafeningly loud in her brain.

Anna wrote something down on Lindsay's chart and then perched herself on the edge of the bed. "Have you ever heard of Rohypnol?"

"I don't think so."

"Roofies? That's what Rohypnol is—also known as the date rape drug."

"What?!" Lindsay said. The shock of Anna's statement made her sit up, a reaction she immediately regretted. Woozy lines crisscrossed her vision, and a wave of nausea overtook her. As she lay back and recovered, it slowly began to dawn on her just how little she really knew about her charming dinner companion.

"That's what we found in your system," Anna said. "When they brought you in, I honestly thought you were having a stroke. You were slurring and disoriented and didn't have motor control. But that wasn't it. Somebody slipped you the proverbial Mickey. Who the hell was that guy you were you with, anyway? The dreamboat who rode with you in the ambulance? Did you hire an escort service or something? There's no way that guy lives in Mount Moriah. I'd have noticed."

"What would you have noticed?" Warren asked.

Lindsay and Anna both jumped. Somehow, Warren Satterwhite was suddenly standing at Lindsay's beside, seeming to have materialized out of nowhere.

"Warren!" Lindsay said. Again, her own voice seemed impossibly loud to her.

Although there was concern in his eyes, there was a hard set to his jaw that immediately let her know he was in full police mode. Standing beside him was Officer Freeland Vickers, a pudgy, chinless lump of a man whose eyes held a perpetual gleam of good humor.

"Hi, Warren. Hi, Vickers," Anna said. "I was just bringing the patient here up to speed on the past few hours of activity."

"What's going on?" Lindsay asked. "Did something happen?"

"What happened to you was a crime, and we're lookin' into it," Vickers explained. "Drugging somebody is assault. Rohypnol is a controlled substance."

"Is she up to answering some questions?" Warren asked Anna.

Anna looked at Lindsay. "Are you?"

Lindsay tried not to show how upset she was at Warren's aloofness.

"Do you have to be the one who asks the questions?" Lindsay asked him. "Isn't there some kind of law against investigating somebody you're involved with? Um, or were involved with?" Having been drugged was bad enough, but the prospect of telling Warren all the details of her "non-date" with Adam was a million times worse.

"There's no law against it, no. If we prosecute, it would come up at trial, but only if it can be shown to have interfered with the investigation. Anyway, there isn't much choice. Summerhays is on vacation," he said, referring to the chief of the New Albany force. "And Prendergrast's kid broke his leg pretty bad playing football yesterday. They're upstairs right now. Vickers can do it instead, if you want. That's why he's here. Or I can get somebody from the Mount Moriah force, though none of them are detectives."

"Fine," Lindsay said miserably.

"I know it's uncomfortable," Warren said, "but given that this may relate to the Swoopes investigation, I'd prefer to do it personally."

The mention of Swoopes' potential involvement cleared some of the cobwebs from Lindsay's head. She realized that even if she could avoid talking to Warren directly, sooner or later he'd listen to the recording of her interview and hear everything she said. "Is it okay if Anna stays?" she asked. She was suddenly fearful of being left alone with Warren and Vickers. She felt like she herself was the criminal, rather than the victim.

Warren nodded and took out a digital recorder. "Please state your name."

"Lindsay Sarabelle Harding."

"Now please tell me everything you know about Adam Tyrell. Like when and where did you first meet him?"

"That day when I needed my tire changed," Lindsay said.

Warren's eyes narrowed, his professional demeanor giving way briefly to a jilted boyfriend's jealousy and hurt. "*That* was the guy?! You never told me that you saw him again after that. How long was this going on? Were you seeing him while we were together?"

Vickers loudly cleared his throat. "Let's start the recording again," he said, gesturing to the recording device. "I don't think it picked the sound up right that time."

Warren snapped himself back into detective mode and began the interrogation again. This time, his emotions remained firmly in check.

After Lindsay finished recounting the story, she felt more foolish than ever. How could she have let her guard down? How could she have allowed herself to be alone and vulnerable with a stranger she barely knew? Worst of all, however, even though she glossed over the details, she could see the pain register in Warren's eyes as she related her encounters with Adam.

When she was at last finished, she said, "I wish I could help more, but it's all so hazy. I don't remember anything after the car stopped." She was suddenly seized by a deep terror. She turned to Anna and lowered her voice to a whisper. "Did anything, you know, happen? When I was blacked out?" Her words hung heavy with the unspoken implication.

Anna took hold of her hand. "No. I did an exam."

Lindsay let out the breath she'd been holding. "Where's Adam now? Did you bring him in for questioning?"

A look passed between Anna, Vickers, and Warren.

"He's gone," Anna said. "He came in with you and he seemed really concerned. In fact, he was the one who called 9-1-1 in the first place. He said you'd had too much to drink. The attending physician was just going to pump your stomach and leave you to dry out overnight. It was Jesper," Anna said, rolling her eyes at the mention of her ineffectual colleague's name. "That woman would gladly put a Band Aid over somebody's broken leg if it saved her time and effort. Anyway, I happened to look at the board on my way out and saw your name. I couldn't believe you'd just had too much to drink. I've seen you drunk," Anna smiled. "And this was different. Unfortunately, one of the idiot interns thought Adam was your boyfriend and told him we were running a tox screen on you and the cops were on their way to question him. Next thing you know, he disappeared."

Lindsay shook her head. "I know you're going to think this is crazy, but is there any chance Adam didn't do it? Why would he go through all the trouble of drugging me, but then not do…whatever he was planning to do? He had me alone in the car. The roads between Mount Moriah and New Albany are pretty deserted on Sunday nights. If he was going to attack me, he could've done it then."

"Maybe he chickened out," Vickers offered. "You looked real sick when we first got here. Maybe he overdid the dose, thought you were gonna die, and got scared."

"What about his mother? She may still be upstairs recovering from her surgery. Maybe she knows something," Lindsay said. She dropped her head into her hands. "Oh god. What if there isn't a mother?! I never even checked to make sure she was real."

Vickers patted her shoulder. "Don't feel bad, Miss Lindsay. You're not the first person who got her head turned by a smooth talker with a pretty face."

Warren shot him an ice-cold look. "Anna, can you check the records to see if there were any patients named Valerie admitted for GI surgery?"

Anna shook her head. "'Fraid I can't. Only the administrators and medical records staff can do system-wide searches like that. We only have access to our own patients' records unless we get special system permissions. It's to protect patient confidentiality."

Warren turned to Vickers. "Go down to Medical Records. If they tell you we need a warrant, call Judge Severson at home. Get them to check different names, and get a couple of our guys to start checking to see if the diagnosis description rings any bells with anybody just in case Valerie was a nickname or something." His phone began to ring, and he removed it from his pocket.

"I'm sorry, Warren," Lindsay said. "I know this all sounds bad. But it really wasn't like that."

Warren, however, had already stopped listening. He pushed the button to answer his phone and stepped to the other side of the curtain. Lindsay closed her eyes, wishing she could evaporate into thin air.

"It's really over between me and Warren isn't it? He thinks I cheated on him with Mike and Adam. He hates me."

"I'm sure he's just worried about you," Anna said.

Lindsay opened her eyes. "I think he might've forgiven me for all the other stuff, but I kind of went on a date with a hot stranger a week after we broke off our engagement."

Anna scrunched up her face. "Yeah, that's not ideal."

"What time is it, anyway? Somebody needs to call Simmy and my dad to let them know what happened," Lindsay said.

"It's five a.m.," Anna said. "Don't worry. We already called Simmy. And Dunette is going to take her to her dentist appointment at nine and then they'll come over to visit. Your dad was here up until about an hour ago. I made him go home and get some sleep. I didn't think you'd wake up so soon. I'll call him and let him know you're okay. You don't need to worry about anything but feeling better. Speaking of which, I need to check to see if a room has opened up for you yet. I want you to stay, at least until the cobwebs clear. We should really just start keeping a room open for you here." Anna brushed a stray curl from Lindsay's eyes and smiled at her.

Lindsay smiled back, closed her eyes and let her scattered thoughts be swept along in a current of dreamy semiconsciousness. She was awakened a short time later by the sound of the curtain around her bed being pulled back. Warren stepped to her bedside. His jaw had a grim set to it, and his face had gone extremely pale.

"I thought Vickers might have come back," he said.

"I don't think so," Lindsay said. "I think I fell asleep."

Warren turned to leave, but she stopped him. "Are you okay? You look like you've seen a ghost."

"I'm fine," Warren said. "It's not me I'm worried about."

"What then?"

Warren hesitated, but Lindsay reached out and took hold of his hand. "Tell me."

Warren looked down at their joined hands and said quietly, "That call I took before was my friend, the SBI fingerprint technician who always turns things around quickly when I ask her. I sent her some prints we lifted out of your car earlier tonight. You remember Terry Addison?"

"The con man who pretended to be the building inspector?" Lindsay said. Despite her brain fog, she instantly recalled the name of the man who passed himself off as Weaponless Doer. "What was he doing in my car?"

"I'm trying to tell you that I think Adam Tyrell and Terry Addison and W. Doer are all the same person. Nobody else's prints were in there. Yours, mine, Simmy's, and that set."

"But how can that be? You showed me his mug shot from when he was arrested in South Carolina. That heavy guy with the long hair and the goatee. It wasn't Adam."

"This is Terry Addison's passport picture. It was taken about five years ago. Does he look familiar?" Warren held out a piece of paper with a photo printed on it. The man was younger, heavier, with longer hair and a goatee, but it was almost certainly Adam Tyrell. He also bore a passing resemblance to the mug shot of long-haired, heavy-set Terry Addison Warren had shown her when they began looking for W. Doer.

"I think that's Adam," Lindsay gasped. "But, how can that be?"

"He's been living in Slovakia. That area's the plastic surgery capital of the world, apparently. People fly in from all over. A new nose, a haircut, a shave and a whole lot of diet and exercise, and Terry Addison becomes Adam Tyrell."

"But what about Doer? John said he was hideous." She frowned. When she looked into Warren's eyes, she immediately read his thoughts there. "You think he was disguised, don't you? I told y'all I thought it was Swoopes in disguise, but it wasn't. It was Adam." She looked away, disgusted with her own stupidity. "What the hell is this, an episode of Scooby Doo?"

"I remember you saying that once before," Warren said with a sad smile. "I compared you to Velma, and you got mad at me."

She mirrored his wistful smile. "You saved it, though. You said you liked the smart ones. Guess you were wrong about me being smart, huh? I'm not even sure I'm one of the good guys."

"We're still the good guys," Warren said. He dropped her hand, his expression becoming grave. "This guy's gone through a lot of trouble to get close to you, and I promise we're going to find out why."

Chapter 18

Three days had passed since Lindsay had returned home from the hospital, and there was still no sign of Adam Tyrell's whereabouts. The night of their Olive Garden dinner, he'd returned the Mercedes he'd been renting to the car rental company and checked out of the hotel where he'd been staying. Despite an exhaustive search through credit reports, criminal records, tax filings, and work histories, the police could find no record of Adam/Terry from the time he completed his parole requirements more than a decade earlier until the time he popped up in the Mount Moriah Medical Center parking lot a few weeks previously. A thorough search of the hospital's records had turned up no sign of a patient matching what Lindsay knew about his mother, "Valerie." He'd spent time in foster care, and, although the records were spotty and incomplete, there was nothing to indicate that any of what he said was true.

The police had tried to keep the details of the investigation close, putting out pictures of Adam Tyrell taken from the hospital's surveillance cameras in the media and saying only that he was wanted for questioning in relation to a fraud investigation. Lindsay tried to stay as busy as possible, taking hours-long runs each day, pushing herself almost to the point of exhaustion. She returned from one of these marathon runs in the late afternoon to find Mike sitting in a chair in her living room with his feet up and her book about the Lumbee Indians in his hands.

"I thought my fancy alarm system was supposed to keep riffraff like you out," Lindsay teased, wiping her sweaty face with a hand towel.

"Rob let me in," Mike replied.

"Rob was here?"

"Yeah, he brought over some Chinese dumplings while you were out running," Mike said, without raising his eyes from the page. "Simmy put them in the fridge."

Lindsay looked at him curiously. "Comfortable?"

He put the book down and rose to his feet. "Oh, sorry. I stopped by with some more stuff for Dunette to sign. And Rob was here with the dumplings, so we all ate some. And then Dunette and Simmy took Kipper to the dog park in New Albany. Dunette said she'd pick up your dry cleaning, too. I guess they called to say they still have some of your stuff from before Christmas, and they were going to donate it to Goodwill if you didn't get it today. And then they're going to get some groceries."

"And you decided to stay behind and brush up on your Native American history?"

"Don't look so shocked. I'm not just a pretty face, you know." He smiled, propping his reading glasses on his head. "Speaking of which, you look nice. I like how your t-shirt matches your running shoes."

"Uh, thanks." She couldn't help but be amused at the way Mike always managed to find something about her to compliment, even when she was disheveled and sweaty. She wiped the back of her neck with her sleeve. "So you're just here, reading history books and...looking pretty?"

"Actually, Owen's coming over in a minute. He left his basketball uniform in my car and he has a game tonight." He paused. "And there's something else. Something important. I wanted to see you."

"Oh?"

He studied her face for a moment. "You're wondering about it, too. Aren't you?"

"Wondering about what?" she said.

She walked back to the kitchen with Mike trailing closely behind her. Since she got back from the hospital, he seemed to have found reasons to drop by her house more frequently than was strictly required by his unofficial role as Dunette's legal counsel. All of her friends had been wonderfully supportive and subtly protective of her, but Mike's efforts had outstripped them all. He was constantly checking on her to ensure that she was physically and mentally at ease, bringing her little gifts, and finding excuses to talk to her. Warren's jealous assertion about single men doing favors for their female friends flashed through her mind.

She glanced back over her shoulder at Mike. His forehead was creased in concentration. She wasn't sure what he was getting at with all this talk of them both "wondering" about something, and she was worried that he might be about to make some grand declaration of love for her. Her mind flitted briefly to Warren's initial proposal of marriage. She'd been rushing to the hospital, doped up on pain medication, wondering if her mother and Simmy would survive their injuries. Why did the men in her life completely lack the ability to choose the right moment for romance? Then again, she thought ruefully, her own skills in negotiating the rocky terrain of romantic relationships were sorely lacking. In the past year, she'd managed to go out with a teenage Zoroastrian, ruin her relationship with Warren not once but twice, and have a brief flirtation with a convicted con man who drugged her on their first quasi-date.

"I've been thinking," Mike said. "What if Adam wasn't the one who drugged you?"

Lindsay splashed some water on her sweaty face and poured herself a glass of water, relieved that she'd misjudged Mike's intentions. "Who else would it have been? The police have already questioned the Philpots and all the wait staff at Olive Garden," she said. "Even if I wanted to believe it was somebody else, none of those people changed their appearance with plastic surgery, invented a fake mother to get to know me, assumed a fake identity to get into my house, and then ran away from the hospital once the jig was up. And none of them has a criminal conviction for fraud."

"Look me in the eye and say you don't think there's more to all of this," Mike said. "That you don't want to find out if it ties together somehow." Their gazes locked for a long moment. Too long.

Lindsay turned back to the sink. "Even if I did, what can I do about it? Every time I get involved in something like this, I almost get myself killed. I think I've met my quota for self-destructive behavior this month."

She felt his hands resting gently on her shoulders. "I know. But isn't there a part of you that wants to do it anyway? And a part of you that knows until we get to the bottom of this, you won't be safe?"

She turned to face him. "We?"

They were standing close together, only inches apart, her face tipped up toward his. "Just let me know if there's anything I can do. I'll hire a private investigator. A bodyguard. Whatever you want," he said.

The yearning in his eyes was almost palpable. It would be so easy to put her arms around him. To feel the safety of his warm, strong embrace, the flattery of being wanted so desperately. She remembered the zap of electricity in the kiss they'd shared on the Outer Banks, an impulsive act she'd tried to banish from her mind. He was so close now. Dangerously close. Why did he always smell so damn good? He was right there in front of her, and she wanted so badly to be rescued from herself, to give in to the illusion that happiness and safety could be had so easily.

The back door clicked open. Mike took a step backwards as Lindsay spun back around towards the sink.

"Am I interrupting something?" Jonah asked. He stared them down with his very powerful "disappointed pastor" look.

"No!" Lindsay practically shouted, almost dropping her glass of water.

"Good, because if you're not too busy, I'd like to talk to you about something important. But if y'all are in the middle of something, I can come back. I know what it's like to get interrupted in the middle of something." He looked at Lindsay pointedly.

"No need. I'd better be on my way anyway," Mike said, seeming to sense Lindsay's discomfort.

"But you can't leave," Lindsay said. "What about Owen's uniform?"

"Would it be all right if I just left it here for him? He'll be here in a minute."

"Uh, sure," Lindsay said. She wasn't sure if she was up to having an important conversation with her father, but she didn't see how it could be avoided.

Once Mike had left, Lindsay and Jonah took a seat on the back porch steps. It was still early enough in the evening to avoid mosquitoes and the air was a perfect 70 degrees.

"So, you wanted to talk to me about something?" Lindsay prompted.

"Yes. But first, how're you doing?"

"Oh, hanging in there, I suppose," Lindsay said with a wan smile.

"You've got a lot of people who care for you, you know. I see how your friends look out for you. Speaking of which, what was that all about?" Jonah asked, pointing his thumb over his shoulder toward the kitchen.

"Dad, don't start."

"I'm not starting. I'm worried about you. I don't want you to rush into anything. I know how much you and Warren cared for each other, and it's gonna take some time to get a handle on what you're gonna do now. Teresa said he's been beside himself since y'all broke up. And you've gotta take care. Especially with what all has been going on outside of that."

"You and Teresa talk about us?"

The thought of Jonah and Teresa discussing her relationship with Warren had been weighing on her ever since she'd found out about their romance, but having it confirmed was still disturbing. Disturbing and yucky.

"We're your parents. We both just want you to be happy. Honestly. That's all I want for you. You're my girl."

Lindsay studied her father's face. She'd been steeling herself for a full-on haranguing about her breaking her engagement with Warren, or going out with a dangerous man who turned out to be a criminal, or being caught in a compromising position with Mike. Or possibly all of the above. Her romantic choices had always been one of the many trip-wire topics in their relationship, along with anything regarding her mother, her liberal views, and her more-than-occasional use of colorful language. She'd witnessed several seismic shifts in this long-standing dynamic over the past year, and she was ashamed to admit that most of the moves toward reconciliation had been undertaken by Jonah. He'd gone out of his way to try to cut her a bit more slack, and to hear her side of a story before giving his own opinion. And now he stood before her—perhaps concerned, perhaps even disappointed—but still full of affection. It would take awhile to get used to this mellower, less judgmental version of her father.

"Thanks, Dad. That means a lot to me."

"Don't thank me just yet. I don't think you're gonna like what I have to say next. I've been turning this over in my mind, praying on it, knowing what a terrible time this is for you. But then I thought about how upset you were about me keeping my relationship with Teresa a secret. I realized you and I do that too often—keep things from each other. That's not what I want from you, but I've been doing it, too."

Lindsay tried to anticipate what her father was going to say next, but she drew a blank. With this kind of build up, it was clearly something of monumental importance. She tried to keep an open mind. "I know I've been too secretive. Old habits are hard to break," she said.

"Okay, then hear me out. Like I said, I know this is a bad time, but I have news I hope will bring some joy into our lives. I know you'll probably think it's too soon, but well..." he cleared his throat. "I'd like to ask Teresa to become my wife."

Lindsay popped to standing, as if the porch had suddenly turned white-hot. Her first reaction was to stomp inside her house and slam the door. Or maybe yell at her father for rubbing salt in the wound of her own failed engagement and selfishly following his own bliss while she was still in fear for her life. She wanted to shut down and lock her father out—out of her house, out of her life.

"You want to marry Warren's mother?" she said, almost growling the words.

"She's a good woman, Lindsay. A good Christian. I've waited a long time to find somebody who loves me back."

Lindsay paced up and down in front of the porch, breathing deeply. The energy she'd spent being angry with her father over the years could've powered a small city. Despite all her work experience dealing with human emotions and frailties, it was still so hard to apply what she'd learned to her own life, not just to her patients at the hospital. She took a deep breath and faced her father. It was time to stop humming along with the choir, and really sing.

"Okay," she said finally.

Jonah had been watching her anxiously as she paced, his shoulders pulled forward like he was bracing for a blow. Now he relaxed. "Okay?"

"Yep. I want you to be happy, too. That's what families are about—wanting what's best for each other. Teresa's lucky to have you."

"Really?" he said uncertainly.

"Really." She smiled at him. The more she spoke, the better she felt. She began to believe the words as she said them. "I'm glad you told me. You shouldn't have to hide something that makes you happy. And you deserve happiness. You spent so long pining over Sarabelle, being faithful to her even though she's never going to change. Teresa and I haven't been what you'd call close, and the whole thing with Warren is just going to make this awful and weird for me, but you're right. Teresa Satterwhite seems like a good woman. I can pretty much guarantee that she'll never rob my house, or show up drunk to a church picnic, or steal your Billy Graham Bible." She held out her hand to him. "I'm sorry if I made it hard for you to tell me."

Jonah jumped up, gathered her into his arms, and spun her around the way he'd done when she was a very young child.

"Dad! Your back!"

He set her down on the ground but kept his arms around her. "I don't care. This is worth a hundred slipped discs."

"Uh, hi."

They turned to see Owen loping around the corner of the house in his loose-limbed, teenage way. He regarded them curiously and raised his hand in greeting.

"Oh, hey, Owen," Lindsay said. "We didn't hear your car pull up."

"Yeah, where's your Doberman alarm? I was knocking on the front door. Usually he'd be barking like a maniac."

"He's out with Simmy and Dunette," Lindsay said.

Owen continued to look at Jonah. "My dad said he left my uniform here? And that you had Chinese dumplings? I can come back if you're busy, though, or, you know, just grab the dumplings and the uniform and take off."

Lindsay realized that Owen must think he'd caught her in a compromising position, standing in the arms of a strange man. Was she fated to always have her relationships with men, even with her own father, misconstrued?

"It's okay," she said. "This is my dad. Jonah Harding, meet Owen Checkoway. He's Mike's son."

"Pleased to meet you, young man," Jonah said, extending his hand.

"My dad was just giving me some good news," Lindsay explained.

"I'd better hit the road," Jonah said. "I've got some jewelry shopping to do."

Lindsay involuntarily touched her ring finger, which was still slightly pink and chapped. "Maybe get her a platinum ring? Platinum is a safer bet than gold."

Chapter 19

"Do you want anything else? Dunette made some sweet tea," Lindsay offered. Owen was sitting at her kitchen table, polishing off the last of a mound of two dozen of Rob's dumplings.

"No, thanks. I'm good," he replied, chewing. "Those were awesome." He popped the last dumpling in his mouth and rose to put his plate in the dishwasher. "Hey, do you have time to look at my trig homework? It's due in the morning. Anna said you're really good at math."

"Sure," Lindsay replied. "She might've oversold my skills, though. Trigonometry isn't something I use every day."

"You've gotta be better than my dad. He's awful at math," Owen said. He took his laptop out of his schoolbag and flipped it open.

"How're things with Jess?" Lindsay asked, taking a seat next to him at the table.

"Pretty good. I haven't seen her as much since her grandpa died. She's really sad about it."

"They were really close, huh?" She paused. "Did she ever talk to you about being given power of attorney for him?"

He turned away from his computer screen for a moment to shoot her a quizzical look. "No. That's a pretty weird thing to ask."

"It's a pretty weird thing to do, too. Don't you think?"

He shrugged. "I dunno. Maybe. I mean, it's not like he could trust his daughter. Jess's mom is really nice and everything, but she just does anything anybody tells her to do. And Jess's dad would probably have either stolen all the money or messed it all up somehow. I don't think Mr. Boughtflower trusted anybody except Jess. There's always so much pressure on her to be, like, the family star. She's so good at so many things, but it's like it's never enough. Like she's afraid they won't like her if she's not perfect. I think it was even like that with her grandpa."

"It can be tough to feel like you have to be perfect all the time," Lindsay said.

"Yeah, I think that's one of the reasons we're together. I kind of get that. My dad was always like that with my mom. He thought she was the most perfect person ever. Like if she cooked something, and it was nasty, he thought it was good. I don't think he was just saying it, either. I think he really made himself believe it, like it was wrong to be like, 'She's a really great person and I love her and whatever, but she can't cook worth a damn.' I know he really loved her, but sometimes I wonder if he really even knew her, you know? Like how can you *know* somebody if you never even let yourself see the bad parts of them?"

Lindsay gawked at him. From the first time she'd met him, she'd been struck by what an old soul he was. He always seemed to provide the ballast to the hot air balloon of his father's heedless enthusiasms. Now she was astounded anew by the casual way in which he'd illuminated so many essential truths about the people around him. She still didn't understand what motivated her parents or fueled their relationships. But this kid who'd experienced the trauma of losing his mother to a devastating illness? This kid was the Dalai Lama in sweatpants.

Owen opened the on-line practice exam he'd been asked to complete. "Anyway, Jess and I don't really talk about family stuff that much, that's just kind of like my opinions."

"This might seem like a weird question, too, but did she ever mention anything about a place called Burnt Island or the Lumbee Indians?" Lindsay asked. She didn't want to lose the opportunity to find out more about the Boughtflower family's past.

Owen gave her another quizzical look. "Well, she did a report on Henry Berry Lowrie for North Carolina history last semester. He was a Lumbee, right?"

"What?!" Lindsay asked, shocked to have stumbled so effortlessly onto a mound of pay dirt. "Do you know what it was about?"

"Yeah. We had that class together. That's how we met. We had to pick a famous person from North Carolina history. She did Henry Berry Lowrie. He was, like, a vigilante or something. He and his gang pulled off a bunch of small heists against the rich planters and stuff, but then he pulled off this one huge job and disappeared. Stole a ton of money and was never seen again, so he

157

became kind of a legend. And they never found the money. It was a really good paper. She got an A."

While he was talking, Lindsay had gone to the kitchen counter and began paging through one of the Lumbee history books she'd ordered from Amazon, looking for the section on Henry Berry Lowrie. "Did Jess say why she picked that topic? Was it part of your curriculum or something?"

"Nope. She had to get special permission from the teacher to write about the Lumbees, but she usually gets her way, you know? She's really persuasive."

"And you don't know why she picked Henry Berry Lowrie?"

"Nope. Probably just because he was really interesting. Like a cool Indian swamp pirate or something. I did Nina Simone. She was pretty cool, too, but I only got a B."

Lindsay turned the information about Jess's interest in Lumbee history over in her mind. She'd been so focused on finding out about Boughtflower's involvement in the Battle of Hayes Pond that she hadn't fully explored the connection to Henry Berry Lowrie. Could it be that the money Boughtflower thought of as cursing his family was the missing Lowrie fortune? And could the "hidden body" refer to Lowrie himself? Could something that happened so long ago really trouble a man's dying days the way Boughtflower's had been troubled? There was no doubt in her mind that whatever secret Boughtflower had tried to tell her was inextricably connected to the history of the Lumbees. There was also no doubt that there was a lot more to Jess than her flawless face.

"Do you and Jess have trig together, too?" Lindsay asked.

Owen took one of his basketball shoes out of his gym bag and begun to lace it up. "No, she's in Calculus. She's really good at math. If she wasn't busy tonight, I would've gotten her to help me with this."

Lindsay furrowed her brow, remembering back to her first meeting with Jess. The notebook she'd seen in Jess's purse had looked like trigonometry or geometry problems, not calculus. As if Jess were trying to triangulate something, or solve for a missing angle. Surely Jess couldn't like math so much she did trig problems in her spare time?

"What about astronomy? Are you in that class with her?" Lindsay asked.

"Mount Moriah High doesn't have astronomy," Owen said, raising his eyebrows at her. "What's with the third degree?"

"Sorry. It's nothing really. I'm trying to get to the bottom of something Boughtflower said. Anyway, I just thought Jess might be taking that."

Owen shook his head. "Nope, she's got Calc and theater and a couple blow-off classes. She graduates the week after next, so Calc is really her only hard class this semester."

Although Lindsay found it more than a little fishy that Jess would lie to her about having trigonometry and astronomy homework, she let the matter drop. She was aware that she was already asking an unusual number of questions, many of which must have seemed odd to Owen, and she didn't want to completely freak him out. "Have y'all decided what you're going to do when she finishes?" Lindsay asked.

"We're staying together. I'm gonna try to graduate early, and then move to New York next January. I'll apply to NYU and Columbia, and maybe Hunter as a backup school."

"You're moving to New York for a girl you've only known a couple of months?" Lindsay asked. She tried to keep her tone neutral, but realized that she sounded exactly like the kind of adult she would've avoided when she was a teenager.

Owen, however, took her concern in stride. "I think I want to do something with international NGOs, so New York is probably the best place in the world to do that. And Jess wants to be an actress, so she's gotta be in either New York or L.A. She's really, really good at acting. She can do all kinds of accents and fake cry with real tears and make herself look like a totally different person and stuff. She even had a meeting today with some casting agent or model scout or something. I dropped her off in Raleigh after school. I've gotta pick her up later, after my game."

"She's meeting a casting agent in Raleigh?" Lindsay asked. Compared to Mount Moriah, Raleigh was a bustling metropolis, but it wasn't exactly an ordinary stomping ground for talent agents and casting directors. "Do her parents know about that?"

Owen shrugged nonchalantly. "Probably not. They're pretty high strung. Anyway, she's an adult, you know? She can make her own decisions."

"I guess," Lindsay said, frowning.

"This is the part I don't get," Owen said, pointing to a shape on the screen. "The rhombus where the diagonals bisect each other?"

Although Lindsay's thoughts were distracted, she managed to help Owen work through the most difficult problems, relieved that her math skills weren't as rusty as she'd feared. As she worked with him, she could see the astuteness of something Anna had once said to her—Owen was the kind of kid you just wanted to feed. Lindsay was far from the motherly type, but there was no doubt Owen had a unique blend of maturity, appreciativeness, and vulnerability that just cried out to be cared for.

"What will your dad do if you move to New York with Jess?" Lindsay asked, as Owen packed up to leave. "He'll be stuck here by himself. Or will he go off on another travel adventure?"

Owen looked perplexed for a moment. "I think he'll stay," he said, smirking.

"Don't you think he'll get bored, though?"

"Not with you around." He patted her on the head, looking down at her with an affable expression. "You'll keep things interesting for him."

Chapter 20

When Dunette, Kipper, and Simmy arrived home a short time later, they found Lindsay at her kitchen table with her laptop, several open books, and handwritten notes spread out all around her.

"What on earth are you doing, honey?" Simmy asked.

Lindsay briefly explained her theory about there being a link between the mystery surrounding Boughtflower's will and the Lowrie Gang, and her belief that Jess had been withholding some knowledge about it.

"There's got to be a connection," she insisted. "Everything Boughtflower said fits with this story. Since the end of the Civil War, Lowrie's gang had been doing all these low-level robberies, stealing candlesticks and rustling livestock. Then all of a sudden, in 1872, just as the pressure is really mounting, they pulled off this huge, daring heist. It's like something out of a movie. They stole almost $30,000 in gold from a safe in the sheriff's office and the stores of some well-to-do merchants in town. There's only one more confirmed sighting of Lowrie after that, and then he vanishes. I've also been looking up some information on the Boughtflowers, too. George Boughtflower, Otis's grandfather, set up his first factory in Burlington in 1880. He didn't have any relations there— just appeared out of the blue with enough money to open a factory. There's a missing body, stolen money, and it all took place in and around Burnt Island Swamp. If Boughtflower's ancestors had something to do with Lowrie's disappearance and then used the stolen money to start the family business, maybe that's what he felt so guilty about. Maybe he wanted to see that the Lowrie descendants, the Lumbees, get the stolen money back."

Dunette frowned. "I'm about the only person in Robeson County who's not related to Lowrie," she said. "And if what my granddaddy told me about my family is true, I'm about the last person the Lowrie money should come to."

"What do you mean?" Lindsay said.

Dunette looked uncertainly at Simmy and Lindsay. "I don't really like to say."

"Dunette, if you know something that might help, you've got to say. Don't you think it all ties together too neatly to be a coincidence?" Lindsay asked.

Dunette lowered her eyes to the table. "Don't nobody know this. I don't think Angel even knows. My great-great granddaddy was Donahue McQueen."

"Donahue McQueen?" The name was familiar to Lindsay, but the significance wasn't immediately apparent. She paged through one of the books in front of her. "Was he one of the Lowrie gang members?"

"No. He was the man who killed Lowrie's brother-in-law, Boss."

Lindsay found the account of the killing and quickly scanned the details. Shortly after Lowrie's disappearance, McQueen, who was half Lumbee and half Scottish, had shot Boss to collect a $2,000 bounty. Boss, who in addition to being Lowrie's brother-in-law was also his right-hand man, had been laying by the fire with his brother's family when McQueen shot him through the cat hole that'd been cut in the door. The Strongs chased McQueen away and buried Boss's body out in the swamps to try and keep him from collecting the reward, but he got the money anyway. After more than eight years as an outlaw, Boss was dead and buried before his twenty-second birthday.

"I can see why you're not too proud of that particular ancestor," Lindsay said, smiling kindly at Dunette. "But remember you're looking at somebody whose mother is currently in the penitentiary. Again. We're not them."

Dunette smiled back. "I know. But it's hard enough being a Lumbee when nobody understands who we are, but on top of that, I'm a half-black, black sheep Lumbee. Part of me feels like I know what it must've been like for Donahue McQueen, why he hated Henry Berry. Henry Berry came from the ultimate Lumbee family. They had more money and land than a lot of the whites, and Henry Berry married the prettiest Lumbee girl in the whole county. They were *the* Lumbees. But Donahue? He was just a half-caste. He tried to be white, but whites didn't want him. Then he tried to be

Lumbee, and they didn't want him either because he'd always acted like he was too good for them." She sighed. "When you're mixed race, things can get confusing."

"Like the woman who converted to Mexican," Lindsay said, remembering the earlier conversation she'd had with Angel about Lumbee identity.

"You know Sheila Locklear?" Dunette asked, looking at Lindsay out of the corners of her eyes.

"No, sorry. I was just thinking of something Angel said. Anyway, do you know what happened to McQueen after he collected the bounty?" Lindsay asked.

"He left the county. Had to. Went out West for awhile, and then up North and got married. Eventually, I guess karma caught up with him because he got shot coming out of his house one day. His grandson, my mother's father, moved back to Lumberton when he was grown. He was the one who told me the truth about our family. My father was an Oxendine, you see—a *real* Lum—so he didn't like anybody to know that he'd married Donahue McQueen's great granddaughter. To tell the truth, I'm not sure his parents would've let him go ahead with the marriage if they knew. Lumbees have long memories. My granddaddy told me anyway, though. He thought it was important to always be honest about things, because a secret like that will eat you up inside."

"I wish my family had been a bit more open about our family tree," Lindsay said ruefully, thinking about the events of the previous December. The secrets that Simmy and her Aunt Harding had kept had almost destroyed them all.

"I sometimes wish I didn't know the truth," Dunette said. "Sometimes I think it was too big a burden to know that one of my relatives was a murderer."

"What's past is past," Simmy said. She had been drumming her fingers impatiently on the tabletop while Lindsay and Dunette spoke, and now she rose from the table. "I don't see why y'all are so interested in dredging all this up anyway. Let sleeping dogs lie, I say. Especially when the sleeping dogs are dead, and they're gonna give you tons of money." She grabbed her cane with one hand and a bottle of wine with the other. "I'm going to bed," she announced.

"It's not even eight o'clock," Lindsay said. "And you haven't had dinner."

Simmy held up the wine bottle. "Dinner's right here. Good night."

Once they'd heard the door to Simmy's room close, Lindsay turned to Dunette. "I wonder if the thing I said about family secrets upset her. I wasn't blaming her."

"No, she's been like that all day," Dunette said. "That's why I took her out on all those errands this afternoon. I could tell she was fretting, and Mike was making it worse. He's a good man, but he's always so wound up. It's like having a big puppy around. Anyway, Simmy puts up a good front, but I think this thing with you almost getting hurt by that man has set her on edge. She wants you to live your life to the fullest. She doesn't want you to have to be afraid, so she doesn't want to show that *she's* worried. Half the time, I believe she thinks she's living here to watch over you rather than vice versa."

"Really?" Lindsay said. She realized she'd been so wrapped up in her own fear of being harmed that she hadn't thought at all about how her experience might've affected Simmy or anyone else.

Dunette nodded. "Sugar, underneath all her big talk, she's as soft as an old featherbed, and she really cares about you. I guess that's always how it is with the ones we love. We want them to live big and take chances, but we don't want them to fail or get hurt. So we spend all our time worrying over 'em." Dunette swatted her hand dismissively. "That's people for you. We're as dumb as mules."

"She should eat something," Lindsay said, rising from her chair.

"You sit down. I'll fix her some cheese and crackers on a plate."

As Dunette prepared Simmy's snack, Lindsay chewed her thumbnail thoughtfully.

"The story about Boss Strong and Donahue McQueen also has a hidden body, and I suppose the bounty could be considered stolen money? And the Burnt Island thing would still apply," Lindsay said. "Maybe it's that. Maybe it's Boss's story."

"But why would that make Boughtflower want to give me the money? Like I said, you'd think I'd be the very last person on the list."

"Good point," Lindsay agreed. "And you know what else I still don't get? Boughtflower said stealing the money caused 'everything that happened afterwards' to his family. He said it like they were cursed or something. But as far as I can tell, his life was pretty good. I mean, he'd had a successful business, sold it at a profit, lived in a mansion. His daughter and granddaughter, at least, seemed pretty devoted to him. What was so bad?"

Dunette shrugged. "Money can't buy happiness."

Dunette finished preparing Simmy's snack as Lindsay scribbled on a blank piece of paper, reading aloud as she listed all the important information she could think of:

- Boughtflower believed his fortune came to him dishonestly and was cursed
- He felt guilty about hiding a body and stealing money. He wanted to give it back to "Burnt Island people"
- He attended the KKK rally at Hayes Pond in 1958
- He said someone else was helping execute his dying wishes
- He had his secretary (an Irish woman) seek out Dunette
- He gave Jess power of attorney and charged her with selling his house and liquidating his assets
- Jess hid her actions from her parents
- Jess has an unusual interest in astronomy and math
- He left his fortune to Dunette to rectify some past wrong
- He left Jess a key and a star map in his will

Next to these, she listed the questions she still had and the potential answers:

- Whose body was hidden? Lowrie? Boss Strong? Somebody else?
- What is the stolen money? The $30K? Something else?
- Why Dunette?
- What is Jess hiding?
- Who was helping Boughtflower execute his wishes? Jess? The Irish secretary? Someone else?

- Is it coincidence that all of this is going on at the same time as the stuff with Adam???

Dunette leaned over Lindsay's shoulder to look at the list. "You think Jess is up to something? And that there's a connection between all this and what happened with Adam Tyrell?" she asked.

"I don't know. I'm just trying to get my head around everything that's been going on. There are so many pieces, and I don't even know the puzzle I'm trying to solve. With the Boughtflower stuff, we don't really even know if a crime has been committed, or if this whole thing with the will and the money is all just down to a bitter old man's whims."

"I don't like this," Dunette said. "I'd feel better if you'd let the police do their thing and the lawyers do theirs. You're like Kipper with that pair of Simmy's slippers with the bows on them. He just can't leave them in the closet where they belong."

Lindsay sighed. "I wish I could let this go. Believe me. But I can't help it. Until it gets figured out, my mind just won't drop it."

Dunette shook her head and stepped along to Simmy's room to try and convince her to eat something.

Lindsay had just turned the piece of paper over to begin making notes on the other side when her cell phone rang. She didn't recognize the number but answered anyway, thinking it might be some update from the police on the search for Adam Tyrell.

"Hello?" she said.

"Lindsay?"

She recognized the voice instantly. It was Adam Tyrell himself. She was so startled that she nearly threw the phone onto the floor.

As if reading her mind, he said. "Please, don't hang up. I know what you must be thinking, but the police have got it wrong. Please, hear me out. I need your help. I think Jess is in trouble."

Lindsay said nothing. She couldn't. She was too stunned to speak. Her mind raced. She thought about calling out to Dunette and Simmy, but what could they do? Even if they were able to summon the police while she kept Adam on the line, she knew there'd be no way they could set up a trace on her cell phone line quickly enough. The New Albany police would have to put in a call to a State or Federal agency with more sophisticated capabilities, which would then have to try to pick up the signal. All of that would take time, hours perhaps. It had never occurred to any of them to set up a trace for calls coming in on her phone. They had no reason to think Adam would call her. She glanced at the Caller ID screen and, with a shaking hand, jotted down the phone number he was calling from, not quite trusting the automated call log on her phone to save it. At least the police could track down the call information after the fact. If he was using a cell phone, perhaps they could triangulate his location based on the cell phone towers the call bounced off of.

"Lindsay? Are you still there?"

"Yes," she whispered, her voice sounding hoarse.

"Listen," he said, speaking quickly, slightly out of breath. "Boughtflower tried to tell you about me before he died. You know how he said someone was working with him, helping him? That was me. He hired me about a year ago to track down Dunette and make sure she got his money. He had a secretary, too, helping him—a woman from County Mayo in Ireland. Her name was Ellen, but I'm sure that was a pseudonym. I found out that she'd been skimming off money from Boughtflower almost the whole time she worked for him. When I showed him the proof, he fired her. I thought she went back home, but I think she's back. I think she's trying to kidnap Jess."

"What?" Lindsay said. Her mind suddenly shot to Jess's strange "casting agent meeting" in Raleigh. "Why would she want to kidnap Jess?"

"There was something else of value that Boughtflower entrusted Jess with getting to Dunette. Jess was waiting until the stars were aligned so she could get it and hand it over."

"What is it?" Lindsay asked.

"I don't know. All I know is that it's worth a lot, and that it's something tangible. It's hidden somewhere down in Robeson County. Boughtflower said it was marked with a cross."

"What, like X marks the spot? Like pirate treasure?" Lindsay said dubiously.

"That's all I know," Adam replied.

"Why should I trust you? You still haven't explained why you were spying on me. If your job was to find Dunette, why were you still around after she was hired? And why did you drug me?"

"I'm not the one who drugged you, and I wasn't spying on you," Adam said with a weary sigh. "I was trying to protect Dunette. I dressed up as Doer because I needed a way to search your house and check you out. The way you hired her so suddenly, right after Boughtflower let her go and right after you just happened to come into his room. Well, it seemed suspicious."

"You were suspicious of a chaplain visiting a patient in the hospital?" Lindsay asked incredulously.

"Being suspicious is my job."

"Wait," Lindsay said, thinking she'd picked up on a further hole in his story. "How did you even know I'd hired Dunette? Doer showed up at my place the same day as Simmy and I met with her."

"I was following her, okay? And then when I saw you meeting, I got suspicious. Can't you see how that might look a little weird to an outsider?"

"Well, if you rifled through all my stuff and stalked me, presumably you were able to discover that I'm not some kind of criminal mastermind who got a Masters in Divinity, another degree in counseling, and then spent four years working in hospitals just to worm my way into Otis Boughtflower's will."

"You really are funny," Adam said.

"Shut up," Lindsay snapped. "Why didn't you stop messing with me once you knew I was kosher? Why stick around after he died?"

"Boughtflower paid me to see that his wishes were carried out. That job doesn't end until the money is in Dunette's hands."

"What about drugging me? If you didn't do it, who did?" Lindsay demanded. Although she was trying her best to project an aura of skepticism, she had to admit that she was starting to be convinced. She'd always felt that there was far more going on than met the eye, and his story seemed to clear up many of the mysteries she'd been laying out to Dunette just moments before.

"I don't know. That's what worries me. I thought one of the Philpots might be working with Ellen. That might've made sense since they all wanted to get their hands on the money."

"Not Jess," Lindsay observed.

"Exactly. If she wanted the money, she could've abused her power of attorney and just taken it."

"So you think it could've been Yancy or Margo?" Lindsay asked.

"Like I said, I don't know. I can't think that either of them would be involved in kidnapping their own daughter. So, if they were in league with Ellen before, they might not be anymore," Adam said. "I've got to go."

"Wait, I need to know something else. Why did you pick Weaponless Doer as a name? Why *that* name?"

"I'm sorry about that. I guess I was trying to be clever. I'd done a lot of research on you, and was fascinated by the whole Leander Swoopes thing. That was really stupid."

At Adam's admission, Lindsay felt a strange lightness. If what he said was true, then the events of the past few weeks really didn't have any connection with Leander Swoopes. There was still much to fear for Owen and Jess, but *that* fear—that deep bone-chilling fear that had almost overwhelmed her—could be put aside. She could almost feel the focus of her energy shift from trying to protect herself to looking out once again to the world beyond herself.

Adam had stopped talking, and Lindsay heard what sounded like muffled voices in the background. "Look, Lindsay, I've really got to go. I just needed you to know the truth. Try to help Jess if you can. I'll do what I can, too, but it's more difficult now that I've had to go underground."

"If what you say about Ellen is true, why didn't you tell the police instead of telling me? Jess could be in real trouble," Lindsay said. But when her question was greeted by silence, she realized she was already talking to dead air.

Chapter 21

"Then I asked him why he called me instead of the police," Lindsay said.

Two hours had passed since her call with Adam ended. She was sitting in her favorite chair in her living room, and Warren and Freeland Vickers were both on the couch, taking rapid notes. No one could reach Jess or Owen, and with each passing minute, fears for their safety grew. Lindsay had left Simmy and Dunette in her kitchen, trying to soothe Mike's nerves as he waited anxiously to hear from his son.

"What did Adam say?" Warren asked. His face was haggard, his expression strained. He looked like he'd aged at least a decade since the last time Lindsay had seen him at the hospital a few days before.

"Nothing," Lindsay answered. "He'd already hung up."

As soon as Lindsay had hung up with Adam an hour earlier, she'd called the police to relay the contents of their conversation. Her next call had been to Mike, who had been at the Mex-Itali with Anna and Drew. When she passed on Adam's warning about Jess, Mike had immediately placed a call to Owen to find out if he was with her. Mike had been calling and texting his son every 10 minutes ever since then, but hadn't had an answer. It was now almost 11 p.m. The last time anyone could account for Owen's whereabouts was almost three hours before, when his coach said he'd left the high school after his basketball game. He'd texted his father to say he was on his way to Raleigh to pick up Jess, and that he'd be home later. Warren told Lindsay that Jess's parents, too, had been unable to reach their daughter.

"You don't have any idea why Adam would call you instead of the police?" Warren asked.

"No. All I can think is that he was afraid he'd be found if he called y'all. Obviously, he's gone through a lot of trouble to hide." Lindsay paused. "Do you think he could be telling the truth?"

Warren studied her expression. "Do you?"

Lindsay frowned. Her interactions with Adam played through her mind like a highlights reel. His dazzling smile. Those twinkling, cinnamon-colored eyes. The seductive smell of his skin. She swept those images aside and turned her focus inward. Leaving aside his flirtation and good looks, what did she really know about Adam? What did she really believe? At last, she answered. "I wish I knew. All I can say for sure is that I wanted to believe him, but something seemed…off. This is weird to say, but he reminded me of Sarabelle."

"What about her?" Warren asked. "Something good or something bad?"

"You mean the manipulative con artist side of her or the charming persuasive side?" Lindsay said. "I can't put my finger on it. It's just that when I think of him, I think of Sarabelle."

Vickers' phone rang. "Sorry, honey," he said to Lindsay. "Gotta take this. I'll be right back."

Lindsay watched Vickers as he shuffled into the hallway, and then she turned back to Warren. "Have you been able to turn up anything else about Adam?"

"Mostly just what Prendergast told you on the phone last time he gave you an update. For now, the FBI is helping us because of the potential Leander Swoopes link, and they've put us in touch with the authorities in Bratislava and Berlin, but if he was living there, he was going by a different name than any of the aliases we know. He entered the U.S. from Paris a few months ago on his Terry Addison passport, so he definitely was in Europe. We just don't know where, or for how long. The website entry for his security consultancy was only put up within the past few months. One thing we were looking at was the source of the Rohypnol he used, or we thought he used, to drug you. It's prescribed legally in a lot of Western European countries, so it would've been pretty easy for him to come by over there. But if what he told you is true, then that might be a dead end."

"What about Yancy Philpot? He works at Kroger, right? Maybe he has access to the pharmacy there," Lindsay speculated.

"I've already looked into that," Warren replied. "They don't stock that drug, and even if they did, that place is locked down tighter than a prison ward."

The words "prison ward" chimed like a bell in Lindsay's head. "Oh my god," she whispered. "Lydia Sikes's son." The connection between Adam and Sarabelle suddenly seemed to come into clearer focus.

"What?" Warren said.

"Nothing. Well, something. I don't know." Lindsay rose from her chair and began to pace. "This doesn't make any sense, but can you see what you can find out about Lydia Sikes's son? I don't think I mentioned it to you, but Lydia's son, Christopher, wrote to Sarabelle in prison a few weeks ago."

"And," Warren said, "you're thinking he has something to do with this?"

"I know it doesn't make sense, but Adam was weirdly curious about my mother."

"But if he thought you might be running some scam on Boughtflower, it would make sense to try to find out more about your criminal connections, right? And anyway that letter writing must've happened before this whole thing with Boughtflower and the will. I don't see a connection."

Lindsay was quiet for a moment. Strong as her hunch about the connection between her mother and Adam had seemed in her own mind, she had to admit that when it came out of her mouth, it sounded like a wild speculation. She tried out another theory. "Okay, then. What if there is no son? What if it was just someone posing as her son?"

"Maybe the Irish secretary? Or one of the Philpots?" Warren asked, seeming to read her mind. "But what interest would they have in getting in touch with your mother?"

Lindsay removed her glasses and rubbed her eyes. "You're right. It doesn't make sense. I'm losing it."

"Your instincts have been known to solve some pretty tricky problems before, finding connections other people miss," Warren said, with a sad smile.

"That may be, but overall, I'd say my instincts have a pretty lousy track record."

There was a moment of strained silence. Warren stared down at his notebook, but he didn't really seem to be reading what he'd written there. Lindsay wanted to reach out and take his hand. She

172

wanted to ask him if he knew about Teresa and Jonah's planned engagement, and what he thought of it. She wanted to show him that Simmy had taught Kipper how to moonwalk. More than any of that, though, she wanted him to put his arms around her and tell her he still loved her. Instead, they sat mutely, and she thought back to the previous summer. They'd started their relationship under such terrible circumstances—the investigation of a murder, and now here they were, trying to track down two missing teenagers. Maybe their love had always been doomed.

Vickers walked back into the living room.

"Prendergast wants our help over at the Philpots'. He said the father is pretty out of control. Wants the National Guard to go after his daughter or something. He took a swing at one of the uniforms. Prendergast had to threaten to arrest him to get him to simmer down. Also," he said, turning to Lindsay. "You were right to pick up on something funny about what Adam told you. The Philpots cast some doubt over what he said about the Irish secretary, Ellen. They never heard of her, or anybody stealing money from the old man. Said the old man didn't even have a secretary."

"But Dunette can corroborate that," Lindsay countered. "She talked to an Irish woman on the phone who said she was his secretary. That's who made all the arrangements for her to work for Boughtflower."

"Besides that, the Philpots never knew about Jess having power of attorney," Warren said. "But we know for a fact that's true. Maybe they just knew less about his affairs than they thought."

Vickers shrugged. "Well, somebody's lying. That's all I'm saying."

The three of them walked into Lindsay's kitchen. Although the room had almost doubled in size as a result of the renovation, it still didn't feel big enough to comfortably hold Lindsay, Simmy, Dunette, Mike, Warren, Freeland Vickers, and Kipper, especially with Mike nervously pacing the floor, seemingly unable to remain still.

As soon as the trio entered the kitchen, Mike approached Warren and Vickers. "You're going to do something, right? Don't tell me that this is one of those 'we've gotta wait 24 hours before we can report them missing' things," he said.

"Absolutely not," Warren reassured him. "That's sometimes a guideline, but I don't know any police department that follows that as a rule, especially not when a minor might be in trouble. I've already called down to Robeson County. They're searching the area around Burnt Island Road and the area along the Lumber River that used to be called Burnt Island. Hotels in Raleigh are being contacted as we speak. We've alerted every county between Robeson and Raleigh, in case they're somewhere en route. We're putting together information to get an AMBER alert issued on Owen."

"What about for Jess?" Dunette asked. "She's the one who Adam said was in danger."

"We can't do an AMBER alert for her because she's 18, but we've put her description out," Warren said. "I know you're worried," he continued, addressing them all. "It's not just the New Albany and Mount Moriah forces working on this. We're in touch with county police, the FBI, and the SBI. We're not taking this lying down. But we have to remember that it may still be nothing. Teenage couples go temporarily out of touch all the time."

"Not Owen," Mike shot back.

"I know," Warren said. "Like I said, we're not taking this lying down. We'll be in touch. Just stay put and call me if you think of anything else."

As soon as the sound of the police vehicle died away, Mike grabbed his jacket.

"Where are you going?" Lindsay asked.

"To find my son."

"Didn't you hear what Warren said?" Dunette asked. "They're on it."

"If it was your daughter, would you just sit there and wait for them to get in touch?" Mike said.

Dunette cast her eyes down to the table.

"What are you going to do?" Lindsay asked. "Drive to Raleigh and look in every hotel?"

"No. I'm going to fly to Robeson County and find the Burnt Island."

"What?!" they all said in unison.

"I'm not just going to sit around here all night and wait for something to happen," Mike said. "From what I can tell, there are three possibilities. One, they're in Raleigh with a casting agent, and they've decided for some reason not to return calls and texts. Two, they're together somewhere having sex or doing drugs or something else that prevents them from returning calls and texts. Or three, they've been kidnapped and taken to Robeson County to get whatever this valuable thing is that Jess is supposed to know about."

"Those aren't the only possibilities," Lindsay countered. "They could be anywhere. Anything could've happened. Besides, what if you end up just getting in the way of the police? I'm sure they don't want you getting involved. And even if someone did take them to try to find this alleged treasure, they could've done that to lead us into some kind of trap. We have no idea who we're dealing with."

"Which is exactly why I'm going," Mike said, his voice breaking with emotion. "My son could be down there, being held hostage by some psycho."

"I'm going with Mike," Simmy said, rising from her chair.

Now it was Mike's turn to say, "What?!"

"You heard me," she said. "Somebody's gotta do something. Look at what happened with Leander Swoopes. They knew how dangerous he was. Every policeman on the Outer Banks knew he was on the loose, and he still got away."

"You can't go," Dunette said. "You can barely walk from the house to the car without getting dizzy. How much use are you gonna be if something kicks off? What're you gonna do? Hit the bad guys with your cane?"

"Well, if anybody's coming, they'd better come. I'm leaving for the airport now," Mike said. "It's a two-seater plane, so there's only room for one."

"Maybe Dunette should go with you," Lindsay said. "She at least knows her way around Robeson County. You're not going to do much good for anybody if you just end up down there driving around in circles all night. Speaking of which, how are you going to drive around at all? You don't have a car down there."

175

"There'll be one waiting for me. I already called ahead and made the arrangements while you were talking to Warren and Vickers." He turned to Dunette and said impatiently, "Are you coming?"

"Uh-uh. I'm sorry, but I can't. I have to take a knockout pill just to get on a regular plane. No way am I getting in some little tin can with wings with somebody who just learned how to fly a few weeks ago. What about Kipper?" Dunette suggested. "Maybe he could track Owen's scent."

Kipper looked up expectantly at the sound of his name.

"Oh, for Christ's sake, he's not a bloodhound," Mike said, grabbing the sides of his head with his hands. He turned to Lindsay. "If anything happens, if there's any news, text me or get somebody to radio me from the airport. I probably won't have voice call reception."

Mike grabbed his jacket and headed out the door. There was a brief moment of silence as the three women sat there gaping at each other.

"What are you waiting for?" Simmy said to Lindsay.

"It's too crazy," Lindsay countered. "Besides, if I go with him, Warren will never forgive me. It'll be like I'm saying I don't trust him to do his job. He said to stay put. He already thinks that I chose Mike over him once."

"Screw that," Simmy said. "Since when do you sit around doing what you're told? Mike's your friend, and his son might be in trouble. Owen and Jess are just kids. You're one of the bravest people I ever met. Are you gonna let Swoopes take that away from you? Are you gonna spend the rest of your life hiding? Go." She made a shooing motion. "Go! We'll be fine."

Lindsay heard the sound of Mike's car ignition turning over. It hit her like the sound of a starting pistol. She dashed out the door, just in time to climb into the passenger's seat of his car as he backed down the driveway.

"What are you doing?" Mike said, not even glancing in her direction.

"What does it look like?" she said. "You know this could end really badly, right?"

"Why do you think I have to go?" Mike answered.

Chapter 22

Lindsay had never before been in a small plane, and Mike's plane was smaller than anything she dreamed could safely take to the air. The entire fuselage was hardly bigger than the body of her Honda. She wasn't usually a nervous flyer, but she quickly realized that all of the things she normally liked about flying—the snacks, the seat-back TVs, the excitement of arriving at a new destination—were not going to form a part of this particular airborne experience. The cabin was cramped and the noise of the engine would've been earsplitting without the headphones she and Mike wore.

For his part, Mike hadn't spoken to Lindsay at all from the time he began his preflight checklist until he started his preparations for landing. He gripped the controls, grimly flipping switches. The only sound came from the voices of other pilots and ground staff that would occasionally burst in over the plane's radio. She was relieved, however, not to have to try and make small talk when it was all she could do not to scream in terror every time they hit a jolt of turbulent air.

They moved through dense banks of clouds that would suddenly open into blackness and then give way again to clouds. They seemed to be suspended between dimensions— rocketing through a place where distance and time moved at a different pace from the earth they'd left behind in Mount Moriah. Lindsay saw from the clock mounted to the control panel that only a little over an hour had passed since they'd been standing in her kitchen with Dunette, Kipper, and Simmy. It seemed so much longer than that. And could it really have been only a few hours earlier that she and Owen had been sitting at her kitchen table working on his trigonometry homework?

She stole a sideways glance at Mike. His jaw was set at a severe angle; his eyes moved rhythmically between the windscreen and the instrument panel. She had the strange urge to reach out and hold his hand. The lack of communication, coming from the always overly-garrulous Mike, heightened her surreal feeling. The minutes ticked by, seeming to go both too fast and too slow. The only task she'd been given was to monitor Mike's and her cell phones for any calls or texts from Owen or the police. Every time she looked at them, she willed them to transmit news that the teenagers had been found safe and they could turn around and go back home. But the screens remained as empty as the dark sky surrounding them.

At last, a voice cut in through the silence. "Bladenboro arrival. Information Kilo. Wind two zero zero degrees, zero five knots. Visibility two kilometers. Scattered clouds 1000 feet. Fog 100 feet. Temperature 15, dewpoint 13. No significant change expected. End information Kilo."

"Is that the air traffic controller?" Lindsay asked.

Mike didn't reply to her but instead said, "Bladenboro approach. Piper Cherokee Echo Papa Echo Golf. Fifteen miles northwest, inbound. I have weather information Kilo."

When no one responded, Lindsay asked, "Is everything okay? Why isn't the air traffic controller saying anything?"

"There isn't one. That was a recording," Mike said. "That's the airport." He pointed into the dark gray mist in front of them. His voice, piped in through her headset, seemed strangely intimate. "There's nobody there this time of night and we're probably the only ones around, but I'm telling everybody on this frequency what we're up to just in case. We don't want to be approaching for landing at the same time as somebody else."

"Where is it? I don't see anything," Lindsay said, peering down through the darkness and patches of fog. She could feel the plane descending quickly; the tell-tale lightness in her stomach was much more palpable than it was on a commercial flight. As they dropped, however, she still couldn't make out anything that resembled an airport. She expected to see a lit-up strip of runway, a control tower, *something*. The area that Mike had pointed to had a few lights, but looked no different than the small clusters of houses they'd been passing during the entire flight.

"If no one's there, how are we going to land? Who's going to turn on the lights?" She looked over at Mike, who was continuing to push forward on the controls. He made a series of quick movements, clicking the radio numerous times in rapid succession.

Suddenly, two rows of lights blazed through the rolling mist. "Did you do that?"

"Yes. Little airports like this have a system that lets pilots control the lights by clicking the radio. Seven clicks turns on the lights. Now be quiet, please. I'm not very good at landings yet and the visibility here isn't ideal."

Lindsay gripped the sides of her seat and gritted her teeth. Her mind flashed back briefly to her cozy house, to the comforting warmth of her cheerful, yellow kitchen. She could be there right now, but instead she was strapped into a glorified model airplane on the hunt for a potentially-dangerous kidnapper with a man who "wasn't very good at landings yet." She shut her eyes. She didn't pray, exactly—she always hesitated to call in favors from God just because the going got rough. Instead, she did what she often did during her hardest days at the hospital—took a moment to recognize that God was there, had always been there, and would always be there. There was no need to ask for anything. She knew deep down that anything she needed had already been provided, and she held on tight to that belief.

The plane smacked down hard and popped back into the air. Lindsay's eyes flew open as they thudded down a second time, this time sticking to the ground. They shimmied from one side of the runway to the other until Mike at last muscled the plane under control. Lindsay's body had been thrown around like a ragdoll during the landing.

When they finally came to a stop near a hangar at the edge of the runway, Mike unbuckled himself and then leaned over to unbuckle her. "Sorry about that," he said. "Are you okay?"

Lindsay realized that she'd been holding her breath. When she blew it out, she felt almost dizzy from pent-up emotion. "Yeah, I'm okay," she said through clenched teeth. "Let's go."

"Grab that bag behind your seat," Mike ordered. "That's our survival pack, in case we ever crash land. We might need some of that stuff."

Lindsay grabbed the duffel bag, unzipped it, and quickly rifled through the contents. It contained two headlamps, a first aid kit, a distress flare, and foil packets of food and water. Lindsay's breath caught again. They were really going to do this. They were going into the woods, chasing after a kidnapper. Events now seemed to be unfolding much more quickly and uncontrollably than she'd planned. The fear she felt on the plane paled in comparison to what she was beginning to feel now. They hurried over to the airport's lone building—a tiny structure smaller than Lindsay's house. A red Chevy Malibu was parked in front of it.

"This must be the rental car," Lindsay said. "But if there's nobody here, where do we pick up the keys?" Mike opened the driver's side door and pointed to the ignition, where a set of keys dangled. "Weren't they afraid it'd get stolen?" Lindsay asked.

"By who?" Mike gestured to the wide expanse of nothingness that surrounded them. They climbed into the car and Mike typed "Burnt Island Road" into the car's GPS. "Twenty five minutes— fifteen, probably, if we ignore the speed limits. I guess we'll start there," he said, gunning the engine and zipping out onto the main road.

"Are you sure about this?" Lindsay asked. She gripped the door handle as Mike took the car around a sharp curve. "Warren said the Robeson County Sheriff is already out looking in that area, and along the river in the place that was the Burnt Island Swamp."

"Do you have a better idea?" Mike snapped.

"Well, I think we should at least let the authorities know we're out here."

"Since when are you such a rule follower? It's okay for you to go all vigilante when it's your own family's lives at stake, but with mine, you're suddenly a Girl Scout?"

"That's not fair," Lindsay replied. She'd never known Mike to be sharp with anyone. In fact, she'd never really seen any other side to him than the devoted, frenetic ball-of-energy persona that he usually presented to the world. She had years of experience watching people change drastically when put under pressure, though, and she was an expert in cutting such people a lot of slack. She took a deep breath and said calmly, "If I didn't care about you and Owen, I wouldn't be out here in the middle of the night with you. All I'm saying is that I don't want to be tromping around a swamp in the dark and end up getting shot by a cop who mistakes us for kidnappers."

Mike lapsed into a sullen silence and gripped the wheel more tightly.

Lindsay allowed a few tense minutes to pass. She looked anxiously out the window as the black shapes of trees whipped past. She hadn't spent much time in this part of the state, but she knew from reading about it that the land was only habitable because of extensive efforts over the centuries to drain the swamps and build up patches of dry land. Despite those efforts, much of the region was still at or below sea level, and densely forested. Countless ditches and small creeks cut through the landscape, all draining toward the slow-moving Lumber River—a body of water, she recalled with an ominous shiver, which had originally been known as Drowning Creek.

"I know you're afraid the police will try to stop you, but I think you know I'm right," she said at last. "We need to work together. The last thing Owen needs to hear when he's found is that his dad did something reckless trying to save him and got hurt or killed."

Before Mike could speak, the sound of his phone's cheerful rock-and-roll ringtone filled the car. The phone was sitting in the center console, and as he reached for it, he swerved off the road. They had been going so fast that he almost lost control of the car as he fumbled with the buttons.

Lindsay grabbed the phone from his hand. "Pull over before you crash!" she commanded. The number that showed on the screen wasn't Owen's, but she thought she recognized it.

"I feel like I know that number," she said.

"Just answer it! What if it's Owen?" Mike said frantically.

Mike steered the car on to the grass verge as Lindsay answered the call on speakerphone.

"Dad!"

"Owen, is that you?" Mike said.

"Thank God," Lindsay whispered.

"Are you okay?" Mike asked.

"I'm okay, but Jess isn't … a snake. Her ankle … pretty out of it. I don't think … further." Owen's voice was cutting in and out. His voice sounded thin and frightened—nothing like the laid-back, self-assured teenager they knew.

"Where are you?" Lindsay asked.

"Woods ... called the police ... looking for us ...the cross... need to hide ..."

"What does it look like where you are? Owen? Owen?" Mike said, but the line had already cut out. Mike grabbed the phone and immediately tried to call his son back.

"The cellular subscriber you are trying to reach is not available at this time," intoned a woman's silky voice. "Please try again later."

Mike cursed under his breath and frantically dialed and re-dialed the number. Lindsay, meanwhile, took out her phone and dialed Warren's number. He picked up on the first ring.

"Warren, Owen and Jess are in trouble. I think they're being chased by someone, and Jess has been bitten by a snake," she said. She quickly recapped Owen's call and explained where they were. By now, Mike had put his phone back down and they were again speeding along the deserted two-lane road.

"I know," Warren replied. "I just got off the phone with the Robeson County Sheriff. Owen tried to call 9-1-1, but the calls kept cutting out before they could get any information from him. The dispatcher was able to track the call based on the cell towers, though, and they think the calls came from somewhere a few miles north of the areas they're already searching. They're getting more people out looking now that we know for sure they're down there somewhere. I'm on my way down, too. Did Owen give you any more information about exactly where they were?" Warren asked.

"No. Just that they were in the woods," Lindsay said.

"I'd tell you not to do anything stupid, but it sounds like I'm too late for that," Warren said somewhat testily. "So just be careful, okay? I'll tell the cops down there that you're on your way. If you're heading to that area, you'll probably run into the guys out looking for them anyway. Link up with them, okay? Don't try to do this on your own."

"I love you," Lindsay blurted out. She had no idea where the words had come from.

There was a long pause before Warren replied. "Be safe."

Lindsay hung up and stared at the phone for a second, mouthing his words back to herself. *Be safe?* She realized that part of why she'd said what she'd said was that she wanted to hear the words reflected back to her right then. She was scared and worried, afraid for Owen and Jess, afraid that she and Mike might get themselves in over their heads. When they were dating, she rarely told Warren she loved him, but she'd reached out now. Sure, they were just words, but those words were extraordinarily comforting to say and to hear. *Be safe?* That had been his response to her declaration of love. Were they always doomed to do this reverse polarity dance of reaching out and pulling away at all the wrong times? She angrily pocketed her phone. There was no time to think about her relationship with Warren; she had to focus on helping Mike find Owen and Jess.

She looked at the little blue dot moving across the screen of the GPS, trying to get her bearings. The GPS indicated that they were racing along Route 211. She'd studied the Google Map image of this area a dozen times, trying to match the terrain to the historical area that had been known as the Burnt Island. The whole region was populated with names that referenced that time—Burnt Swamp School, Burnt Island Tires and Brakes. Some of these stood in areas that the Lowrie band would've recognized, but in this ever-shifting lowland landscape, who could say where the old Burnt Island began and ended anymore? Very few of the old structures remained. Poverty, hurricanes, and the ravages of the warm, damp climate ensured a constant battle against decay.

"The cross!" Lindsay suddenly yelled. "Turn left!"

Without hesitation, Mike followed her direction. He only asked why after they'd turned onto Old Whiteville Road.

"There's a big church on this road. I've seen it on Street View. You'll see it in a second. Oh my god, why didn't I think of it sooner?" Lindsay said. She was already texting Warren to let him know about her hunch. She wasn't yet certain enough to call the Sheriff and redirect the search efforts—after all, the authorities were basing their search on cell phone triangulation. Real data. All she had was the seed of an idea. Still, she asked Warren to let the Robeson County searchers know what she and Mike were up to. The idea of being shot in the woods like a deer was still very much at the forefront of her mind.

Mike pulled into the parking lot of the Antioch Baptist Church, a complex of red brick structures that stood on a lonely stretch of road across from dense forestland. "The cross," he whispered. They emerged from the car, their backs facing the church. Sure enough, across the street from the church stood a 10-foot tall white cross on a U-shaped patch of grass carved out from the surrounding forest.

"This church building is fairly new, but this congregation dates back to the 1800's," Lindsay said. "It was originally called Burnt Islands Baptist Church."

"Do you think this could be the place?" Mike asked. "X marks the spot?"

"I really don't know. But I think it's worth a look, don't you?"

They circled the large church building first, trying doors and peering in windows, looking for any trace that would suggest anyone was inside. The interior, though, was pitch-black, other than the glow from the illuminated EXIT signs. They could see nothing to suggest that the teenagers had been there.

They walked across the street, towards the cross. It was now nearly 1:30 in the morning. The air was thick with moisture, and mist clung to the trees like cobwebs. Though the low clouds blocked out the moon and stars, they reflected the terrestrial lights and made the wide expanse of the church parking lot abnormally bright. Still, as they approached the woods' edge, they could see that the light would quickly disappear if they entered the forest.

They passed under the outstretched arms of the cross, looking along the ground for any signs that Owen and Jess had been there recently. Lindsay leaned on the cross, momentarily resting her weight against it.

"Owen said something about needing to hide. How will we find them if they're hiding in there?" she wondered aloud.

No sooner had she given voice to those words than the regular pattern of nighttime forest sounds—croaks and creeps and chirrups—was disturbed by the sudden noise of a flock of birds alighting from their roost deeper within the forest. The tiny birds irately chirped their distress as they swept out into the air over Mike and Lindsay's heads. They circled the high steeple of the Antioch Baptist Church before diving back into the canopy.

Lindsay turned to Mike. "I'm not really one for signs from heaven, but I'm also not one to stand around and wait for God to drop a big, flashing neon arrow out of the sky."

They strapped on their headlamps. Mike slung the duffel bag over his shoulder and began to move quickly ahead.

"Mike!" Lindsay called. "Slow down and look where you're going, okay? Do you think the snake that bit Jess is the only nasty thing out here?"

The role of the prudent protector was an unaccustomed one for Lindsay. Usually, she was the one running headlong into danger, heedless of risk, while her father or Warren cautioned her to look before she leapt. An old thought returned, one she'd had before, when she first met Mike. If the two of them ever got together, which one would be the grown-up?

She followed along after Mike, picking her way over tree roots and underbrush. Despite her warning, he'd barely slackened his pace, instead crashing ahead like he was being chased by a grizzly. They couldn't have penetrated more than a half a mile into the forest, but it felt like they'd traveled to another world. The land was almost completely flat; the trees close-packed and interspersed with an understory of bushes, fallen branches, and scrubby pines. Even in the dark, Lindsay could sense slight differences from her own familiar forest in the Piedmont. Although pine trees were plentiful here, even the smell was not quite the same as the fragrant pine forests that surrounded Mount Moriah. It was spring, but the air around her had a murky, earthy smell, like an unventilated basement.

Mike had now moved out of her range of vision. She was alone. Although she often ran on forest trails during the daytime, staggering through the woods in the darkness was an entirely different proposition. There was no discernable trail, meaning that every step required an unaccustomed degree of thinking and planning. These nighttime woods felt looming and oppressive, like a vast ocean that might sweep in and drown her. She suddenly became aware that if her headlamp went out, she'd be able to see nothing at all. Nothing except the shadowy visions conjured up in her imagination.

Lindsay stopped walking, out of a mix of caution and tingling fear. Pausing allowed her to take stock of her surroundings. Although she'd initially been glad that she was wearing running clothes that allowed for easy movement, she was beginning to wish she'd dressed more appropriately for the terrain. Her running shoes and leggings were spattered with sandy mud and soaked through, and her thin running vest wasn't doing much to ward off the chilly evening air. She heard rustling in the trees overheard and looked up, but she could see nothing beyond the halo of light given off by her headlamp. Still, she felt certain that the birds had alighted from and returned to a spot somewhere near where she stood. She turned off her headlamp, closed her eyes and listened. There was no sound except the rustle of the birds overhead and the rhythmic vibrations of insects.

She leaned against a tree, took her phone out of her pocket and checked the signal. One feeble little bar of service. On a whim, she tried calling Owen, but the line wouldn't connect. She typed out a text telling him she and Mike were in the forest and pressed Send. It seemed to go through. It was a long shot, but often a text could be transmitted when a call wouldn't go through. She felt she had to try. Next, she dialed Mike and then Warren, but faced similar disappointment with the lack of connection. This whole thing was ridiculous. How was stumbling around blindly in the woods going to help? They still didn't really know what had happened with Jess and Owen. Had they been kidnapped or were they just lost? And what would happen if she and Mike got lost? They'd be diverting police resources away from the search for Jess and Owen. Although she'd been stealing glances at the compass app on her phone as they went and still felt confident that she could find her way back to the road, she couldn't guarantee that she'd be able to keep her bearings if she went any deeper into the woods. She turned around. It was time to put an end to this.

Suddenly, the sky almost directly over her head exploded in a burst of orange light. The flare from Mike's emergency pack. The deciduous trees weren't yet in full leaf, so it was possible to make out a bit of the arc of smoke the flare had given off before it exploded. Lindsay hurried in that direction, calling out Mike's name. She'd gone only a few yards before she heard her own name being called.

"Lindsay! I found them!" She could see the light of Mike's headlamp bouncing through the trees as he rushed out to meet her. He caught her up in his arms and buried his face in her hair. "They're alive, but Jess is in bad shape."

He took her hand, half dragging her along. To speed her up, he hooked her arm over his shoulder and wound his arm around her waist, which, due to their height difference, allowed her to propel herself along as if she were in a three-legged race.

Mike began speaking quickly, in something akin to his usual mile-a-minute style. "Somehow I *knew* where they'd be. Like, I felt it. Maybe it was the birds. Maybe it was God. You'll probably think this is crazy, but I was praying to Saint Anthony. He's the patron saint of lost things, and Drew and I were raised Catholic. Our mom was big on saints. Monica, if somebody was having marital problems. Francis, if the dog got sick. That kind of thing. Anyway, I just started calling out and they were right in front of me. Jess has been bitten by a snake. I think she's in shock. But they're alive."

They came to a large tulip poplar. Jess lay against the trunk, with Owen crouched over her. As Lindsay got closer, she could see that he had opened the first aid kit Mike brought and was rummaging through the contents.

Owen looked up at them, his face streaked with dirt. He seemed to be on the verge of tears. "I don't know how to help her."

Lindsay crouched down next to him and put her hand on his back. She smiled reassuringly.

"Jess, honey, can you hear us?" Lindsay asked, gently stroking the girl's silken cheek. Her fingers trailed down to Jess's neck, where she could feel a weak but steady pulse.

Even in the yellowish light of Lindsay's headlamp, Jess looked ghastly pale. Her eyes were closed, and her breath was rapid and shallow. Her eyelids fluttered briefly at the sound of Lindsay's voice, but she didn't seem able to respond. Lindsay had taken the basic first aid and CPR training that was free to all hospital employees each year, but she, like Owen, wasn't entirely sure about the correct treatment for a snake bite. Owen had already removed the mud-covered ballet-style shoe from Jess's grotesquely-swollen foot, and rolled up the ankle of her pants. Lindsay shined the light from her headlamp on Jess's ankle. There were two clearly-defined puncture wounds surrounded by a sickening crimson and purple bruise. Large, pus-filled blisters were rising along the edges of the colored area. The whole area was spattered with mud, increasing the wound's grotesque appearance.

"Oh my god," Mike whispered, covering his mouth with his hand. "Do you have an idea what kind of snake it was?"

Owen shook his head. "We didn't see it. She just stepped on a pile of leaves when we were running and felt something bite her. She kept going for a while, but then she fell behind. I lost her for a few minutes in the dark and when I backtracked I found her like this."

"Probably a coral snake," Lindsay guessed. "I think that kind of venom can take awhile to kick in." She had a vague recollection that a bite victim should be kept still as much as possible to prevent the venom from travelling through the body and causing shock. Well, too late for that, she thought grimly. She looked more closely at Jess's ankle. The swollen flesh was being compressed by the tight hem of the girl's blue, metallic cigarette pants. Lindsay's mind flashed back to her experience with her engagement ring.

"Do y'all have anything sharp?" she asked. "I think we should cut the bottom of her jeans; they're cutting off her circulation."

Mike produced a Swiss Army knife from his pocket, and Lindsay began carefully cutting away the fabric from the bottom of Jess's leg. As she worked, she glanced at Owen and asked. "What happened? How did you end up out here?"

"I was on my way to the hotel in Raleigh to pick her up, but I got a text saying to meet her in an alley near the hotel instead. I thought she was just trying to save me from having to park and come in, so I didn't think anything was weird. But when I got to the place, she stepped out of the shadows with Adam Tyrell, that guy who drugged you."

"What?!" Lindsay and Mike said in unison. Lindsay almost let the knife slip. She took a deep breath and tried to keep her hands from shaking.

"He was kind of disguised, like with a hat and glasses, but I recognized him from the news and stuff. Jess said he had a gun and we needed to do what he told us. He told Jess to tie me up with duct tape. She kept crying while she was doing it and saying she was sorry. Then they put me in the trunk of my car and we drove for what seemed like a really long time. The next thing I knew, Jess was letting me out of the trunk and telling me we had to run and hide."

"But why would he kidnap you? I don't understand the connection," Lindsay said.

"I don't know, either," Owen replied. "There wasn't any time to talk. I don't understand it at all. I thought I was going to give Jess a ride home from Raleigh, and next thing I know, I'm running through the woods escaping from some psycho. I don't know how Adam found Jess or how she escaped. We just ran into the woods, and then she got bitten, and we ran a little while longer, and then she collapsed. I carried her as far as I could."

"It's okay. You did all the right things. You're alive, and that's all that matters right now," Mike said, putting his hand on Owen's shoulder.

"Oh god," Lindsay said. "Whose phone did you call from before?"

"I don't know," Owen replied. "Adam took my phone when they tied me up. I found this one in Jess's pocket after she fainted. It's not hers, so I guess it's Adam's."

"That's why I recognized the number. It's the one he called me from. I even wrote it down, but I still didn't recognize it," Lindsay said. Her mind was racing. Adam had kidnapped them. All along, it had been Adam! If she'd just been paying closer attention, she could've recognized the number, and told Warren about Adam's involvement while they still had phone service.

Up until that point, Mike had been pacing back and forth in a tight circuit, but now he stopped in his tracks. "We're going to have to carry her out of here. Somebody might've seen that flare. Maybe the police, but maybe not. I don't think we can wait. She really doesn't look good. And if the police didn't see it and Adam did... Either way, we can't stick around."

"Do you know the way back?" Owen said. "I didn't pay attention."

Mike's eyes widened in panic. "No. Oh my god. No."

"It's okay," Lindsay said. "I can find it. You two lift her and I'll lead the way."

They hurriedly packed up the first aid supplies. Mike took hold of Jess under her armpits and Owen stood between her legs and lifted her under her knees.

"On the count of three," Lindsay said, "One, two, *three*."

As they hefted Jess into the air, she gave a moan of pain and her eyes opened momentarily. "Don't let him take it," she said.

"Do you mean Adam? What's he trying to take?" Lindsay asked, but Jess had already slipped back into unconsciousness.

Chapter 23

Although Jess's unconscious body was a dead weight, Owen and Mike were strong enough to move quickly through the forest. They moved so quickly, in fact, that Lindsay could hardly keep pace. Adrenaline spurred them ahead. Lindsay reckoned that it was less than a mile from the tree where they'd found the teenagers back to the church. Every few dozen yards, she checked her phone to be sure they were headed in the right direction. Luckily, the app continued to work despite there still being no signal for calling or texting. They'd been traveling for about 10 minutes when Lindsay finally saw two bars of service appear in the top corner of her phone's screen.

"I've got a cell signal," she said triumphantly.

She began to dial 9-1-1 as she continued to walk. Before she knew what was happening, her foot caught on a fallen branch and she found herself sprawled face down on the damp ground at the base of a tree. She rolled onto her back, clutching her knee to her chest. She had torn the meniscus in that knee the previous summer, and the hard blow immediately aggravated the underlying injury. She clutched her knee and gritted her teeth, trying not to cry.

Owen and Mike quickly laid Jess down and hurried over to Lindsay.

"Are you okay?" Mike said, lifting her into a half-sitting position.

Lindsay ignored the question. The wind had been knocked out of her and she struggled for breath. "My phone," she gasped. "The call was connecting."

Owen lifted it from the mud where it had fallen. "Hello? Hello? This is Owen Checkoway. I'm in the woods, and I'm with Jess Philpot and Mike Checkoway and Lindsay Harding." He paused, listening to something the dispatcher said. "Actually, I don't know where I am. Hold on." He handed the phone to his father.

"Yes, this is Mike Checkoway. We're in the woods, making our way toward Antioch Baptist Church on Old Whiteville Road. Jess has been bitten by a snake; we think a coral snake. They were kidnapped by Adam Tyrell. Hello? Hello?" He looked at the phone's screen. "Damn."

"Do you think she heard what you said?" Owen asked.

"I hope so."

Owen looked at Adam's phone. "The battery's gone on this one. I was using it as a flashlight before when I was trying to help Jess."

Mike looked at his own phone. "Nothing. Let me see if I can put it on roaming. Maybe I can pick up another network."

From her place on the ground, Lindsay could see that Jess's lips had started to take on a bluish tinge. Her closed eyelids looked shiny and swollen. "There's no time," Lindsay said, her voice tight with tension and pain. "Just take her and get to the road as fast as you can. Take my phone. Keep going north and east and you'll hit the road. It's gotta be only another ten minutes or so."

"We're not leaving you out here by yourself," Mike said, pushing a stray curl out of Lindsay's eyes.

"You have to. I'll slow you down."

"But you might get lost without the compass."

"I won't get lost because I'm going to stay right here. When you get to civilization, tell them I'm about a quarter mile from the road, southwest from the cross. They shouldn't have any trouble finding me. I'll be listening out for them. Go!"

"I'll carry you and Owen can carry Jess," Mike said.

"That's crazy," Lindsay said. "She's in bad shape. She could die if you don't hurry. I'm fine."

While they were speaking Owen had already pulled a granola bar and a little foil pouch of water from the duffel bag and put them down next to Lindsay. "She's right, Dad," he said. "The longer Jess is out here, the worse it's going to be for her."

"Here, take my phone then," Mike said.

"And take this, too." Owen pulled a handgun from his pocket. Lindsay and Mike both recoiled from it, startled.

"Where did you get that?" Mike asked.

"Jess had it tucked into her waistband," Owen replied. "She must've taken it from Adam."

"I don't want it," Lindsay said. "I'd probably end up shooting my foot off. You two keep it."

"Take it for protection," Mike urged. "What if Adam's out here? Owen and I have each other for protection."

"No, I don't want to hold a gun ever again." Lindsay thought back to her conversation with Rob. She'd turned it over in her mind a hundred times since then. Maybe God had spared Swoopes's life for her sake. Or maybe she was just a terrible shot. Either way, she realized that guns just weren't something she wanted in her life. "I couldn't shoot somebody just to save myself. I couldn't live with the guilt if I did."

"When we get back, I'm going to buy you a Taser, okay?" Mike said, with a half-smile. He squeezed her shoulders and kissed her gently on the top of her head. "You look really beautiful when you're being stupidly idealistic."

"Dad, we've got to go," Owen said.

Mike nodded and carefully eased Lindsay into a more comfortable sitting position. He took off his jacket, put it over her shoulders, and then rose to his feet. He and Owen lifted Jess from the ground and, with only a quick backwards glance, headed off through the forest. Lindsay listened for a few moments until the sounds of their footsteps faded and she was alone. Again, the beam of her headlamp revealed nothing but the tangled forest. She scooted to a drier patch of ground, mindful of places where snakes might be hiding, and took a deep breath. The fall had left her shaken, but when she pulled up her leggings to examine her knee, she was relieved to see that it wasn't in as bad a condition as she feared. She flexed and relaxed it a few times and found that the initial, excruciating pain had subsided.

Looking around the dark forest, she wondered if she'd made a mistake by not going with Owen and Mike. Maybe if she hurried, she could still catch up with them. Instead, she twisted open the little plastic spout on the pouch of water Owen had left for her and drank it down in one big gulp. She then proceeded to work her way through the granola bar. She hadn't eaten anything since lunch and was suddenly starving. When she finished, she pocketed the trash and she hugged her knees to her chest. Mike's jacket was so large on her tiny frame that she was able to zip her whole huddled body inside it. She kept the beam of her headlamp on and ducked her head inside the jacket. It illuminated the space—her own little flashlight in her own little tent.

In the stillness, Lindsay fought the urge to bargain with God. It was something she'd seen so many times with her patients. Christian, Muslim, Jewish—it didn't matter. The instinct was universal. When people were frightened, they'd propose all sorts of deals to their Maker. *If you just let me live, I'll be a better person. If I just get out of this okay, I'll go to church every week.* She didn't want to engage in that. Instead, she took deep breaths, inhaling the damp scent of the springtime forest—simultaneously decaying and regenerating. She just had to trust. Mike's rash plane journey, a giant roadside cross, a flock of shrieking birds, and a desperate prayer to Saint Anthony had led them to Owen and Jess. If that all happened according to some divine plan, then God certainly had a whimsical streak, not to mention a pretty warped sense of humor.

She heard a nearby rustling that sounded like footsteps. She popped her head out of her coat tent and listened carefully. Nothing could be heard but the sound of her own shallow breathing. It was so easy to get lost in space and time out in a place like this. There was nothing around her to mark the location, no hint of modernity.

In the gloom, she could almost see the events of the previous century play out before her. She could envision the fateful night of the big heist. The Lowrie gang gathered around a campfire in the murky depths of the forest. After years of abuse and persecution, after the terrible years spent enduring the deprivations of the war and its aftermath, they'd pulled off a major coup against the county's elite. All eyes would be on the quietly charismatic Henry Berry, his young deputy, Boss, at his side. Although they were all young men, they'd be careworn from their years as outlaws, unshaven and poorly-clad. The men would be celebrating their clever victory, counting their treasure, making plans for Henry Berry's escape from the lawmen that so relentlessly pursued him. She pictured Donahue McQueen—the red-headed, half-Scottish Lumbee who never quite fit in—hiding nearby, preparing his ambush.

"Who's there?" she heard a familiar voice, very close by.

Her heart thudded in her chest as she scrambled up to a standing position. She reached up to shut off the light and ducked behind a tree, trying to decide if she should run or scream.

The beam of a flashlight raked over her body. "Lindsay? Oh my god. What are you doing out here? Are you okay?"

Although she couldn't clearly see who was speaking to her, she recognized the voice immediately. Adam Tyrell was directly in front of her, not ten yards from where she stood.

She decided it was no use trying to escape. Even without her injury, she was utterly exhausted. The tank of adrenaline that had been keeping her moving all night was down to fumes. "Adam," she said simply. She was surprised at the evenness of her own voice. It was almost as if she was now too tired to be scared anymore.

He quickly covered the space that separated them, and his form came into view. His temple sported a large purple bruise, and a crust of dried blood had formed on his perfectly-chiseled cheekbone. He wore a tight-fitting jacket, which was open at the front. In one hand he carried a heavy flashlight. In the other, a shovel. As he leaned toward Lindsay, various scenarios played out in her head. *He'd strangle her and then use the shovel to bury her. He'd kill her with the flashlight or the shovel and then leave her body in the open for wild animals to devour.*

"How did you get out here? Did she hurt you?" he asked, setting down the shovel and laying a gentle hand on her shoulder.

Lindsay regarded him with a perplexed expression. He seemed so concerned for her. Why was he approaching her in this careful, solicitous way if he intended to harm her?

"What are you talking about?" she asked. "Did who hurt me?"

"Jess," he said. "I think she has Owen. That's why I'm out here. I'm trying to find Owen. I think she took him."

"I don't understand what you're talking about."

Adam shook his head. "Sorry. Of course you don't. I was totally wrong about Jess. You know how I said I thought she was in danger? Well, it turns out she *is* the danger."

"You kidnapped her. Her and Owen. He told us that you tied him up and put him in the trunk," Lindsay said. Again, she was surprised at how calm her voice sounded.

"What?! No. You have to listen to me, Lindsay. I told you I was trying to help Jess, right? To keep her safe so she could carry out the rest of Boughtflower's wishes. Well, I found her at a hotel in Raleigh where she'd arranged to meet Ellen. I went to the room and found Ellen dead. When I saw that, I finally figured it out. It was Jess. She'd lured Ellen there, not the other way around. She was the one who drugged you. She set this whole thing up. When I went to the hotel room, Jess pulled a gun on me and forced me to help her kidnap Owen. She made me drive her down here and then she clunked me on the head. I can't believe she didn't kill me. Maybe she thought I was dead. I don't know."

"I don't believe you," Lindsay said. "That doesn't make sense. How did you know what room they'd be in? And how did you get into the room? Why would Jess need to take you and Ellen out? She has power of attorney. If she wanted the money, she could've taken it for herself at any time."

"I don't think she just wanted the money. You know how I said there was one more thing she needed to do? One more thing she needed to get hold of? Well, I found out what it is."

"You're a liar," Lindsay said, edging away from him.

"I know I lied to you, and I'm sorry," Adam said. "I was just doing my job. I know that's not an excuse. But I'll prove myself to you now. Come on, I'll show you what I'm talking about. I'm on my way there now. We need to stop Jess before she gets it."

"I don't think she's in a position to get anything," Lindsay said. "She was bitten by a snake. Owen and his father have taken her to get help."

"Are you sure?" he asked, fanning the beam of his flashlight over the surrounding woods.

"Of course. I just watched them go. She was in bad shape. She looked like she was dying."

"Is it possible she was faking?"

"No," Lindsay said.

It wasn't, was it? She'd seen the puncture marks and the blisters. She'd felt Jess's thready pulse. Her mind flashed back to what Owen had said about Jess's acting skills, about her ability to change her appearance and fake emotions. And his description of how he'd lost track of her in the woods for a few minutes right before she collapsed. Lindsay quickly dismissed the idea. Nobody could fake something like that. She held onto that belief, and onto the thought that Mike was still carrying the gun. Even if what Adam said was true, surely Jess wouldn't be able to overpower him and Owen?

"Well, let's hope not. There might still be time then for us to get the letters," Adam said. He started walking purposefully in the opposite direction of the road, back the way they'd come.

Lindsay followed him, trailing at a distance both because of her still-tender knee and her continued distrust of him. "If all this is true, we need to go after Mike and Owen and warn them about her. They were carrying her to the road."

"When did they leave?" Adam asked.

"They're maybe ten minutes ahead of us."

"You can go, if you want, but I can't risk it. They've probably linked up with the cops by now. I'd like to avoid getting arrested tonight, if possible. If I can find what Jess was after, it'll prove everything. You can take the proof to the police and my name will be cleared," he said.

"Why can't you tell them yourself?" Lindsay asked.

"I need to go and get the proof first. Besides, keeping a low profile is my bread and butter. Any involvement with the police is bad for business in my line of work. If you'll help me, maybe I can finish my work for Boughtflower and get safely back on a plane out of the States before I have to answer any unpleasant questions about what I've been up to."

"Where are you going?" Lindsay asked.

He turned back toward her. "I'll tell you while we walk."

She hesitated for a moment. She stole a quick glance at Mike's phone. Still no service. Should she follow Adam? Did she have a choice? Owen and Mike were probably nearly to the road by now. Even at a flat-out run without an injured knee, she had no chance of catching them. She could stay in the forest by herself and wait for the cops to find her, but what good would that do anyone? Surely if Adam had wanted to hurt her, he already would've done it. If he'd missed his opportunity after their dinner together, he really couldn't expect a much better scenario for mischief than being alone in the dark woods with her.

She hurried to catch up with him, moving as fast as her injured leg would carry her. "Okay, tell me where we're going," she said.

"Well, I found out at least part of Boughtflower's secret. Jess told me at the hotel. You know how I said whatever he wanted Jess to take care of for him was an actual thing? Well, it's a packet of letters."

"What letters?'

"Do you know who Henry Berry Lowrie is?"

Lindsay nodded. "Actually, I've become a bit of an amateur biographer of his over the past couple of weeks."

"Good. Then you don't need a lot of background. Tell me what you know about Lowrie's death."

"Well, basically, his death has always been mysterious. The sequence of events is that the gang's last big heist was in February, 1872. Shortly after that, Lowrie went missing, never to be seen or heard from again. Some people said he accidentally shot himself while cleaning his gun. Some people think he escaped with the money from the robbery. Then a few weeks later, during the first week of March, Boss Strong, Lowrie's number one guy, was killed by Donahue McQueen, who claimed the bounty and then moved away."

"What do you think it would be worth to find letters that would change history? Henry Berry Lowrie is a hero to the Lumbees, right? And Boss Strong was his right-hand man, as well as his brother-in-law. Well, apparently these letters prove that Lowrie did die that February. It also proves that he didn't accidentally shoot himself. Boss killed him."

"What?!"

"He hatched a plan with Donahue McQueen. They worked together to kill Lowrie, steal the money and then fake Boss's death. They split the money from the Pope-MacLeod robbery and the bounty that Donahue collected on Boss," Adam explained. "They both went off in separate directions. Donahue went to California and then eventually settled in Pennsylvania."

"Wow," Lindsay said, beginning to think that Adam might, in fact, be telling the truth. The image that she'd conjured up just moments before began to shift. She could still envision Boss, Henry Berry's trusted second-in-command, sitting alongside him in the moonlight. Only now, Boss's dark eyes would be surreptitiously darting to the undergrowth just beyond the circle of the campfire's light—to the place he knew Donahue McQueen was lying in wait. He'd be full of false camaraderie, all the while planning to slip off later that night and meet McQueen in secret. As the other men celebrated, he'd be plotting the details of their elaborate plan to fake his own death and murder the man he'd devoted his entire young life to following: Henry Berry, the Robin Hood of the Lumbees, his own sister's husband.

"How do the letters prove all of that?" Lindsay asked, bringing her mind back to the present.

"They were Boss's. He and Donahue split up after they faked his death and agreed never to be in touch again. Boss changed his name and used his share of the money to start up a textile mill."

"Boughtflower," Lindsay said.

"Exactly. Donahue found him. He wrote to him about ten years after they parted, asking for money. He'd spent his share. He was trying to blackmail him. The letters are only Donahue's side of things, so we don't know what Boss's replies said. But we do know that shortly after the second letter arrived, threatening to expose the whole scheme, McQueen was killed." Adam stopped to look at a device Lindsay initially thought was a phone. He held it up for her to see. "GPS. It runs off a satellite." He began walking in concentric circles, scanning the ground as he moved. She followed him, and eventually they found themselves in front of a large, flat rock.

Lindsay regarded it curiously. One thing that struck her when she had stood alone observing the forest was the almost complete lack of rocks on the ground. Anyone who'd ever tried to dig out a garden in the rolling hills of north-central North Carolina knew that you'd find plenty of granite scattered on top of, and embedded within, the thick, red clay soil. Here, however, the rock-free ground was littered with fallen leaves, pine needles, and little else.

"It looks like a tombstone," Lindsay said.

"It is. Boss and Donahue dragged that rock out here to mark the spot where Henry Berry Lowrie is buried. It was mentioned in the letters. Apparently, Otis Boughtflower inherited the letters from his grandfather and spent years trying to find this place. He finally found it sometime in the 50s and buried the letters here, too. Jess managed to work out the coordinates based on the directions her grandfather left. He'd mapped it all out using a star chart and a rough longitude and latitude, but it wasn't exact. You know I said she had to wait until the stars aligned? Well, that was literally true. She waited until the right time of year based on when he'd buried the letters and then mapped it all out using the chart. She transposed that into GPS coordinates and *voila*." He gestured with the shovel. "Why don't you have a seat over there? I'd better start digging if I'm going to be out of here before the police find us."

Lindsay leaned against the trunk of a dead tree near the rock. "This is unreal. Why would Jess want the letters so badly? Did she want to destroy them? Or sell them? I bet they'd be worth a lot of money to a lot of people."

"You're right. I've already made a few calls about it. They'd be worth a fortune to collectors."

"They should be in a museum," Lindsay said, raising an eyebrow at him, "not with a collector."

Adam nodded. "You're probably right." He stopped digging and leaned on the handle of the shovel. "Hey, I need to ask you something. I know it's a little weird to bring this up right now, but I was wondering." He moved closer to her until his body was squared with hers, her back pressed against the trunk of the tree behind her. "If it hadn't been for all this other stuff, do you think you and I could've had something? I mean, I feel like we had a connection." He took hold of her hand as he spoke.

"I don't know what to say," Lindsay sputtered. She looked down at their joined hands and then back up to his face.

He focused his penetrating gaze on her. "Come on. Admit it. We had something."

As usual, that sultry gaze caused a tingling sensation to zip up Lindsay's spine. This time, though, it didn't feel like sexual attraction. It felt more like fear. There was something empty in his expression, almost reptilian. His grip on her hand was far too tight.

"I don't really know you," she said at last, trying to edge a little further away from him. "Um, going back to the letters, I don't get why Boughtflower wouldn't have just destroyed them when he first saw them. If his grandfather was such a scumbag, wouldn't he have wanted to disavow any kind of relationship and hide the family's connection to Lowrie?"

Adam dropped her hand abruptly, turned his back to her, and began digging. "You tell me. You know a lot about being related to scum. Take your mother. She's lowlife scum, and yet you faithfully write to her and visit her."

"What?" Lindsay said. She was so taken aback by the vitriol of his words that she felt like she'd been punched.

"Your mother," Adam said, turning around to face her. In the harsh beam of Lindsay's headlamp, his features seemed to have twisted into a grotesque caricature of the mild, handsome face she recognized. "She supplied the gun that Leander Swoopes used to kill Lydia Sikes," he continued. "She knew where he was and she helped to hide him. She was willing to trade so many people's lives—even yours—for her own. She's scum. Human scum. But you did everything in your power to help her get a light sentence. With good behavior, she could be out in less than two years. With Leander Swoopes missing and maybe dead, no one will ever really be held accountable for Lydia Sikes's death."

Chapter 24

Lindsay took a step backwards. "Adam, you're really freaking me out."

"Am I?" He smiled. "I was right. This is so much better."

"What are you talking about?" She began to back further away from him. Despite the lingering soreness in her knee, she was prepared to run if necessary.

Adam seemed to sense her plan. He leaned down and drew a gun that had been strapped to his ankle. "Have a seat and I'll tell you all about it." A thought suddenly seemed to occur to him. "Actually, better yet, you can come over here and dig. That'll be ironic. Since you're such an expert on Lumbee history, you probably know that that's what started the whole Lowrie war in the first place. Henry Berry had to watch while the Home Guard made his father and brother dig their own graves before they were shot."

Lindsay's brain raced, trying to assimilate what was happening. Clearly, all the debates she'd been having with herself about Adam's character were now resolved. He was, without a doubt, the bad guy. It only remained to try to figure out why. Her earlier conversation with Warren flashed back into her brain. Christopher Sikes. Who else but a son would care so much about the death of a woman who, by all accounts, had been little mourned? Now that she'd put the pieces together, she felt that, on some deep level, she'd always known. There was a connection between them all right—Leander Swoopes had cut his path of destruction through both their lives. But how had this made Adam decide to kill *her*?

"Come on, Reverend," Adam said, holding out the shovel to her. "Tick-tock. Time's a'wastin'."

Lindsay looked around, the beam of her headlamp raking its yellow light across the trees and bushes that surrounded them. What were her options? She'd never before understood how someone could be forced to dig their own grave. Why, if you knew you had only moments to live, would you want to spend them in abject terror, performing humiliating physical labor for your soon-to-be killer? If you were going to die anyway, why not die with dignity, standing on solid earth, refusing to comply? Why not make your killer at least have to put in the effort to bury you after the deed was done?

But now she understood with painful clarity. It was human to hope against hope. The digging could buy time. After all, she'd had close shaves like this before, and both times, she'd escaped with her life. Maybe she could somehow use the shovel to disarm or disable Adam. Maybe, any second, the nighttime sounds of the forest would be split open by the sound of a police helicopter coming to rescue her. Maybe there was a SWAT team perched in the trees even now, just waiting to get a clear shot at Adam. She wondered if Henry Berry's father and brother had made a similar, frantic calculation when the Home Guard's guns had been turned on them. As they, too, hoped against hope that their salvation would come.

Lindsay rose, took hold of the shovel, and dug the blade into the sandy soil. "Why do you care so much about my mother?" she asked.

"Because nobody cared about mine," he snapped.

"Lydia Sikes," she said quietly.

He nodded.

"I didn't know she had children."

He laughed a bitter, mirthless laugh. "There wasn't much coverage of her life, was there? In all the news coverage—and believe me, I've read it all—she's only mentioned in passing, if at all. The reporters couldn't get enough of the pretty, young minister who rescued her mother and great grandmother. Every story painted you as the hero. But my mother? She was just some junkie slut who had it coming. If they ever showed a picture of her—and only a few of them did—it was one of her old mug shots where her hair is all messed up. I've heard you talk about Leander Swoopes or about your mother a dozen times, but you've never once mentioned her name. For all your legendary curiosity, it never occurred to you to find out anything about her."

"How would you know if I talked about her or not? And what do you mean you've heard me talk about Swoopes and my mother? I never gave a single interview about what happened. I had no interest in publicity, and I definitely don't consider myself a hero."

Lindsay was openly crying now. She wished she could turn off the tears; she didn't want to give him the satisfaction. But she was hungry, frightened, tired, confused, and in pain. And more than anything, she was furious with herself. She'd been a fool. At every turn, she'd drawn the wrong conclusion, made the wrong choice.

Adam shined his flashlight in her face, seeming to take pleasure in her distress. Looking at him she wondered if these were the same kind of cold, pitiless eyes that would've shone out from the face of the snake that had bitten Jess.

She wiped her cheeks with the back of her hand. "You put something in my house when you went in as Doer, didn't you? Bugged my phone or something?"

"Now there's a bit of the spunky heroine I've read so much about! Yes, I put a listening device in your kitchen. Pretty much undetectable to your average Joe Policeman. Although I'd argue that the New Albany and Mount Moriah forces, especially Detective Warren Satterwhite, are well below average. For weeks, I've heard every word you said."

"And picking that name, Doer, wasn't a coincidence," she said.

"I hoped you'd figure it out, and that it would remind you. Maybe cause you to take a moment to think about the woman he murdered, but it didn't."

Lindsay plunged the shovel into the dirt with force and wiped her tears away with the backs of her hands. "Not a day goes by that I don't think about Swoopes. Your mother wasn't his only victim."

"She's the only one who died. Why her? Your mother was with Swoopes for years. *Years*! And he didn't kill her. My mother was with him for a couple of months and she's dead. And what about you? I've read the police reports. You had him right there, helpless on the floor in front of you. You could've ended him there so easily. Made him pay for what he did. But you let him get away!" His eyes glittered in the light of Lindsay's headlamp. "Did you know that we'd just gotten back in touch? Just a few months before she died. She was trying hard to get clean. Right before she met Swoopes, she'd been in rehab and things were going well for her. I was keeping tabs on her, so I knew she'd really made a change. Not all of what you know about me is fake. I really do have a security consulting business in Europe. It's a great way to get people to hand over their computer passwords, even the keys to their damn houses! These people are so rich they never notice if money goes missing. Or sometimes, I'll set it up to look like they've had a data breach before I came to work for them. Then I get to be the savior and they get to be the dupes."

"So you want to be the savior? You still can be. You have the ability to track people down. Why not help the authorities track down Swoopes?" Lindsay said.

"The authorities?! They had him! He was in prison and they let him out on a plea deal. They're worthless."

Lindsay had trouble mounting an argument on that point. She, too, had often been angry when she thought of how the criminal justice system had failed in the case of Leander Swoopes. She also wondered where the authorities were at that very moment. She and Mike had managed to find Owen and Jess in this vast forest, but the police didn't seem anywhere close to finding her. She half wondered if they had even started looking.

"So you got in touch with your mother?" Lindsay asked, changing the subject.

"Yes. We made plans to meet up over Christmas. I hadn't seen her since I was 10 and they cut off her visitation rights." His features softened for a moment but then became rigid once again. "But then Swoopes came into her life. He got her doing drugs again. And you know what happened in the end," Adam said.

"I'm sorry for your loss. I truly am. That's an awful way to lose someone." She turned toward him, the light from her headlamp illuminating his twisted, red face. He looked nothing like the handsome man she'd first met in the hospital parking lot a few weeks before. Instead, he seemed to her like an angry child trying desperately not to cry.

Adam narrowed his eyes. "Take off your headlamp and throw it over here," he commanded.

Lindsay complied. The only light now came from Adam's flashlight, which was pointed at her head, along with the barrel of his gun. The pit she was digging was plunged into black. She dug in silence for a few moments, and then said, "I don't get it. Why come after me? You and I are on the same side. We both want to get Swoopes."

"I'm on my own side," he replied.

"What was all that stuff about feeling a connection? Why did you say that?"

"I just wanted to see how far you would go. I was guessing it would only take one date to have you believing my every word. When I took you out, I could practically smell how desperate you are for affection. But I underestimated you a little. Since you're a minister and a bit of a prude, it probably would've been two dates before you would've thrown yourself at me." He gestured with the gun. "Don't forget to dig."

For awhile, the sharp slice of the shovel digging into the ground was the only sound. "Don't worry," he said, breaking the silence. "I'll get Swoopes. And everyone who played a part of letting him get away. Your mother, Warren Satterwhite— everybody who had a hand in how my mother was treated. You were just the low-hanging fruit."

"Why did you lie to me about Jess being the mastermind behind all this?" Lindsay asked. Even in her state of near-panic, knowing that her life was about to end, her curiosity burned more intensely than ever. If she was going to die, she didn't want to die with loose ends.

"In a way, she was," Adam answered. "She was planning to get Owen to take her down here to get the letters. That's why she started dating him, because he had a nice car and seemed willing to be her personal chauffeur. But first she had to figure out exactly where the star chart led. Thanks for that tip, by the way. You and Simmy and Dunette explained the details of the will so clearly, and I listened to every word you said. With that information, it was easy to convince Jess. She was so patient in setting everything in motion, but I got her to trust me in a matter of hours. She really thought I was working for her grandfather. How else would I know what was in the will? She led me all the way here and gave me all the information I needed to 'help her.'" He smirked.

"Good for you, psycho. You outwitted a teenage girl and a chaplain," Lindsay muttered.

"What did you say?" Adam said, narrowing his eyes at her.

"I asked why you dragged me all the way out here," Lindsay lied. "You could've killed me the second you found me, or for that matter, when you drugged me and had me alone in the car."

"Dumb luck with the drugging," he said. "I couldn't get your piece of junk car to start again. The keys wouldn't stay in the ignition. And the Philpots had seen us together. It was too risky to do anything then. I would've had to drag your body along the road and then walk home. So I called 9-1-1."

His casual use of the phrase "your body" gave Lindsay a slight shiver. That's what she'd be soon—a dead body. "And you hoped they'd believe that I was drunk. Maybe pump my stomach and let me dry out overnight," Lindsay said, remembering how, without Anna's intervention, that's exactly what would've come to pass. "Why tell me any of this if you're only going to kill me?"

"Like I said, this was more...amusing. You really are unbelievably gullible. But also you're fun to talk to. I haven't been able to talk to anyone about any of this. And you are funny. So, let me answer your questions. That'll be my parting gift to you.

"Really, it's my job to keep an eye out for opportunities," he continued. "That's how I make money. This Boughtflower thing, which you and your friends discussed in such great detail in your kitchen, struck me as too good to pass up. Like I told you before, I already know of a buyer for the letters. He deals in this kind of thing. And, as to why I dragged you all the way out here, call it what you want. Poetic justice. Curiosity killed the cat. I wanted to see how far I could take you. I'm honestly a little disappointed in how easy it was to string along the supposed righteous minister hero. I'm a bit of an expert in desperate women, but you might win some special prize. You're not a hero at all. You're just like a little puppy, coming back every time even when you've been kicked."

By now, the hole Lindsay had been digging was nearly knee deep and about three feet in diameter. Despite her tender knee, she climbed out and stood alongside it. She looked Adam squarely in the face, suddenly resigned. There would be no last-minute reprieve—no escape, no salvation.

"You know what?" she said. "Dig your own damn hole. My life hasn't been a picnic either, but that's not an excuse. It's hard, but every day I work toward trusting people and being open to life."

"Are you preaching to me, Reverend Harding?"

"Yes, so listen up, because this is my last sermon. You can let the bad things that happen to you make you hard and resentful and mean. That's your choice. I've got my affairs in order, both on earth and beyond."

"Oh, that's right," Adam said, seizing the shovel violently from her hands. He threw it to one side and pushed her to her knees. "I forgot for a second that you're this holy saint. The newspapers loved that, didn't they? Well, don't think you can scare me by telling me I'm going to hell. I don't believe in any of that crap."

Lindsay was slightly breathless from the pain of putting weight directly on her injured knee, but she looked straight at Adam. If she was going to die, she would do so staring her killer in the eye, with her self-respect intact.

"I don't believe in hell, either. Not in the way you mean, anyway, with fiery pits and Satan with a pitchfork. But it seems like you and people like you are already stuck in a place that must feel like hell. That's a pity."

"My mother believed in hell," Adam said quietly. "I remember when I was a kid, she talked about it all the time. It terrified her. She died scared." Then more loudly he said. "Are you scared, Lindsay? If not for yourself, what about for your mother? Or Warren?" He pointed the gun right between her eyes. "How does it feel to be in my mother's shoes, Lindsay? How does it feel to know you're going to die like she did?"

Lindsay continued to stare straight ahead. Her focus was no longer on Adam or the gun. It turned inward, folding in and in until she could see the spark of life inside her own soul. Open-eyed, she prayed that her body would be found quickly. That her friends and family wouldn't be kept in suspense about what had happened to her. She prayed that Dunette would take care of Simmy and Kipper, and take Simmy to visit Sarabelle in prison sometimes. That Mike wouldn't beat himself up about leaving her behind in the woods. She prayed for his happiness, and the happiness of all her friends. She hoped Jess would come to see Owen as the extraordinary young man he was. She prayed that Warren would find someone who could love him the way he deserved to be loved. That her father and Teresa would make each other happy. She held them all inside her prayer, letting her heart fill so full with the burning embers of their love that she thought she might burst into flame.

She heard a soft whooshing sound. A dull thud like the thump of a fist against a pillow followed, and suddenly Adam was falling backwards. The beam of his flashlight arced upwards and then fell, its light shining out into the forest. She heard his body hit the ground, and a strange, wet gurgle emerged from his throat. She knelt where she was for a moment, her heart pounding so loud she was sure it could be heard for miles around.

"Lindsay!" a voice called out. "Get away from there!"

She scrambled to her feet and retreated into the tree cover. As she ducked behind a cottonwood tree, she could make out the shape of a large man emerging from behind a tree on the opposite side of the small clearing. He ran past the hole she'd been digging, holding a crossbow out in front of him, pointed at the supine body of Adam Tyrell. He kicked Adam's body with the heel of his boot. There was no movement. He grabbed the flashlight from where it had fallen and shined it on Adam. Lindsay gasped when the light illuminated the shaft of an arrow standing straight up in the middle of Adam's chest. The man reached down and pocketed Adam's gun.

He pointed the flashlight to the tree where Lindsay was concealed. "It's okay. He's dead. You can come out."

She edged cautiously from her hiding place. As she approached, the man turned the flashlight upwards, so it lit up his face from below. "It's me," he said.

There before her, wearing a camouflage cap pulled low over his brow, stood Warren's brother-in-law, Gibb White. The up-lit shadows cast by the flashlight made him look like a creature out of a horror movie, but she wouldn't have cared if Dracula himself stood before her. She'd never been so relieved to see anyone in her whole life. She stumbled toward him, collapsed against his chest, and burst into tears. Gibb allowed her to rest against him and sob.

When at last she began to quiet down, he asked gently, "What in the Sam hell are you doing out here?"

Lindsay gulped air. "He was going to kill me. Thank you for saving my life."

Gibb looked at his feet, seeming embarrassed by her gratitude. "I didn't set out to do it. I was up in a blind, waiting for some feral hogs to come back to their nest. We'd been out for a couple hours, but hadn't seen 'em yet. Porter and his brother went back to the cabin to get 'em a couple hours sleep. They gotta drive back in the morning. I was just gonna give it another couple minutes, but I saw some lights. I'm sorry it took me so long to get a shot off," he said, looking back over his should at Adam's body. "You were both moving around so much, and I didn't like to take a chance on missing, what with him having a gun in your face."

"Thank you," Lindsay said again. They were the only words she seemed able to form.

"Is he the one you left Warren for?" Gibb asked, glancing back over his shoulder.

"Huh?"

Gibb looked down at his shoes again. "Well, Tanner had heard that her friend Janella saw you at the Olive Garden with some new man. Janella said y'all were pretty cozy, so I just figured…" he trailed off. "Anyways, it's none of my business, but I thought that wouldn't be too good if you left Warren for this guy and then he tried to blow you away. 'Cuz I've known Warren Satterwhite a lot of years, from even before me and Tanner got together, and he's the type of man who would never hurt a woman. Not like that."

"I know," Lindsay said. "Warren's a good guy."

Chapter 25

"I wondered if I'd find you here."

Lindsay looked up, startled at the sound of a voice. She'd just finished conducting the hospital's Wednesday evening service—her first service since returning to work after six weeks off—and was gathering up her things to leave. Her homily had been on thankfulness, and it had been one of her most heartfelt ones. Over the past year, she'd been lied to, robbed, threatened, and nearly killed at least half a dozen times—all traumatic events that would leave her permanently changed. But even so, during the prayer and meditation time, she'd found herself genuinely thanking God for her life. Yes, she'd been given a pretty raw deal in the mother department. Yes, she'd had way more than her fair share of run-ins with murderers and lunatics. Yes, she'd broken up with the man she'd hoped would provide her a chance at living a normal, stable, adult life. And yes, she was experiencing yet another in a seemingly endless string of really bad hair days. Still, she *was* grateful for her life, pain and all.

"Jess!" Lindsay said, stepping off the dais to greet the girl.

Jess made her way up the aisle on crutches, the bottom of her empty pant leg pinned up. Lindsay tried to keep from looking at Jess's missing limb, but it was nearly impossible. It was as if someone had torn the airbrushed cover of a magazine, marring the perfection of the model.

"It's great to see you," Lindsay said. "How are you feeling?"

"Pretty good. These things are a pain in the ass," Jess said, tilting her head toward one of her crutches, "but I'll get fitted for my prosthesis in a few weeks. Then I'll be bionic." She smiled, her lovely features lighting up with what appeared to be genuine amusement. Jess eased herself into a seat in the front row of chairs, and said, "I wondered if you had time to talk?"

"Sure," Lindsay said. "Do you want to go to the cafeteria or something?"

"No, this is good. Kind of fitting, since this is where you and I met. I feel like it all kind of started here, you know?"

Although Jess had been transferred to Mount Moriah Medical Center almost two weeks before to complete the final stage of her rehabilitation, Lindsay hadn't seen her. She had only returned to work part-time, and whenever she'd tried to stop in for a visit, Jess always seemed to be at a physical therapy appointment or surrounded by a gaggle of visiting girlfriends.

Lindsay had been following the aftermath of that fateful night's events closely, and she knew that the police had interviewed Jess several times to fill in details of their investigation. The story that emerged finally allowed her to piece together a coherent narrative from the scattered fragments of the Boughtflower family story. Boughtflower's confession—the hidden body, the stolen money, the cursed fortune—at last made sense in light of the story of Boss Strong and Donahue McQueen's duplicity. As Boughtflower's health worsened, he had come to believe in the necessity of righting his family's historical wrong to the Lumbee people, their own ancestors. He came to regard the Boughtflower fortune with distrust and perhaps even disgust, believing that it had been an evil influence over his life and the lives of his forebears. So, he sought out Donahue McQueen's most direct living descendant, Dunette, to ensure that the money would leave his family's hands forever.

After Lindsay and Jess revealed what they knew of the story to the authorities, and the forensic examination surrounding Adam's death was over, a team of archeologists from UNC had descended on the site. Following weeks of preparation and careful excavation, the team pulled up a corroded metal box. It was fastened with a rusty lock of the same make as the key that Jess had been given by her grandfather. When they opened the box, though, all they could say was that it appeared to have contained papers at some point. Water and sandy soil had penetrated the rust-eaten fastenings and hinges. Frequent flooding and wet conditions since the 1950s had taken their toll, and nothing remained of the documents that could've proven the veracity of the tale.

Before he died, Boughtflower told Jess that, when he visited Maxton in 1958, he'd intended to return the letters to a relative of Henry Berry's and make amends. He maintained that he and his wife had gotten caught up in KKK rally accidentally, and that he was mistaken for a Klansman solely because he was an outsider. Lindsay found that claim more than a little dubious—after all, the rally had been widely advertised in advance. If she had to bet money, she'd say that Boughtflower's desire to give the money to the Lumbees stemmed more from his belief that his fortune was cursed than any altruistic sentiments. However, she kept her opinions to herself. Jess maintained that her grandfather fled, not out of cowardice, but out of fear that the letters would be destroyed in the melee. Like the contents of Boss Strong's letters, Boughtflower's participation in the Battle of Hayes Pond—as an aggressor or as a victim of mistaken identity—was yet another secret that died with him.

Whatever the truth, after the events at Hayes Pond, Boughtflower changed his mind and buried the letters in a box near Henry Berry's grave marker. He'd been told the rough location of that marker by his father, but it took him weeks of searching to find a stone that matched the description he'd been given. In those pre-GPS days, he had devised the star map as a way of marking the location for anyone who might go looking in the future.

The archeologists, however, had as of yet discovered no trace of the alleged grave of Henry Berry Lowrie. Since Boughtflower had only found the marker, and never tried to locate the body, it was possible that the stone he had so carefully devised a map to was simply the wrong one. The team from UNC said they would continue to search the surrounding area, in case the stone had been moved or the topography had naturally shifted. However, based on what they'd found so far, it appeared that if Boughtflower's story were true, he had waited too long to unburden his family of it.

When Dunette found out that the letters that might have cast her great, great grandfather in a different light had likely been lost forever, she took it in her stride.

"The mystery is part of what makes Henry Berry special," Dunette had said.

Lindsay's mind railed against accepting that so many questions would remain forever unanswered, but deep down, she realized that, this time, no amount of searching or rumination was likely to yield satisfactory answers.

"I suppose you're right," she agreed. "It'd be like if somebody came up to you and said, 'Here's the Loch Ness Monster. He's been living in my pool all this time.'"

"Exactly, and even if I believe Boughtflower's story," Dunette continued, "it wouldn't make Donahue McQueen a hero, just a slightly smarter scoundrel. I think there's a reason they didn't find Henry Berry's body out there, and that's because it's not there. He got away."

"So you don't believe any of it?" Lindsay asked. "The letters? The betrayal? The grave?"

"Explain to me how Henry Berry hid from the law for more than ten years, escaped from prison Lord knows how many times, and then he's gonna go and get himself murdered right when he's about to get away with his biggest ever robbery? And his own brother-in-law, who'd stood by him through the war and all the tough times that followed did it?"

Lindsay, too, was inclined to doubt Boughtflower's version of events. He clearly loved Jess and wanted her to think well of him. Perhaps that, more than a desire to tell the truth, influenced his version of events.

"Anyway," Dunette continued, "However that family came by that money, I thought about Boughtflower's will long and hard. It'd sure be nice to have all that cash. I could quit working and concentrate on my nursing classes. Heck, I could just up and quit work, period. Buy a little house somewhere and live out my days. But I don't want that money now any more than I wanted it before I knew all this. Maybe Boughtflower wanted to do some good by giving it to me, or maybe he just wanted to pass the curse on to me. I'm of the same mind as he was in the end—wherever it came from, that money was stolen and it's cursed. Look at all the trouble it's caused. If it does end up coming to me, I've already talked to Mike about creating a scholarship fund and donating to some charities in that part of the state. That's the only reason I don't just drop my claim on it right this minute. Because if the Philpots end up with it, Yancy'll probably just buy hisself a new truck and a big house and a trip to Las Vegas. Too many people died in the Lowrie War for me to let that jackass spend Scuffletown's money on box seats at NASCAR."

Another mystery that the investigation had cleared up was the identity of the shadowy Irish secretary, Ellen, whose ghostly presence had cast a pall over the whole affair. Even knowing that Jess played no part in the crimes, Lindsay had expected to hear of the discovery of the woman's body at a Raleigh hotel. Ellen, she presumed, had met her end at Adam's hands. In fact, Jess had revealed that there was no such person. Ellen had been Jess's invention, designed to conceal the fact that she'd been conducting business on her grandfather's behalf long before she came of age. For years, "Ellen" had dealt with landscapers and accountants and others in Boughtflower's employ—always conducting business by phone or email. Jess had come by her convincing Irish accent while rehearsing for a school play during her freshman year. When Boughtflower started needing more live-in care around the same time that Jess became legally allowed to handle his affairs, "Ellen" moved away.

Lindsay pushed aside these recollections and took a seat next to Jess in the front row of the chapel. "Your surgeon told me you'll be discharged tomorrow," she said.

"That's the plan. I thought it'd be weird if we saw each other out somewhere before we had a chance to talk," Jess said.

"Oh?"

"I guess I wanted to apologize or explain. I dunno." She began picking at a label sticker that was affixed to the metal support on one of her crutches.

"You don't have anything to be sorry for, Jess. You got away from Adam. And you saved Owen's life. You certainly don't owe *me* any explanation. All I did was bumble into the situation following Mike. If anything, I should apologize to you. It was me that Adam came looking for originally."

"It's not that that I feel bad about," Jess said. "My grandfather told me that he'd asked for your help. He was worried that he'd given me more than I could handle, but he didn't know who else to ask. He didn't have any friends, and my parents would've been useless. He felt like we could trust you because you were a minister and because he'd read in the paper that you were some kind of big hero. But I didn't listen. I ignored him and was trying to take care of everything all by myself. I kind of resented the idea of having somebody else get involved. I didn't want anybody's help."

"That's understandable. You'd already handled so much. I heard how you'd been running things for your grandfather for a long time. That's a lot for a young person to handle."

"I guess," Jess shrugged. "Everyone's always just expected me to be, like, wise beyond my years or something. But I totally messed everything up. I'd always been so careful. First, I hid how sick my grandpa was because he didn't want anybody to know. Then I started doing all the money stuff for him when he couldn't do it anymore. I never told anybody. Not my parents or my friends. Not even Owen." She looked up at Lindsay, her lovely amber eyes filled with tears. "But then I went and told Adam or Terry or whatever the hell his name was everything practically as soon as I met him. Because of that mistake, we all almost died and I lost my leg. It's all my fault. I just can't believe how dumb I was."

Lindsay rested her hand gently on Jess's forearm and allowed her to cry for a few moments. "Adam was an expert manipulator. The police said he spent his entire life scamming people. He fooled everyone, even really experienced, powerful businesspeople." She added ruefully, "If it helps, at least you didn't share a basket of unlimited breadsticks with him."

Jess wiped her face and smiled. "True."

Lindsay paused, remembering how Adam had compared her to a pathetic puppy. "But I do know how you feel. It's awful to have somebody abuse your trust like that. It can make you question everything."

Jess nodded. "Adam just seemed so honest. He came up to me when I was coming out of my acting lesson one day and arranged to meet me at the hotel in Raleigh. It was his idea to tell everyone I was meeting an agent because that would be a plausible cover story. I believed, like, *everything* he told me, even the stuff that I should've known was a crock. I really thought he was a private investigator working for my grandfather. He just knew all this stuff that I didn't think anybody else would know, like about the will and Dunette and you. I completely bought it. And I totally should know better. If I've learned anything in my life, it's the hotter the guy, the more likely he is to be full of crap." She paused. "Owen's the exception, but only because he doesn't know he's hot."

"How are things going between you and Owen?" Lindsay asked.

"Oh, you mean because of the whole 'only dating him to get a ride to Robeson County' thing? Yeah, I apologized to him about that. It kind of started that way—using him to get stuff, you know? But as I got to know him, I realized he was actually a really amazing person. I told him I was sorry for using him, and he forgave me. I made sure to emphasize that everyone would think he was a total jerk if he broke up with the girl whose leg just got chopped off."

"Smart move," Lindsay said with a smile. She hoped that Jess's sharp sense of humor would continue to carry her through in life. "So, I still don't know how you escaped from Adam."

"Well, when I heard what Adam had to say, that seemed like the solution to lots of stuff. I thought I'd just meet him in Raleigh and then get him to drive me and help me with stuff, so then I wouldn't even need to involve you or Owen or anybody. Once he got me to Raleigh, though, he freaked out because Owen came inside after he dropped me off. I'd left my bag in his car. Adam was like, 'What if he saw me?' And I was like, '*Relax*. I'm sure he didn't see you, because if he had, he probably would've flipped because your picture has been all over the news.' And he was disguised anyway with a hat and glasses, but he was being really weird about it and asking me how much Owen knew, saying stuff like, 'I know you told him something about me.' He was being so aggressive, so finally I just said, forget this. I'll get Owen to drive me. That's when Adam turned on me."

"And made you help him kidnap Owen?"

Jess hung her head. "Yeah. I always thought if I was ever in a situation like that, I'd be all heroic, like, 'You can torture me, but I'll never betray my friends.' But truthfully, as soon as he showed me he had a gun, I fell apart. I really thought he was going to kill me, and I just went into some kind of robot obedience mode. He told me to call Owen and get him to come back to Raleigh. Then he made me tie him up and help put him in the trunk." Jess got a far-off look in her eyes. Tears pooled at the corners of her eyes once again. It was obvious that the shame of capitulating to Adam so quickly weighed on her enormously.

"But you got away," Lindsay quietly reminded her. "And you saved Owen."

"Yeah. Adam had my arms tied up but not my legs. When he bent down to open the trunk and get Owen out, he took his eyes off me for a second, so I kicked him really hard in the balls. Then when he was on the ground, I kicked him in the face."

Lindsay's mind flashed back to her own narrow escape from Leander Swoopes, which also involved a well-placed kick. "Nice work," she said.

"I know, right?" Jess said, perking up slightly. "As long as you can kick guys in the crotch, who needs karate?"

"You were really brave. I'm sure you would've made your grandfather even prouder than he already was of you," Lindsay said.

"I hope so," Jess sighed. "I'm disappointed about the letters, though. That was so important to him. And my dad is being really stubborn about the will, and because my dad says we should fight it, of course my mom is just like, 'Whatever you say, Yancy.' He says the money's for my college and medical expenses, but I keep trying to tell him I don't need it. I'm still gonna be an actress." Her voice was defiant, but the tip of her nose reddened and the tears that had gathered began to roll down her cheeks. She wiped them away with the backs of her hands and looked plaintively at Lindsay, her mask of strength and determination momentarily slipping.

Lindsay reached out and took hold of one of Jess's hands. "I know everyone probably keeps telling you it's going to be okay, and it is. I promise it is. But it's all right to be sad. It's all right to be really, really pissed off," Lindsay said. "It's great that you're staying positive and being brave, but what happened to you sucks. It's terrible that you lost your leg because of what Adam did to you."

Jess nodded. They were quiet for a long moment while Jess quietly sniffled. At last she said, "Thanks for saying that. I guess this is kind of your job, right? Talking to people who've had crappy stuff happen to them?"

Lindsay squeezed Jess's hand. "Sometimes. Sometimes I get to celebrate with them when the crappy things turn out all right after all."

Jess smiled and dabbed at her face with a tissue. "Well, I'm gonna be one of those people. I *am* gonna be an actress. And I *am* gonna be successful. Adam Tyrell can suck it, and so can that damn snake. I read that amputation is really big right now because of that cancer guy in *The Fault in Our Stars* and that South African runner who killed his girlfriend. And Paul McCartney married that girl who didn't have a leg. So there's definitely money in disability if the rest of you is good looking." She tossed her head, sending a ripple through her long, glossy hair. "Really, my dad just wants the money because he's greedy."

"I'm sorry. That must be hard," Lindsay said.

"Well, I suppose it's kind of my grandpa's fault for being such a prick to him and my mom. They probably feel like they deserve *something* for all those years of putting up with his crap."

"He was never short with you?" Lindsay asked. It was something that had baffled her, having seen Boughtflower's personality in action.

"No. He had this weird superstition about me. Like, he'd always known the story about how his family came to have the money to start their factory. His mom died young and his dad was an alcoholic. I guess my great grandpa was an asshole to everybody, and that being jerks kind of ran in the family. So when my grandma got pregnant, my grandpa started freaking out about it. Because of 'the curse' or whatever. He decided to reveal all the stuff in the letters and give the money back. But you know what happened with all of that. Then his wife left him and his health started tanking. He got super fat. When my mom came back to live with him after her mom died, I guess he didn't trust her. He treated her like she was stupid, which, I guess she kind of is."

Lindsay allowed the disparaging comment about Margo to pass without comment. It had taken her until she was 30 to begin seeing her parents as full human beings. She couldn't fault Jess for oversimplifying and seeing her mother through an unflattering lens.

"Anyway, then my mom got pregnant and married my dad while they were still in high school and all the stuff with the miscarriages happened. I guess my grandpa was a total wreck back then. He was drinking a lot and he thought he was dying, so he sold his company. Nobody outside our family knows it, but he gave all the money from that sale away to charity. Then I was born." She pointed to her face. "Magic. He thought it was because he gave some of the money away. Apparently he thought I looked just like Rhoda Strong, the Queen of Scuffletown, which is silly because nobody even really knows what she looked like. Anyway, he was like, 'You getting born was the first good thing that happened to our family since the whole Lowrie thing went down.' He thought it was an omen. But it's not easy, you know? Being, like, supernatural." She rolled her eyes and made little wavy motions with her hands.

"It sounds like everyone had a lot of expectations for you," Lindsay said.

"That's what's cool about Owen. He doesn't try to control me at all. He wants what's best for me, but he kind of just lets me be the way I am, you know?" Jess smiled, but she looked slightly pained. When she spoke again, her voice wavered slightly with emotion. "A lot of guys would've freaked out because of the leg amputation. I'm gonna need a couple more surgeries and the doctors said I can't drive for at least *another* year." Her hands unconsciously went to the knee that no longer had a leg below it. Her eyes took on a faraway look. "But Owen's like, 'Whatever, you're still you.' He's just... there for me."

As if on cue, the door to the chapel swung open and Owen and Mike entered.

"Hey, sorry, are we interrupting something?" Mike asked. "The nurse in the rehab unit said we could find you here."

"No, we were just talking," Jess said. "I'm ready." She turned back to Lindsay. "I asked Owen to bring me take-out from the Mex-Itali. I'm so bored with the food in here."

Owen held up two plastic bags with Styrofoam containers in them. "You and my dad can join us if you want. I got a ton of food. We're gonna eat outside in the meditation garden. It's really nice out there."

"Have you eaten?" Mike asked Lindsay. When she shook her head, he said to Owen, "Why don't you and Jess head out there? We'll catch up with you in a minute."

Owen and Jess walked out together, leaving Mike and Lindsay standing side by side near the front of the chapel. Mike looked around. "Can I help you pack up, your, uh, Bible or something?" he asked.

"I'm basically finished. I just need to drop some stuff off in the office and then I'll be ready," Lindsay said.

"I was surprised to hear that Jess was down here. There are a lot of ways to describe her, but 'devout' isn't really a word that would spring immediately to my mind."

"She had a few things on her mind. I guess she thought I might understand better than some people."

"I'm sure that's true," Mike said. "I know she was grateful to you for coming to the rescue."

"I don't know why she would be. I just followed you out there, and I was totally ready to believe it when Adam said she was a criminal who would double-cross her own grandfather and parents," Lindsay said. "I was pretty useless." This seemed to Lindsay to be yet another instance of her getting credit where none was deserved or wanted.

"Stop beating yourself up," Mike said. "You were right to suspect she was up to *something*. You just didn't know what."

Lindsay had had about a thousand versions of this conversation with her friends and family since the events of that night. Simmy had been especially patient in listening to Lindsay's circular ruminations and keeping her from getting too caught up in her dark thoughts.

"So, you're back to work. How are things going with you?" Mike asked.

"Good. Dunette's been a star. She took me and Simmy to our physical therapy appointments when my knee was all messed up, walked Kipper, just everything. She lets Simmy experiment on her with beauty products, and she doesn't seem to mind being subjected to whatever crystals or chanting or bitter herbal teas or heaven knows what Simmy's dabbling in from week to week."

"She's a pretty amazing person," Mike agreed.

"I don't know what we would've done without her, and I don't know what Simmy's going to do when she starts nursing school in the fall. But Simmy's health is so much better now that we can't really justify having her there so often. She's got her own life to live, too."

The truth was that the little household they had formed had kept Lindsay sane over the previous weeks. The cheerful banter of Simmy and Dunette, coupled with Kipper's solid, reassuring presence, had been like a layer of insulation, muting the menacing noise of the outside world and quieting the even more destructive voices inside her own brain. Somehow, just having Kipper, Dunette, and Simmy around had managed to shield her from the trauma she had experienced and keep her from shutting down again.

"Yeah, last time I saw Dunette, she mentioned something about Angel urgently needing her help?" Mike said, raising an eyebrow.

Lindsay laughed. "Angel convinced her to join the choir at her church. She's got her eye on one of the tenors, but apparently one of the other altos is trying to beat her to him. She needs Dunette as her wing-woman."

"Ah, yes. Sounds like a matter of national importance." His face softened. "I'm sorry I haven't been around much lately," he said. "Owen doesn't show it, but he was really shaken by what happened. He needed me."

"You don't need to apologize. He's your son. Of course you had to make sure he was okay," Lindsay said.

Although she could barely admit it to herself, she had been acutely aware of Mike's sudden near-absence from her life. It seemed like suddenly everyone else had someone who ranked above her in their priorities. Rob had always had John, but now Anna had Drew, and her father had Teresa. Even Simmy and Dunette had formed a bond separate from Lindsay. And Warren? Who knew where she ranked in his list of priorities? Probably somewhere just below flossing. Although it was only natural that she shouldn't be the center of everyone's world, she wished she would at least be at the center of someone's.

When she thought of Warren, she remembered how he had been the one to drive her back from Robeson County. There were only two seats in Mike's plane, and he'd flown back with Owen the morning after their ordeal. During that whole long drive, she and Warren had avoided talking about anything serious, instead keeping the conversation incongruously light. They joked about becoming stepsiblings if Jonah followed through on his plan to propose to Teresa, and speculated about whether Gibb would remain such a henpecked husband now that he was being celebrated as a bona fide action hero. It was as if they were both skating quickly across thin ice, afraid that any slowing of forward momentum would cause them to crash through into the frigid lake that lay beneath.

Over the weeks that followed, Warren visited Lindsay occasionally, bringing updates about the case. The visits had been brief and cordial, with no indication on his part that he'd pledged his undying love to Lindsay over meatballs marinara at the Mex-Itali only a few months before. At times, she wanted to scream at him, to ask him how he could just sit at her kitchen table and pet Kipper and nibble Chex Mix as if they'd always just been good buddies. Didn't he want to come to her rescue and hold her tight against his chest, the way he had done so many times? Couldn't he still feel the buzz of energy in her presence that Lindsay felt in his? Or had he simply pulled the kill switch and shut off the current that used to flow between them? In the end, she said none of these things. She, too, sat across from him like an old friend, cordially eating Chex Mix.

Mike interrupted her thoughts of Warren, saying, "I've also been working on a mediated settlement for the Boughtflower money. I think I've finally gotten everyone to agree that we'll create a trust for Jess's education and medical expenses, and that the rest will be invested in community projects in Robeson County."

"That's great," she said. "How did you manage to convince Yancy?"

Mike blushed, his eyes dropping to the floor. "Um, I gave him my plane."

"You what?!"

"Don't tell anyone, okay? He didn't seem like he was going to budge, and I really didn't think it would be good for anybody for this to go to trial. At one of our pretrial meetings, I overheard him mention to his lawyer that he always wanted to fly. So, I said I'd give him my plane and pay for him to take flying lessons if he would agree to drop his claim on the money. He knew from the beginning that his chances of winning were really slim, so he decided to take the sure thing and agree to my proposal."

"So you just bribed him with your plane?"

Mike shrugged. "I'd kind of outgrown it, anyway. I think I need something bigger. Maybe a four-seater. Then we could all go for rides together. Or maybe a six-seater, so there'd be room for Kipper and Simmy."

"You've got big plans, huh?"

He pushed the chapel door open and smiled at her. "I always have big plans." He paused as she passed close to him. "Did you do something different to your face?"

"Simmy tried out some new lip gloss on me and Dunette."

"I like it. It's really sparkly. Your lips look like the lips on one of those weird dolls all the good moms won't let their daughters play with."

Lindsay smiled at the "compliment." Good to see that some things never changed.

"Lindsay!"

Lindsay looked up at the sound of her name being called in Warren's familiar warm North Carolina twang. Warren stood almost directly in front of her, looking annoyingly handsome in his trademark grey button-down shirt with rolled-up sleeves. Alongside him was his erstwhile Vegas wife, Cynthia Honeycutt. Cynthia carried her purse over her shoulder, but she was still dressed in nurses' scrubs. Scrubs usually managed to make women look formless and frumpy, but Cynthia wore fashionably-tailored hot pink and black ones that reminded Lindsay of Mandarin-collared silk pajamas. Sexy pajamas.

"Hey, Warren," Lindsay replied. Politeness compelled her to add, "Cynthia, this is my friend Mike."

"We were just going out to get some drinks," Cynthia said brightly, shaking Mike's proffered hand. "Wednesday is two-for-one Chianti daiquiris at the Mex-Itali." She rested her fingertips briefly on Warren's arm as she spoke.

Lindsay noted the gesture, and her heart seemed to momentarily swell up, constricting her throat. "I know," she said. "Warren and I used to go there all the time."

A painful silence that not even Southern manners could conceal descended over the group.

At last Warren spoke. "I was here dropping off a drunk who got into a fight over at the truck stop off of 85 and I ran into Cynthia. She was meeting some friends and asked me along. It was kind of a spur of the moment thing." His cheeks colored as he rambled breathlessly through the explanation.

"Why don't y'all join us?" Cynthia asked, with a coy downward snap of her wrist.

"Unless you and Mike have plans," Warren added, looking pointedly at Lindsay.

"We were just going to have dinner in the courtyard with my son and his girlfriend," Mike said. "To celebrate her being discharged from the hospital tomorrow. Also kind of a spur of the moment thing."

Lindsay turned her head and smiled gratefully up at him. His large frame felt reassuringly solid next to her, like a sun-warmed rock.

"Well, it was nice seeing you, Lindsay. You take care," Cynthia said. "We'd better head out." She seized Warren under the elbow and led him away. He cast a quick backwards glance at Lindsay. His expression looked slightly pained, but Lindsay had no way of knowing the source of his distress. Maybe it wasn't emotional at all. Maybe Cynthia's grip was just too tight.

"You know what?" Lindsay said once the pair was out of earshot. "It's been a really long day, and I have to work in the morning. Why don't you go without me? I'm going to head home. I'll be happier on the couch with Simmy and Kipper."

Lindsay found, to her surprise, that the statement was entirely true. In the past, it was the kind of excuse she would've made to flee from a painful situation and retreat inside the numbing sanctuary of her own psyche. But this time, she found she wasn't afraid of feeling negative emotions. Of course the encounter with Warren and Cynthia had been surprising and upsetting, but she had no plans to curl into a ball and hide from the world. Seeing them together had sucked. But like she'd told Jess, sometimes things do just suck.

Over the past few weeks, something inside of Lindsay had shifted. So many times, she'd simply reacted without listening to the quiet whispers of her inner voice. Saying yes to Warren's proposal, becoming furiously angry at her father and Teresa, following Adam into the forest—she'd done all these things on a sort of emotional autopilot. Now, she was making a habit of turning her ears inward, pressing them against her soul, and hearkening to its quiet voice. And she realized that by doing what she wanted to do, she wasn't necessarily avoiding Warren, or Mike, or anyone. The plain truth was that she really would really prefer to hang out in her own house with Simmy and Kipper. They were halfway through binge-watching the soapy fairytale drama *Once Upon a Time*, and the action was heating up. If she went home now, they could watch four or five episodes before bedtime.

"Are you sure you're okay?" Mike asked.

Lindsay nodded. "Scout's honor. Tell Jess I'll pop up and see her tomorrow before she's discharged."

"You're not bothered by that nurse Warren was with are you? Because you shouldn't be. You're a lot more attractive. Her face is just boring-pretty. Like if you were going to pick a pretty person from central casting, she'd be it. You've got a memorable face. It kind of sears itself into your brain."

"Are you comparing my face to a cattle prod?" Lindsay asked, arching an eyebrow in amusement.

Mike smiled broadly, his green eyes glittering playfully. "Exactly. You, Lindsay Harding, are an unforgettable firebrand."

Historical Note

Henry Berry Lowrie (sometimes spelled Lowry or Lowery), his wife Rhoda Strong, her brother Boss, and Donahue McQueen were all real people and much of the action described in this book, including the incident at Hayes Pond and the Pope-MacLeod heist, is well-documented and true. However, with apologies to my Native American friends and to my historian friends and especially to my Native American historian friends (!), I've taken some major liberties by imagining an alternate ending to their stories. The most radical departure from the facts is the idea that Boss Strong, Henry Berry's trusted friend and brother-in-law, could have worked with Donahue McQueen to betray him. Although that betrayal worked well for the purposes of my story, the whole scenario is purely a product of my imagination. Most of the evidence suggests that Henry Berry either escaped with the stolen fortune or was killed when his gun accidentally discharged in the days following the heist. Personally, I believe he escaped. The gang was sophisticated enough to elude capture for more than a decade, and it seems more than convenient that Henry Berry disappeared so suddenly at the crucial moment following the Pope-MacLeod robbery.

If you want the real deal, history-wise, I highly recommend *To Die Game: The Story of the Lowry Band, Indian Guerrillas of Reconstruction* by William McKee Evans and Malinda Maynor Lowery's *Lumbee Indians in the Jim Crow South: Race, Identity, and the Making of a Nation.* Or, if you want another fictional take on the rise and fall of the Lowrie War, with yet another imagined scenario for what became of Henry Berry, Boss, and Rhoda, check out Josephine Humphreys's award-winning novel, *Nowhere Else on Earth.*

Thanks for reading!

Loved it? Loathed it? Tell the world! Your reviews on Amazon and Goodreads help readers like you to figure out if *The Burnt Island Burial Ground* is the book for them. So if this book was your cup of tea, say so! Or if it was your cup of NyQuil with a Valium chaser, warn the unsuspecting public! Because no one wants to read a book that's gonna make them drool with boredom.

Haven't read the rest of the series and want to find out how it all started? Check out *A Murder in Mount Moriah* and *A Death in Duck*.

Be the first to know when the next book in the series will be released. Sign up for updates on my website: **mindyquigley.com**.

Acknowledgements

Praise be to my stalwart friends, Tanya Boughtflower, Jaime Gagamov, Megan Hohenstein, Jane Goette, and Charlotte Morgan, for reading drafts, providing honest feedback, and generally being ace. Bethany Keenan gets a special thank you. As everyone in your small town knows, you have helped me become a better killer, and for that I'll always be grateful. Thanks to expert plane guy John Baute for sharing his knowledge. Valerie Pate, the Comma Queen, provided top-notch copyediting and feedback. If mistakes remain, it's only because I can never resist making last-minute changes. Gratitude in the direction of Professor Malinda Maynor Lowery for her wisdom and guidance on all things Lumbee. I hope this book inspires people to read the real history of the Lumbees, which is way more interesting than any novel. My Little Spot colleague Allison Janda is pretty awesome, as is our publisher, Nicole Loughan. Love to Alice, who endlessly cheers and encourages me, and to my husband Paul for putting up with all my nonsense.